# AN ERROR IN JUDGEMENT

Nell Bradbourne berated herself for being a fool. Mr. Brandon Manningford had seemed so perfect a gentleman. Surely there would be no danger or even hint of impropriety in accepting his kindly offer to drive her to her aunt's home in his elegant carriage.

Now he made it clear that he had a far different goal. He was plainly and simply abducting her. Of course, it was her fortune he sought—but telling him that she no longer had one might be yet another mistake. For Brandon was the kind of man who clearly had other uses for a woman than wealth.

Being a lady in distress had been bad enough. But now Nell was a lady on the brink of disgrace . . .

---

AMANDA SCOTT, winner of the Romance Writers of America's Golden Medallion (*Lord Abberley's Nemesis*) and the *Romantic Times'* Awards for Best Regency Author and Best Sensual Regency (*Ravenwood's Daughter*), is a fourth-generation Californian with a degree in history from Mills College in Oakland. She lives with her husband and teenage son in Folsom, California.

# THE BATH ECCENTRIC'S SON

*Amanda Scott*

A SIGNET BOOK

To Tom Sawyer for the frame.
To Lady Peel for the gilded edging.

SIGNET
Published by the Penguin Group
Penguin Books USA Inc., 375 Hudson Street,
New York, New York, 10014, U.S.A.
Penguin Books Ltd, 27 Wrights Lane, London W8 5TZ, England
Penguin Books Australia Ltd, Ringwood, Victoria, Australia
Penguin Books Canada Ltd, 10 Alcorn Avenue, Toronto, Ontario, Canada M4V 3B2
Penguin Books (N.Z.) Ltd, 182-190 Wairau Road,
Auckland 10, New Zealand

Penguin Books Ltd, Registered Offices:
Harmondsworth, Middlesex, England

First published by Signet, an imprint of New American Library,
a division of Penguin Books USA Inc.

First Printing, February, 1992

10  9  8  7  6  5  4  3  2  1

# 1

"Murdering him is out of the question, I suppose," Lady Flavia Bradbourne said wistfully as she straightened the frothy lace cap perched atop her snow-white curls. A thin little woman dressed in a wide-skirted gown fashionable twenty years before, she sat in one of the two armchairs flanking the drawing-room hearth, well out of the way of drafts from the tall, narrow windows, her tiny feet propped on a tapestry tool.

"My dear ma'am!" Petite auburn-haired Nell Bradbourne, her dark-blue eyes alight with unaccustomed laughter, turned from the window through which she had been contemplating the serenity of Laura Place with its gently spraying central fountain, and the broad, deserted, rain-dampened length of Great Pulteney Street beyond. Her great-aunt's tone, as much as the words themselves, having successfully distracted her from the brown study into which she had fallen during a pause in their conversation, she shook her head in fond reproval. "You cannot mean it."

"I suppose you are right, but your father's cousin Jarvis seems to be no better than his own sire, and that generation of Bradbournes was sadly lacking, I fear, though the worst anyone ever said of your papa—until last year, at all events—was that he was bringing an abbey to a grange and had no sense. Jarvis, now . . . Well, all I can say of him is that if the world would be better without him . . ." She paused significantly.

Nell choked back a gurgle of laughter. "No, no, Aunt Flavia. You know that that was not at all what I meant when I said I should prefer the world with him out of it. I shan't deny that I haven't wished from time to time that I might make him disappear in a puff of smoke, or that—"

"Oh, I daresay it would not be so easy as that," Lady Flavia said, twinkling, "and poison will not do, for I cannot imagine how one might prevail upon him to ingest it. Nasty-tasting stuff, it must be, for one cannot expect to be so fortunate as to come by one of those mysterious unnoticeable Oriental poisons one so frequently encounters in gothic romances, particularly when one does not know a single mysterious Oriental person from whom one might acquire such a thing. But wait." She held up a hand with the index finger extended for a brief, thoughtful moment before adding, "I believe Sydney Saint-Denis, up on Bathwick Hill, has an Oriental servant. Perhaps he might—"

Nell's laughter could no longer be contained. "Aunt, *will* you be serious for a moment," she implored when she could speak. "We must think of a solution far more practical than murder."

"But, my dear," Lady Flavia protested, "though I may have suggested murder only to make you laugh, you cannot call it impractical. Not with everything in such a tangle, what with your father's losing Highgate in that idiotic wager, and then your brother's duel, and the tragedy that followed. You even suspect that Jarvis had a hand in Nigel's trouble, if not in your father's death, so if he now believes the only way to salvage your reputation from the ashes of theirs is to ally yourself with him, you must know you will never convince him otherwise."

"I know nothing of the kind, ma'am. Indeed, I do not doubt that he will cease to plague me the moment he discovers that I have sunk myself so low as to seek genteel employment."

Lady Flavia stiffened in her chair, and her right foot began to tap irritably upon the footstool, beating time to the cadence of her words as she sakd, "I take leave to remind you, Nell, that that is simply not to be thought of! What would people think?"

"But surely, dear ma'am, they would think even less of a murderess," Nell responded in a teasing tone.

"They would never know," her ladyship said tartly, "and goodness knows, ladies of quite the highest quality have been known to do such things before now—even queens, I believe—though they do *not* seek employment, Nell, genteel or otherwise. Oh, I know I have been talking nonsense, but if you should do such a thing, and in Bath, of all places, people will think perfectly dreadful things.''

"Only that I have not got sixpence in my pocket, which is no more than the truth," Nell said with a sigh. Then, seeing that her aunt was truly distressed and only too ready to continue the argument they had had over and over since Nell's arrival in Bath four days before, she stepped impulsively toward the old lady, kneeling beside her chair and taking one of the thin hands firmly between her own. It trembled a little, but when she squeezed it, the squeeze was returned. "Aunt Flavia," she said gently, "what can it matter what people think? If I do not care—"

"Then I suppose I am not to care either," Lady Flavia interjected. "Well, and perhaps I would not if I believed you will not. But you will, my dear, you will! Oh, and I would too if I were such a zany as to allow you to attempt to earn your living. You were not brought up to it, Nell, any more than I was. Your father was only a baron, of course, and began life as a younger son, for that matter, but your mother was from an excellent family, just as I am, and there is nothing really amiss with the Bradbournes that a little ambition could not cure. Ah, if only Robert and I had been blessed with children!'' She lapsed into a brief reverie, but then, giving herself a shake, added sharply, "To pretend you do not care what people say—what a farradiddle! If you did not care, then why did you come here? Why did you not simply stay at Highgate and let Jarvis frank you as he wished to do? Surely he never asked you to leave.''

"Indeed, and you know he did not." Nell bit her lower lip. "He was all consideration, as only he can be, but when he enters a room, one feels somehow as though a snake has slithered in. I do not know how it is, for to own the truth, he has treated me only with kindness, but even while he remained at Crosshill, one frequently felt his frustration that my papa and not his had inherited the seat of the Bradbournes. When he informed me of his intention of removing to Highgate, pretending to be doing so out of a sense of duty, I could not bear to remain there.''

"I cannot think," Lady Flavia said, "how, with his fine notions of propriety, he expected to move in with you without ruining your reputation. One must suppose he intended to force you to accept his hand.''

"Well, of course he did, ma'am, but it would surprise you to hear how easily, when he sets his mind to do a thing, he is able to explain how it is really the only thing to do. In this case, however, he said only that it was his duty to protect me and also to be near at hand to restore Highgate to its former glory. He talks like that, Aunt Flavia. It quite shrivels one's liver.''

Lady Flavia smiled at hearing such an expression on Nell's lips, but said, "You know, dear, I have been thinking about all this, and I cannot think why he waited nearly seven months.''

"Well, he told me straight off that he had decided to marry me, as though he meant the news to comfort me, but he explained that he did not want to cause more talk than there was already by arranging our marriage while I was in deep mourning, so we would wait until I came of age. I daresay the truth was that he had realized there would be some difficulty about consent and supposed that with Papa dead and Nigel heaven-knows-where, the matter would arrange itself more neatly if he waited. And, too," she added on a bitter note, "no doubt he thought to give me time to realize that no one else would step forward to protect me.''

"He might have thought I would," Lady Flavia said pensively.

"If you will forgive me for saying so, ma'am, since you did not offer to bring me out when I turned eighteen, despite the fact that we had been corresponding for years, Jarvis might be excused for discounting you. Oh, you had never given me cause to expect such a thing of you, but Papa did,'' she added when Lady Flavia frowned, "and I daresay Jarvis will guess that I have found sanctuary with you now, for there is no one else.''

"Sanctuary, indeed," the old lady snapped. "I am very

glad you came to me, Nell, but how you can speak of sanctuary when you mean to cut up all my peace by going out to seek work as a housemaid, I cannot imagine!''

"I have no intention of seeking such a lowly position. Indeed, I doubt I should be any good at it. However, I must say, ma'am, that while I will do nothing a-purpose to distress you, I have seen enough here since my arrival to know that a little extra money in this house would not come amiss.''

"But you refuse to consider what people will say,'' Lady Flavia repeated more urgently. "It simply is not to be thought of that the grandniece of Lady Flavia Bradbourne should seek employment. Indeed, since you are known to be my heiress, Nell, we must thank heaven that your father's passing renders my taking you about to parties quite ineligible, for otherwise people would be like to think I ought to be doing so.'' She leaned forward a little in her chair and said earnestly, "We will sign your name in the master of ceremonies' book, of course, for it would be thought extremely odd if we did not, but you must be sure to continue to wear your half-mourning, my dear.''

"You may be sure that I shall, ma'am,'' Nell said dryly, looking down at her pretty dove-gray-muslin afternoon frock, "for although Jarvis insisted that, as a Bradbourne, I be fully rigged out in mourning clothes cut according to the latest fashion, I fear my other dresses would not impress anyone in Bath.''

"Oh, my poor dear,'' Lady Flavia said, squeezing her hand again. "I am so sorry.''

"Well, you need not be.'' Nell's eyes narrowed. "Look here, Aunt Flavia, though you have rather neatly turned the subject, I cannot allow you to put me off again. Even had I come here intending to hang on your sleeve, which I did not, I must very soon have begun to wonder if you could comfortably support me. To be sure, you live in this wonderful house, and the furnishings in this room and in the hall and dining room are as fine and elegant as any I have ever seen. But most of the other rooms are much more sparsely furnished, and several are as bare as can be. Moreover, although the first meal we shared was excellent, the ones we have had had since then . . . Well, not to put too fine a point on it, ma'am, they have been distressingly meager.''

"You see, my dear," Lady Flavia said in the tone of one making a confession, "I did not know at first how long you meant to stay, and it is one's habit, of course, to feed one's guests as lavishly as one reasonably can."

"Then it is as I had begun to suspect, and you are not nearly as wealthy as I had been given to believe. I did not quite like to ask you about it before, but why did you not tell us long ago how things have been with you?"

"Goodness me, why should I? That one occasionally must eat soup instead of roast partridge is nothing, but to suffer the pity of one's friends would be prodigiously uncomfortable, and to endure the contempt of those who are not one's friends, utterly unbearable. Life is much more pleasant, I assure you, as the wealthy Lady Flavia Bradbourne than it would be for a common old woman living in genteel poverty. Moreover, if by 'us' you mean I ought to have told your father, why, he had more than enough debts of his own without adding any of mine."

"Dear Aunt, what sort of debts have you got?"

"Not debts precisely, or not in the way you mean them—only to the greengrocer, the butcher, the chandler, and others of their ilk. Nothing to signify." An airy wave of Lady Flavia's hand dismissed these trivialities even as she sighed and said, " 'Tis only that the bills appear to increase, even when one sends a bit on account from time to time. It is beyond comprehension."

"But, surely, ma'am, this cannot go on."

"I do not know why it should not," Lady Flavia replied placidly. "It has been going on for years, since prices began increasing so outrageously during the French war. One's income does not increase, you know. Not, at all events, when one lives on a widow's jointure. Indeed, it seems to decrease, for it does not buy near so much now as it did fifteen or twenty years ago."

"But however have you managed to fool everyone for so long?" Nell demanded.

"Oh, really, it is not so difficult." Lady Flavia pulled her shawl more tightly across her shoulders. "I am not destitute by any means, but only must take a certain care, and since one's guests generally do not attempt to go beyond the hall or drawing room and no one thinks it odd that a woman of my years no longer invites friends to large dinner parties, it is not so bad."

"But even so, people must have seen—"

"People," Lady Flavia said firmly, "generally see what they want to see and think what they want to think. Then, too, it gives them a certain cachet, don't you know, to have wealthy friends. They do not wish to discover that one is not so wealthy as they believe one to be. 'Twould be to diminish themselves."

"But surely there must be outward signs of . . . of . . ."

"Of decay?" Lady Flavia suggested. "A decayed gentlewoman—so descriptive a term, beloved of novelists, but rather hateful when it is fact. Fortunately, in Bath, elderly ladies are expected to behave and to dress in an eccentric way. Gentleman too. Indeed, there are several hereabouts who take eccentricity to its limit. One in particular, Sir Mortimer Manningford, has not set foot out of his own house these twenty-five years past. 'Tis said he leaves notes for his servants and sees his heir but once a year for twenty minutes, then shoves him off about his business again. His younger son he don't see at all!"

"Despite such examples as that, ma'am, I doubt your pretext can be so simple to maintain as you would have me believe."

"But it is, my dear. One dines out as frequently as one can do so, of course, and your coming to stay will prove a boon in that direction, for a good many people will wish to meet you. And no one will expect us to entertain either, not with your father dead less than a year. Quite providential, that is."

"Yes, you said so before," Nell said, adding more grimly, "but it will remain providential, you know, only until one of the quizzes for which Bath is so famous discovers the rather untidy circumstances of his death."

"Very true, so we shan't divulge them. To anyone so busy as to inquire, you must say you find the subject too painful to discuss. I, on the other hand, should anyone ask me, will look down my nose and demand in my haughtiest tone to know by what ill-bred impulse he or, more likely, she has dared to pry into a matter that cannot possibly concern anyone outside the Bradbourne family. That will silence the most brazen amongst them."

"No doubt it will, ma'am, but I am not good at dissembling, you know. The first time someone asks me directly, I shall most likely tell the truth."

"Good God, Nell, you will never be such a goose! The next thing you will be doing is to admit that Jasper went aloft on a cloud of debt."

"Well, and 'tis true enough if, indeed, he went aloft at all. Considering the manner of his going, 'tis more likely—"

"Don't say it," Lady Flavia snapped. "For goodness' sake, Nell, promise me you will not let your wretched tongue run away with you. You are welcome to stay for quite as long as you like, if only you will not cut up my peace by telling people you are seeking employment, or by confessing your father's dreadful sins, or by speaking in an equally frank manner about that rapscallion brother of yours. Indeed, you must promise not to mention Nigel at all if you do not wish to see me suffer a severe spasm!"

"But, ma'am, surely if Nigel shot Mr. Bygrave right here in Bath, either everyone knows all about it already or the situation must have been very different from what Jarvis described to us."

"Well, I cannot say about that, of course, but I do know that no one has ever mentioned the matter to me. Of course, if that dreadful duel took place in a gentlemen's club, 'tis possible that no one *would* say anything to me."

"Well, but I am certain Jarvis had more to do with it than he admitted. Papa didn't trust him, you know—said he was a make-mischief. For that matter," she added with a quizzical look, "Papa told me that his uncle Robert was used to say the same of Jarvis' papa, Reginald. Is that not true?"

"Dear Robert," Lady Flavia said fondly, her sharp

features softening. "He was a fine husband to me, though that time of my life has begun to seem a trifle distant, you know. So difficult to look at oneself in the glass and imagine that same reflection wedded to a man in his twenties, which, of course, is the only way one can remember Robert. I have tried to imagine him older, but it does not answer. Jarvis was not even thought of when he passed on, of course, for Reginald was only a boy then, and I do not know what Robert thought of Reginald, but I never liked him. For some reason, he expected Robert to leave him this house, for it was not part of the entail, and he was most put out when he discovered it had been left to me. Whenever he visited us during that dreadful time of Robert's illness, one could see the gleam of calculation in his eyes, so the contents of Robert's will must have come as quite a shock to him." She sighed. "One would think, since Reginald always seemed to have more money than any younger son ought to have, that he would have been glad to have seen me provided for, but he resented it quite as much as he resented your papa's coming into the title and estate."

Nell frowned. "Did he resent Papa? I know Jarvis has long thought it wrong that Papa and now Nigel—both so extravagant—should hold the reins at Highgate, but I thought Reginald doted on Papa. They were always together, you know, for the few years separating their ages made them more like brothers than uncle and nephew. If there was resentment, surely it can have been only on Jarvis' part. He makes no secret of the fact that he disliked Papa and believes Highgate ought to have been his."

"Like father, like son," Lady Flavia said firmly. "Fate is capricious, is it not? To begin, there were three brothers, who by rights ought to have had long lives and dozens of children. Instead, dearest Robert, the eldest, died first, childless. Then the estate passed to your grandfather, who had only the one son—your father, Jasper. The third brother, Reginald, born a mere nine years before your father, produced only Jarvis."

"But where did Reginald get his money?" Nell demanded. "He was always very well to pass, you know."

"I am sure I cannot say," Lady Flavia replied. "He married well, of course, for that is how he got Crosshill, so one must suppose that his wife's fortune was larger than one was led to believe at the time, or else invested wisely. But money, you know, my dear, is not the same as land. And the Bradbourne barony is a very old and respected one. To be Lord Bradbourne of Highgate is no small thing for a man to covet."

Nell grimaced. "But why must Jarvis covet me as well? He does, you know, though he couched it in saintly terms, murmuring in a hushed tone that he had buried two wives already and never really believed he should brave the married state again."

"Don't tease yourself over that. Died in childbed, the pair of them, and the babes with them. Indeed, I should not be at all amazed if Jarvis don't fancy himself another Henry the Eighth."

Nell stared. "Henry the Eighth?"

"He had six, did he not—wives? And only to get a son. If Catherine of Aragon had given him one, that would have been that. Not that he would not have enjoyed himself with Anne Boleyn all the same, but men will be men, after all, and kings even more so, no doubt. No one would have objected very much."

Nell believed herself to be generally quick-witted, but there were times when her great-aunt left her standing, when it took her a moment to catch up. Now, though she would have liked to avoid the tangent altogether, she found herself saying, "But his third wife gave him a son, and he still married three more."

"But she died, my dear, and the boy was feeble. And the next was Cat Howard—not at all suitable. She played him false, which he ought to have expected, for he was getting on by then, but men, you know, always believe themselves up to every—"

"Aunt Flavia," Nell said firmly, "whatever can Henry the Eighth's wives have to do with the point at hand?"

"Why, sons, Nell, to inherit. I thought you understood."

There was a moment of silence before Nell said, "Do you

mean to say that Cousin Jarvis wants to marry me only for the purpose of begetting sons? But surely any female of age and not utterly stricken in years would serve his purpose if that were the case."

"Highgate is still the case, I believe."

"But Nigel owns Highate," Nell protested. "Perhaps I did not make the matter clear when I explained it—indeed, it is all very confusing—but even though Papa lost the wager he made with Reginald, Jarvis made only the one attempt after Reginald's accident to claim Highgate. Then, after the duel, when Nigel was forced to flee the country, he said no more about it."

"He will, my dear. Nigel is on the Continent, after all, and may even be dead by now, for all you know. He does not write to you, does he?"

"No, but—"

"So few men do," Lady Flavia said with a sigh.

"He is still the owner of Highgate."

"If he should be found guilty of murder, he won't be," Lady Flavia said tartly, "and that is precisely what will happen if he has to stand his trial. It may become a matter for Parliament in the end—I know little about such things—but Jarvis Bradbourne stands next to inherit the barony, and his position in a court of chancery could only be strengthened if he were married to you. Like Henry the Seventh, that would be."

"No more Tudors," Nell said firmly.

"I meant only that your marriage to Jarvis would unite the two lines, much the same as when the seventh Henry married Elizabeth of York, and of course your son, if you had one—"

"I wouldn't!" Nell exclaimed, revolted. "I would not marry Cousin Jarvis under any circumstances. Even if I liked him, which I do not, he is too old. I mean to marry a man my own age, not one who will precede me into senility by a dozen years. Jarvis simply must be brought to understand as much."

"Men," Lady Flavia said with an air of vast experience, "generally believe themselves to be not only infallible but also irresistible. And, too, you know, he is a greedy man, so one must consider your inheritance."

"But I have none," Nell protested. "Papa meant me to have a proper dowry, of course, and I daresay that once the estate is running properly again there might be enough for a settlement of some sort or other, but—"

"I meant," Lady Flavia interjected patiently, "the fortune that you will inherit from me, or—to put the matter more exactly—the fortune you are *expected* to inherit from me."

"But you said there is no fortune."

"I said nothing of the kind. To be sure, there is not nearly so much as people think, but my capital is intact, and at all events, Jarvis is no more aware of how matters stand with me than you were. Moreover, whatever else he may believe, you can depend upon it that his father will have told him that this house is a property worth owning, for indeed, my dear, it is."

Nell smiled. "No doubt it is, ma'am, but I must tell you that since I never expected to inherit anything from you, I find it impossible to believe that Cousin Jarvis might expect me to do so. As to anyone else's believing it, you must forgive me for telling you to your head that such a notion is absurd. No one could be sufficiently interested even to wonder about it."

"Innocent, that's what you are," Lady Flavia said, shaking her head. "Only think, my dear, how quickly information flies about in a country village like Trowbridge. Then consider Bath."

"I do not know what you mean, ma'am. To be sure, at home, folk talk about their neighbors, but what else is there to talk about? And what can Bath know of me? 'Tis a very sleepy town, for all that it was used to be so fashionable. I know there are assemblies and concerts, and I should love to have the money to indulge myself in a visit to the shops in Milsom Street, for we have nothing like them at home, but that people should care—"

"That is just the point," Lady Flavia said. "In Bath people live for gossip. No entertainment at the Pump Room or the Assembly Rooms can ever be as interesting as what one's neighbor is doing, or means to do, or has had done to him. If, on any given day, there is not adequate grist for the rumor mill, people have been known to make things up, a fact that irritated the great Beau Nash fifty years ago, and would no doubt still irritate him today. Thankfully, with such a wealth of gossip as there is, such tactics are rarely necessary.''

Sighing, Nell said, ''I do not doubt that what you say is true, ma'am, but it does not change my mind about what I must do. If I were a man, I would be working to prove Nigel innocent of the charge against him. Instead, as you say, I have run away from prattling tongues, knowing looks, and Jarvis, hoping to find sanctuary in Bath. If I cannot do that, at least I will not allow myself to become a burden upon you, and perhaps in time I will yet discover the truth about both Papa and Nigel.''

''The truth is already known,'' Lady Flavia said in a gentler tone than any she had used before, ''and you do no good, child, by deluding yourself to think otherwise. In Nigel's case, there were witnesses, were there not? Indeed, there must have been.''

''All but Cousin Jarvis supposedly as drunk as Nigel,'' Nell said bitterly. ''And what with Jarvis' having been the only reliable witness . . .'' She shrugged and fell silent.

'' 'Tis as I said, then,'' Lady Flavia declared, ''and a pity it is that he was not the victim instead of that Mr. Bygrave, for no one would have caviled at that, and there would then have been no witness, so Nigel might have gone tamely home again. As it is, you can do nothing about his difficulty. Indeed, even if there might be more to the matter than we know,
Nigel brought it on himself, for he is no pattern card, my dear, as well you know. And to be grieving over his problems, instead of looking after yourself is quite foolish. You would be a great deal more sensible to be thinking of marriage.''

''Marriage! But I told you I would not even think—''

''Oh, not to Jarvis, for pity's sake. And Bath, of course, is not precisely as full as it can be of eligible young men,'' she added, "though I suppose there must be some."

"It cannot matter if there are," Nell said, staring at her. "There is no possible way that—"

"Oh, but there is always a way, my dear," Lady Flavia said placidly. "Now, hush and let me think."

"But, Aunt—"

"Hush, I said. This may take a moment or two." And with that, the old lady leaned back in her chair and closed her eyes.

Watching her, Nell was torn between equally strong urges to laugh and to cry. Certain that her aunt had, after the fashion of the elderly, merely decided to take a nap without admitting the need for one, she exerted herself to control both urges and turned to stare out of the window again instead.

A broad ray of sunlight had broken through the clouds, gilding the pale yellow Bath stone from which the houses were built, and making sparkles dance in the puddles dotting the quiet street. The sight was a pretty one, but Nell found little satisfaction in it, feeling irritation instead when the peaceful silence outside was broken by the clatter of iron-shod hooves and carriage wheels on the wet cobbles as a small brown post chaise, picked out in red and drawn by a pair of bay horses, rattled toward her from the north end of Great Pulteney Street.

# 2

The clatter had disturbed one of the three dozing occupants of the post chaise sufficiently to make him push his curly-brimmed beaver hat up off his eyes and peer out of the window, squinting against the glare of sunlight on the wet pavement.

"Yeller houses," the Honorable Joseph Lasenby muttered thoughtfully to himself before the information, slowly processed by his awakening brain, brought him to a startling conclusion. "By Jove, Bran," he said in a louder tone, looking past the gentleman gently snoring beside him to the opposite side of the street, and finding no cause in what he saw there to alter his reasoning, "I believe we've come to Bath! Dash it all, wasn't it Bath where Halstead said you'd find that heiress, the one you said you'd be damned if you'd abduct, wager or no wager? Here, wake up! No, not you," he added with dismay when the large toffee-colored hound taking up most of the floor space stirred and raised its head from his once highly polished boot, gathering itself as though it meant to get up. "Down, sir! Down, I say." The hound sighed and dropped its head again to the booted foot.

Freeing his elbow sufficiently to gain some leverage in the close confines of the chaise, Mr. Lasenby jabbed the gentleman sprawled beside him. "I say, Bran, do wake up." He jabbed again. "There must be some sort of mistake. Tell the lad!"

Brandon Manningford grunted and tried to evade the annoying elbow, but Mr. Lasenby being determined to wake him and the chaise being entirely too small to allow him to move out of reach, it was not long before he opened his hazel eyes and gazed irritably at the other young man. "What the devil do you mean by jabbing a fellow, Sep? You'd be sorry if I retaliated in kind.''

"Dashed right," Mr. Lasenby replied placidly. "You're bigger than I am. Stronger, too, and you might take it into your head to call in all my vouchers—not that that would do you a lick of good. But look here, we're in Bath, I tell you.''

Mr. Manningford continued to regard him with displeasure. "So? What if we are?''

"Dash it all, man, Miss Wembly might accuse me of having the worst memory in all England, but you ain't the one cursed with a grandfather plaguing you to marry money, and I remember plain as day that you said you'd no interest in heiresses!''

"That is not at all what I said," Mr. Manningford informed him testily. "I said I'd be damned if I'd abduct one merely to win another wager with Halstead.''

"Nothing mere about four thousand, Bran! Dash it, I'd know what to do with it. And it ain't as though abducting an heiress is beyond your line. 'Tain't nearly so bad as some things you've done. Why, you once rode a bear into a dinner party, and another time, you put that same bear to bed with a total stranger. And how about the time you told that fellow you was going to pay him some ridiculous sum for a horse he wanted to sell you, and that all he had to do was to take your note of hand to a certain banker? That poor toad ended in Bedlam or some suchlike place.''

"You never get that tale right," Manningford complained, straightening in his seat and rubbing the place where a crease in his heavily starched neckcloth had irritated his throat. His hat had long since fallen to the floor, and as he bent to rescue it, he patted the dog's head, adding, "Fellow tried to cheat me, so I gave him a note to a banker who happened to be guardian for a nearby insane asylum. Is it my fault the coper assumed the note requested payment when instead it said, 'Admit bearer to your asylum'? Served him right. But, Sep, that prank and the others with Old Nolly are buried in my misspent youth, and at my worst, I never abducted an heiress. Ill-bred thing to do, that is, not to mention its being a hanging offense. You surprise me.''

"Why?" Mr. Lasenby demanded. "The wager was Halstead's notion, not mine. I thought the idea bacon-brained from the start, even if she is as rich as Croesus. Not that I've the least notion how rich that might be," he added thoughtfully. "Didn't know Croesus, did I?"

"I don't suppose you did, or you'd have borrowed money from him," his friend retorted. "But forget the heiress, will you? If you will exert that feeble brain of yours, you will recollect that Bath is also where my esteemed father resides."

"So he does," Mr. Lasenby acknowledged, much struck. Thenm, after another, visible mental struggle, he added, "You said years ago you didn't mean to ask him for another groat, so I still can't think why we've come to Bath unless you changed your mind about that heiress. Not that you could pull it off, of course."

Manningford smiled, but the expression altered to a sharp wince when one wheel of the chaise struck a hole in the road. He looked out the window to see that they had passed from Laura Place into Argyle Street and were approaching Pulteney Bridge.

Spanning the River Avon and built end to end with small shops, the three-arched span was the only work in Bath by Robert Adam, once England's leading architect, but just then Manningford remembered only that it was too narrow and was glad there was no traffic. As the chaise lurched over another hole, he pressed a hand against his aching head. "Blast. My brain feels like someone's got loose inside with a hammer and anvil."

"You drank the devil of a lot of brandy last night," Mr. Lasenby pointed out. "Ought to have stuck with the port, just as you ought to have stuck to faro instcad of turning to the wheel. It ain't never been lucky for you, Bran." Regarding Manningford curiously, he added, "You lost the devil of a lot of money last night. Dash it, after all you've lent to me, it must be low tide with you. You sure it ain't going to be the heiress?"

"I'm sure," Manningford said with a sigh. "I'm too old, Sep, and I hope I have gained sufficient wisdom with the years not to back myself anymore to win idiotic wagers."

Mr. Lasenby looked doubtful. "You ain't so old as all that,

Bran. Same as me, ain't you? Though you'll turn twenty-nine in December, as I recall. Don't hardly make us gray-beards.''

Manningford shrugged. "Boredom ages a man, Sep. I fear I've become a sober citizen, tired of pranks and nonsense.''

"Certainly you have." Mr. Lasenby looked pointedly at the hound on the floor. "Perhaps the fact escaped you, but it has not before now been my habit to travel with damp canines in my post chaise. On the hunting field, I'll grant you, or when one goes out shooting, one may without censure be accompanied by one's dog, but not in one's town chaise, my lad. Certainly not in a small enclosed post chaise. Even Poodle Byng would scorn to do such a thing. You mightn't have noticed it, Bran, but your friend there carries a certain odor with him—no doubt we do too, by now—and not one that will add to our welcome, wherever we're bound. Not that I wish to complain, mind you, but—''

"Peace, Sep." Manningford grinned at him. "The poor old fellow stinks like a polecat, but he can't help it any more than he could stop the rain when we let him out to do his business. He's the only thing I won last night that I didn't manage to lose again, and I did not hear you make any suggestions about what I was to do with him if he didn't come with us.''

"Well, you're wrong there," Mr. Lasenby said. "Miss Wembly was quite right about my lamentable memory, but I distinctly—''

"No acceptable suggestions," Manningford retorted, laughing.

"Perhaps not, but if you think I mean to sit here and listen to you telling me what an old sobersides you've become, when you just won that beast on the most ridiculous wager—''

"Fustian. Nothing ridiculous about it. If I'd lost, I'd have had to stand Halstead to a dinner at the Drake in Reading, where they pad the reckoning with every crumb and scrap they can. Likely I'd have ended franking the place for a fortnight. Still, the odds must be shockingly against tossing a pack of cards into the air and having every single card land facedown. I couldn't have known I'd win the best hunting dog in all England, could I?''

Mr. Lasenby shook his head sadly. ''Bran, old fellow, if you think Halstead would stake an even passably decent dog against one dinner, no matter what the odds were, you must be all about in your head. Why, the wine at the Drake is only tolerable, and the caper sauce they served the only time I ever dined there was a joke. That's a fact, Bran.''

Manningford shrugged. ''I like him. Here, fellow,'' he added, holding his hand out to the dog. Raising its head again and looking over its shoulder, the dog politely sniffed the hand and, evidently finding it pleasing, pushed its nose against it. Manningford grinned. ''Good lad. I say, Sep, do you happen to remember by what name Halstead called him?''

''Haven't a notion,'' Mr. Lasenby replied, gazing with disfavor at the dog. ''Knowing Halstead, I should think it would have been something ridiculous, like King or Duke or Chief, don't you? That man's got feathers in his cockloft.''

''Or Prince,'' Manningford said, ignoring the rider. He eyed the dog skeptically. ''He doesn't respond to any of those names.''

''Probably got more sense than Halstead,'' Mr. Lasenby said. ''How about Stinker or Duffer or Tramp?''

The dog put its head down on its paws again.

''There, now, look at that,'' Manningford said reprovingly. ''You've hurt his feelings.''

''Well, if you expect me to apologize, you're fair and far out, for I shan't do any such thing. I've told you what I'd name him if he were mine.'' A shudder crossed Mr. Lasenby's cherubic face at the thought, and he glanced out the nearside window again. They were passing a portion of the city's medieval wall, and when the chaise emerged just then into the opening known as the Saw Close, Mr. Lasenby found himself facing a carved wooden plaque informing passersby that the house it adorned had belonged to Beau Nash, that once-great arbiter of social life in the city of Bath. ''I say, Bran, is it true that Nash's mistress spent the rest of her life sleeping in a tree after his death?''

"Good Lord, Sep, how should I know?"

"Well, you lived here, after all."

"Not then I didn't. Good Lord, he died half a century ago! I do know her name, though," he added with a smile. "Popjoy, it was—Juliana Popjoy. An appropriate name for a mistress."

Mr. Lasenby chuckled, and silence fell between them until the chaise had passed by the beautiful central garden of Queen Square and made its way up Gay Street to the Circus, which, inspired by the Roman Coloseum, had been designed by John Wood the Elder and built by his son in three curved segments so that at each of the three approaches one was met by a sweeping three-tiered facade of columns. The chaise rattled across the cobbled circular central area and turned west onto the steep incline of Brock Street, slowing noticeably.

"Only a short distance now," Manningford said.

"Steep street, this one," Mr. Lasenby observed, shifting his legs away from the dog's pressing weight. "Makes one feel some sympathy for the horses."

"Save it for the chairmen we'll hire if ever we come up on a rainy day," Manningford told him. "One rarely employs a carriage in Bath, and chairmen charge extra to carry one up this hill. But only wait until you see the view from up top."

A few minutes later, when the chaise drew to a halt before the Royal Crescent, crowning the hilltop, Mr. Lasenby agreed that the view was all that had been promised. The city lay behind and below them to the east, while away to the south, under billowing clouds, beyond well-tended grasslands, all the way to the horizon, lay green fields dotted with sheep and parkland lush with trees.

Mr. Lasenby raised his quizzing glass. "Sheep?"

"A ha-ha runs across the grassland there to prevent them from straying this far," Manningford said. He glanced at the door in front of which the chaise had halted. "Doesn't appear that our arrival has been noticed. I hope Father hasn't turned off all the servants again."

"What?" Mr. Lasenby looked dismayed. "Turned them off! Why would he do a fool thing like that?"

Manningford, pushing open the door of the chaise, looked back and shrugged. "He does that sort of thing. No, dog, you wait until I see what's what." He stepped down and said to the postboy, "Someone will come out to get our things and the dog. Then you can take the chaise round back to the stables, where you'll find a bite to eat and a place to spend the night if you don't have to get the horses back today."

Shaking beads of water from his yellow oilskins, the postboy, who was in fact a small weather-beaten, middle-aged man, nodded and reached to take the money Manningford held out to him. "Right you are, sir. I'll have my sup and be getting straight back, if it's all the same to you."

Mr. Lasenby, having followed Manningford to the flagway after carefully shutting the protesting hound inside the chaise, paused now to savor the full impact of the semielliptical five-hundred-foot sweep of thirty houses joined in a single facade designed simply at ground level, elaborately above. "I say, Bran, are these houses all the same inside too?"

"Not at all. In point of fact, if you were to step round to the far end there, by the Marlborough Buildings, and have a look at the backside, you'd see what a sham all this frontage is. From behind it looks like any street of houses in London, growing together cheek by jowl but all different sizes and all in a scramble." Noting that the dog had continued to voice its disapproval of being left in the chaise, he glanced at it and said, "Silence, dog. I wonder what I shall do with you. Here, Sep, stop gaping about and come inside. I must find someone to deal with all this." Extracting a key from his waistcoat pocket, he strode up the stone steps to the white-painted front door.

"Look here," Mr. Lasenby said behind him. "Perhaps we ought to put up at an inn instead. If your father has no servants, we'll be a dashed nuisance to him."

"No, we won't. We needn't even see him." Manningford pushed the door open, revealing a small high-ceilinged entrance hall and, beyond an elaborately framed white arch, a curved stair with a dark wood railing. Two doors stood at right angles to the archway, both white and framed to match. Both doors were closed.

"Porter's chair, but no porter," Mr. Lasenby observed in disapproval, looking around. "Marble walls?"

Manningford shut the front door. "Painted with feathers and twigs to look like marble," he said. "Fashionable forty or fifty years ago, and probably not painted since. That stairway is not stone, either. Only looks like it, and the floor here is wood, not flagstone. Come up to the library, Sep. You'll be more comfortable there while I see if anyone is about."

"What's behind those two doors?" Mr. Lasenby asked as Manningford strode through the archway ahead of him.

"Saloon to the right and dining room to the left," he said. "If anyone is here, they will be upstairs. Come on."

But Mr. Lasenby hesitated. "Look here, Bran, what do you mean we needn't see your father? I've heard tales about the man, but discounted most of them."

"You'd have done better to believe them, Sep."

"What, that he don't see anyone? That he ain't set foot out of this house in thirty years?"

"Not thirty, only twenty-five. You should feel honored, Sep. You are the first guest I've ever brought to stay here."

"But surely you see him!"

"I wouldn't recognize him if I were to meet him coming down these stairs," Manningford said grimly.

"You're bamming me."

"No. He sees only one man, his personal manservant, and how Borland has put up with him all these years, I'll never know."

Mr. Lasenby chuckled. "Perhaps this Borland murdered him years ago and has merely been having you on ever since."

Manningford glanced back over his shoulder. "Don't think that hasn't been suggested by others before you, Sep, but I exaggerated the case. My sister Sybilla—the one married to the Marquess of Axbridge—has pushed her way in to see him once or twice, counting the cost afterward, and my brother, Charlie, sees him once a year. I don't see him at all."

"But did you never try? I should have thought—"

"Only once, when I was nine, but I got no further than the door to his study. He ordered Borland to thrash me for daring to disturb him, and though the punishment was light, I never made another attempt." At the top of the stair he crossed the landing to throw open a pair of double doors, revealing a spacious book-lined room decorated in shades of peach and trimmed with white molding. "The library, Sep, and Madeira or some such thing in the decanter over there. Help yourself while I see what I can discover."

Waiting only until Mr. Lasenby had removed the stopper, sniffed, and begun to pour wine into one of the glasses set beside the decanter, Manningford shut the doors and turned to a second flight of stairs, narrower than the first, leading to the top floor. In most houses in the crescent, the top-floor rooms were allotted to servants. Here, the entire floor had been taken over by Sir Mortimer and his man.

Manningford paused on the upper landing to run a finger inside his neckcloth, rubbing the area that had been chafed in the carriage. Then, absently smoothing a crease, he stood for a moment longer, regarding the closed door opposite the head of the stairs. A narrow corridor led away from the landing on each side, but he felt no inclination to explore either passage. His attention was riveted on the room directly before him, but he felt no fear and little curiosity. Whatever feelings he had had as a child had long since faded, and the man who spent most of his hours in that room stirred interest in him now only as the chief source of the funds he required to live as a gentleman.

He drew a deep breath, stepped forward, and raised his hand to knock, but before he could do so, a door in the right-hand corridor opened and a barrel-shaped man in his late fifties, wearing a dark coat and breeches, emerged from the room, his right index finger pressed firmly to his lips. Shutting the door behind him, he stepped quicky to the landing and murmured in a tone so low that Manningford had to strain to hear him, "Come back downstairs with me, sir, if you please."

Turning to follow him, Manningford muttered back, "I've

put a friend in the library, Borland. Where are the other servants?''

"Gone, sir, most of them. We'd best use the drawing room if you've put him in the library. Saw you from the window, I did, but couldn't get away till now without him getting suspicious, and fair popped my ears trying to hear you come up them stairs so's I could tell you what's happened before you see the master.''

"See him?''

"Yes, sir. I didn't know where to send word to you, and what with Lady Axbridge and the marquess visiting in France, and Lady Symonds being in Scotland with Sir Harry and the children, and what with him saying he don't want to be plagued by Mr. Charles telling him what Mrs. Charles thinks he ought to be doing about everything, well, I—''

"Never mind all that,'' Manningford said in a normal tone as he reached the lower landing and turned to the right. "What can my brother or my sisters, let alone their respective spouses—or myself, for that matter—have to do with anything here?''

"Sir Mortimer's ill, Mr. Brandon.'' His voice, now that he, too, spoke normally, was harsh, but his manner was gentle.

"How ill?'' Opening the door to the drawing room, Manningford stepped inside, and when Borland did not answer at once, he turned and said curtly, "Is he going to die?''

The manservant gave him a direct look. "Would it distress you if he did, sir?''

"I don't know him. How could it distress me?'' On the chimneypiece in the center of the west wall hung a painting of his mother, and he glanced at it now. "My father left us when she died,'' he said, allowing his gaze to linger on the pretty woman in wide red skirts and narrow bodice, her hair powdered and piled atop her head, her right hand emerging from a flow of frothy lace to caress the slender black-and-white dog curled in her lap. "He never left the house, Borland, but he left my brother and sisters and me when I had scarcely turned three. I wish I could believe he did so out of grief at her loss, but I have never had reason to believe he cared for anyone.''

Borland nodded. "I know that, sir. A hard man to know, is the master, and a harder man to love. I, who have served him these thirty-five years and more, can say so without hesitation. Still, he needs you now."

"Me? I think not. I am here only because I've let boredom, generosity, and my old devil, impulse, carry me to a point I swore seven years ago I'd never reach again. The loans are still out, the luck's still against me, and though I'd hoped to recoup my losses last night, I only made things worse. So, since it's little more than a fortnight to quarter-day, and since I haven't come a-begging in all those seven years, I thought—"

"He won't do it, sir," the manservant said grimly, "and 'tis sorry I am to hear you're in straits, for 'twill give him the sort of edge he best likes to have over his opponents."

"Edge? Opponents?" Manningford glared at him. "What the devil are you talking about?"

"He needs help, Mr. Brandon. He has *asked* to see you."

"Then he knows I'm here?"

"No, but I promised to send for you just as soon as I got word of where to send, and he's been that impatient. Every morning he wants to know did I find you yet. I'd have taken you into his study to talk, but he'd be bound to hear us there, and then the fat would be in the fire."

"How so?"

"Shout for me to bring you to him straightaway, he would, and if you refused, the good Lord only knows what would come of it, for it won't do for the master to be losing his temper."

"You afraid he'd turn you off with the rest?"

"I wouldn't go, sir, but I don't deny I fear his rages right enough. 'Twas one of them put him where he is now, which is to say flat on his back in his bed. Another such could carry him right off and aloft, the doctor did say."

"He's seen a doctor? You astonish me."

"Found unconscious on the floor, he was, sir, three days ago. I had been to the receiving office and back, and had to go out again almost directly, and while I was gone, one of the maids heard a terrible crash and rushed into the study to find him lying on the floor, unconscious and looking ever so queer, she said. She set up a screech, of course, and Mrs. Hammersmythe sent for the doctor, not knowing what else to do and fearing he might die. He awakened after they had got him into his bed, and was right furious, of course, that so many persons had dared to enter his rooms. Turned the lot of them off, he did, before ever I had returned, even the Hammersmyths, who've been here as long as I have myself, and how we shall find another housekeeper and butler as capable as what they was, I'm sure I do not know, and so I told him, but I might as well have talked to a fencepost.''

Brandon grimaced. "Something must be done about that."

"Said they won't come back, sir, not if Lady Axbridge were to ask them, but I do think they ought to get their pension."

"What, he cut them off?"

"Turned them all out without a character. A shame it was, and so I told him, but there, I told you the good that did.''

"Well, I don't know what you think I can do about it. If Sybilla were here, she might be able to manage him a little, and she would certainly provide references for the servants who need them, but until she returns from the Continent, I don't see what can be done. I certainly can't write characters for them. A lot of good it would do if I tried. Perhaps Mrs. Charles would—''

"People would shake their heads at any testimonial for a position in Bath what came from a lady living thirty miles away, sir, and she hasn't even met one of the chambermaids who left."

"Well, I'm sorry, then, but I can't think what you expect me to do. Good Lord," he added as a new thought struck him, "Don't tell me we haven't got a cook!"

Borland shook his head. "Cook is still here, sir, and the scullery maid. They don't never leave the kitchen, so I took the liberty of telling her she weren't included in the order, and she agreed to stay, though it was a near-run thing, she being right friendly with the Hammersmyths. If you don't mind waiting until I get Sir Mortimer settled for the night before having your dinner, I'll serve you myself. But you must see him, sir.''

"Very well, I suppose I must, but don't expect any good to come of it. I mean to ask him for that advance, you know, and he is likely to rant at me when I do so, just as he always ranted at you when you served as my envoy."

"You won't get it, sir, but you've only to stay here, after all, at least till quarter-day, and I'll have new servants hired in a pig's whisper, so you'll be comfortable enough."

"But I don't want to spend a fortnight in Bath."

"See him, sir. Let him tell you what he wants of you."

"You tell me."

"I've promised him I won't do that."

"Do it anyway."

Borland smiled. "No, sir. I'm Sir Mortimer's man."

"Very well, then, damn your eyes. Take me to him."

At the door to Sir Mortimer's bedchamber, Borland paused, looking at Manningford as if to give him time to collect himself.

Manningford merely nodded, whereupon the door was opened, revealing a bedchamber decorated in the French manner, with tall aqua-satin-draped windows overlooking the rolling green hills and fields to the south. The walls were hung with blue-and-white-striped cotton, repeating the colors in the floral Aubusson carpet, but the chief article of furniture, the one that promptly drew his attention, was the wide bed with its blue-silk spread and ornately painted headboard and footboard. But it was not the bed itself that interested him, so much as its occupant.

Propped up against thick pillows, his craggy face pale with illness, Sir Mortimer, in a white nightshirt and a cap from beneath which his gray hair hung limply, glared at them with startlingly blue eyes hooded by heavy lids, looking not the least bit pleased to see his younger son. "Wondered where you'd run off to, Borland," he grumbled, his voice weak, his words slurred, as though he had drunk too much wine.

"I've brought Mr. Brandon to you, sir."

"So I see," he replied testily. "Get me some water, man. I'm parched."

Borland hurried to the side of the room, where a ewer and basin sat on a mahogany side table. Pouring water into a glass, he hurried back to the bedside. The old man made no attempt to take it from him, and the manservant held it to his lips so that he might drink.

When he had done so, Sir Mortimer turned his head away from the glass and glared again at his son. "Well, you see why I sent for you. What have you got to say for yourself?"

"I'm sorry you are ill," Manningford said, "but I don't see what it has to do with me. I came up because Borland insisted and because I hoped you might see your way clear to advance me my next quarter's allowance at once. 'Tis only a fortnight, after all, before it's due, and I've had some unexpected expenses."

"Have you now? Thought you'd learned the futility of trying to hang on my sleeve. I suppose it's because Axbridge is out of reach, since Symonds never has a groat he don't need himself, and Clarissa keeps Charlie firmly under her fat thumb. Well, you've dipped your bucket into a dry well, coming to see me."

Having expected the old man to leap into a rage, Manningford was encouraged rather than daunted by his reply. Seeing no good to be gained by denying that he had made any attempt to borrow money from his other relatives, he drew up a chair next to the bed and said calmly, "I don't suppose you mean that you've lost all your wealth, sir, so perhaps you will be good enough to explain to me what you do mean."

"Where do you suppose I get my wealth, sir?"

Taken aback, Manningford replied, "I don't know. No one ever thought to tell me, and I never thought to ask."

"Just came round with your hand held out."

"I suppose I thought it came from your estate at Westerleigh," Manningford said calmly.

"All that's been turned over to Charles long since. I've kept only my private fortune, augmented by certain investments I've made, but the main source no one would guess if he were to speculate from now till the millennium."

"Then I shan't try. Do you mean to tell me?"

"I never meant to do so—never thought it would be necessary—but the case is altered now. My right hand's of no use to me since the fool seizure, but Borland has all he can do to look after me, and I refuse to have my privacy invaded by an outsider, so you are the logical answer to my problem.''

"I suppose you mean for me to manage your investments," Manningford said, "but I know nothing about such things. You would do better to hire a proper man of affairs.''

"The investments are part of it, certainly," the old man snapped, "and since, if you behave yourself, you stand to inherit this house and a tidy fortune when I'm spent, you'll do well to learn how to keep it all and not give me a lot of backchat. I'll see to it you get a proper power of attorney, but that ain't even the heart of the matter. There's still the novel.''

"What novel?''

Sir Mortimer's glare faltered, and he looked away, saying gruffly, "That's what I've been doing this past quarter-century. I write books.''

"Good God, sir, what sort of books?''

"Popular ones, damn your eyes! Gothic romances. And you needn't poker up like that. You've been willing enough to take the profit, damn you; the time has come to do some of the work.''

Twenty minutes later, fiercely indignant and hoarse from arguing, Manningford stormed down the stairs and into the library, startling Mr. Lasenby so much that he spilled his wine.

"By Jove, Bran, look at that! My best waistcoat!''

"I don't give a damn, Sep. We're leaving Bath. But before we go, we're going to abduct ourselves an heiress!''

# 3

By the following morning the last of the rain clouds had departed and the sun shone brightly as Nell walked along the path near the bowling green behind the Sydney Gardens Hotel. There were no bowlers to be seen just then, for the peaceful gardens were nearly empty of people. The air smelled fresh and clean, and the birds sang cheerfully, their songs combining in a chorus from the shrubs and trees lining the smooth, well-raked gravel path, but the only other sound was the crunch of Nell's sensibly shod feet as she walked.

Her great-aunt, having entrusted her with the subscription card that served as a ticket of admission to the gardens, had told her that a significant part of the social round in Bath included a daily stroll along the gardens' paths and promenades, where to be recognized and to be bowed to was confirmation of one's approval by Bath society. For this purpose, however, Lady Flavia had pointed out in her acerbic way as Nell placed the card carefully in her bulky knitted reticule, it was generally considered an advantage to be strolling at a time when there were other strollers about. Nevertheless, in Nell's own opinion, since her primary purpose in visiting the gardens had been to think matters out for herself, her timing was excellent.

Ahead of her, to her right, was a pair of tennis courts, but they too were empty, and she wandered on, adjusting the strings of the unwieldy reticule over her arm and wondering what she ought to do about her future. Remaining with her great-aunt was clearly ineligible unless she could think of a way to contribute to the expenses of the household. And since Aunt Flavia objected strenuously to any plan put forth with regard to Nell's possible employment, she could think of no way to accomplish that end.

She was not, she realized forlornly, much suited to employment anyway. She had been given an adequate education, but she did not think anyone of sense would hire her as a governess, nor did she imagine for a moment that she would enjoy such a position. That was the rub, that she did not, in all honesty, think she would enjoy a menial position, for the simple reason that her temperament was more determined in nature than most employers would tolerate in a dependent. She smiled, remembering her brother Nigel's description of her.

"But I am not obstinate," she informed a scampering squirrel that paused to look at her, sitting back on its haunches, nose atwitch. "Really, I am not. A bit willful at times, I suppose, perhaps even a trifle recalcitrant when I think someone is attempting to take advantage of me, but I should prefer to think of myself as resolute, persevering, or tenacious, rather than just tiresomely stubborn."

It was a game of hers, to think of words, to play with them in her mind, to find exactly the right one to suit the moment. Reading had been her chief joy for many years, and she had also enjoyed writing little tales for her own amusement, but since neither interest could provide her with employment, when the squirrel dashed on, disappearing through a shady grotto into what appeared to be a vast hedged labyrinth beyond, she drew her mind inexorably back to the problem at hand, ignoring a strong temptation to fling her cares aside and follow the squirrel, to explore the labyrinth to her heart's content.

The enormous maze was not the only distraction the gardens offered, for they had been designed in imitation of the famous Vauxhall Gardens in London, with artificial waterfalls, grottoes, thatched pavilions, and even a sham castle with cannon. Ahead of her now, built over a section of the Kennet and Avon canal, diverted to flow through the gardens, was an iron bridge in the Chinese style. She approached it, mentally sorting through a list of genteel occupations, discarding one after another.

Her great-aunt would suffer an apoplectic fit, she was sure, should she apprentice herself to a milliner or a modiste, or try to find a position as a lowly shopgirl. And Lady Flavia would approve even less of anything that smacked of Nell's reducing herself to the servant class. About the one thing she could imagine that might possibly find acceptance in the old lady's eyes was hiring herself out as lady companion to some elderly, albeit not impoverished, gentlewoman.

Stepping onto the bridge, Nell paused a moment in its center to look down at the clear water flowing beneath it, and sighed at the thought of spending her future days at the beck and call of an imperious employer, who would no doubt demand that she fetch and carry and listen to all manner of megrims and complaints. And what if the employer were sickly or, worse, a hypochondriac? Her recent history made it impossible to imagine herself fortunate enough to find employment with a paragon.

On the other side of the bridge the gravel path wound south to follow the canal for a time, and she suppressed her cheerless thoughts for a few moments to enjoy the sight of a sextet of baby ducks who, under the watchful eye of their dignified mother, floating nearby, were flinging themselves from a low rock near the shore into the water, then swimming back, and with their wings aflap, clambering up the rock again to repeat the action with the same gleeful abandon that children might have shown.

Smiling, Nell wandered on, following the path along the canal, stopping briefly to admire a swing wide enough for two people to sit upon. A few yards beyond, the canal disappeared into an underground tunnel, and the path, crossing over it again, joined the hard-packed earthen ride that encircled the gardens, where horsemen exercised their steeds early each morning and others rode to be seen in the late afternoon. Shortly after that she came within sight of the labyrinth again and realized that she had made her way around a full half of the gardens.

The labyrinth at this point appeared to be divided by the ride, with a portion continuing into the shrubbery between the ride and the high wrought-iron fence that separated the gardens from the Sydney Road. She could hear carriage traffic from the road. Indeed, it sounded surprisingly nearer than that.

With something of a start, she realized as she came to the place where the ride passed between the two sections of the labyrinth, traffic was nearer than she had thought possible—for surely carriages were not allowed within the gardens themselves. Yet approaching now from the direction of the main gate was a crane-necked phaeton of the sort the bloods called a high flier, rattling along at speed behind a team of powerful-looking perfectly matched bays.

Nell hitched her reticule more securely onto her arm and drew well aside, for the ride was not intended to accommodate wheeled vehicles or pedestrians—and certainly not both at the same time—and she noted that the single occupant was a well-set-up gentleman with fair hair beneath his high-crowned hat, broad shoulders beneath his well-cut many-caped driving coat, and an irritated expression on his handsome face.

He caught sight of her just then, and his expression lightened as he pulled up his team with a flourish, bringing the carriage to a standstill right beside her. Then, to her complete astonishment, flashing a charming smile, he spoke to her.

"I do hope that you are Miss Bradbourne."

"I am," Nell replied in quelling accents, hoping that gentlemen in Bath did not often accost unknown ladies in public.

He swept his hat from his shining locks and made her a bow. "Sorry to disturb your walk, Miss Bradbourne, but the fact is that I've come here on purpose to find you. There's been—"

"Aunt Flavia," Nell exclaimed, her eyes widening in fright. "Something's happened to Aunt Flavia! Oh, sir, pray tell me."

He looked a trifle disconcerted by her reaction but recovered quickly, saying, "It is nothing dreadful, merely that she asked me to fetch you. I know it is not at all the thing when you do not even know me, but perhaps . . ." His voice trailed off, and he watched her hopefully.

Nell did not hesitate. "Of course I will come with you. Can you give me a hand up? How dreadfully high these carriages are! Oh, sir, what has happened to her?"

He did not answer at once, apparently being too much concerned both with holding his horses and with helping her to ascend to the seat to make explanation. Helping her, in itself, was no easy task, for her skirt was narrow and the step was set high from the ground, intended to accommodate a gentleman, not a lady. At last, however, the deed was done, and Nell discovered that she was not his only passenger when a toffee-colored hound lying on the floor under the seat lifted its head from its paws and gazed curiously at her as she stepped across the gentleman's long legs to take her seat beside him.

"I trust your dog is well-behaved," she said.

"Better than I," he replied. "Hang on!" With that, he whipped up his horses again, and the phaeton sprang forward.

"Oh, sir," Nell cried, "is it not a shorter distance if you turn around and go back to the entrance the way you came?"

"I suppose it is," he replied, "but if you can turn this rig in this narrow ride, you are a better driver than I am, which I take leave to doubt."

She grimaced, saying, "No, of course I could not. 'Twas a foolish thing to say, but I am dreadfully troubled about my aunt, sir. You still have not told me what has happened to her."

"Nor have I introduced myself," he said glibly. "Brandon Manningford, at your service, Miss Bradbourne. You are newly come to Bath, I believe."

"Yes, sir, but though it is pleasant to make your acquaintance, I confess I have no wish to exchange civilities just now. Pray, do tell me about my aunt."

There was more color in his cheeks than she had noticed before when he said, "The situation is not grave, I promise you. Only a slight indisposition. But it frightened her sufficiently that she asked me to go in search of you, and of course I said I would. I can tell you, I was glad to see the gardens were nearly empty, for I had not the least notion what you looked like. As it was, I accosted two other females before you, and nearly a third. Fortunately, I saw that the latter was of such age and countenance as to dismiss any possibility that she might be the Lady Flavia Bradbourne's beautiful niece."

"Her husband was my great-uncle, Mr. Manningford," Nell said, "but I do thank you for your compliment, little though I deserve it."

They were approaching the entrance to the gardens now, and Nell saw that the wiry gatekeeper had opened the gates in order to allow the phaeton to pass through. Manningford raised a hand in thanks, and the gatekeeper saluted him. Once beyond the gates, Manningford negotiated the narrow crescent-shaped entrance road, and emerging into Great Pulteney Street, urged his horses to greater speed before raising his voice above the clatter to say, "You slight yourself, Miss Bradbourne."

"What, in refusing to lay claim to beauty?" She smiled at him, certain he was talking nonsense, trying to take her mind off Lady Flavia until he had delivered her to her side, but she could not let his accusation stand. "I speak no more than truth, sir. Few persons admire carrot-colored hair or the temperament that is thought to accompany it, and while soft curls are desirable, thick wiry ones that tangle like a blackthorne hedge at the least motivation to do so are not. Furthermore, I am much too small for beauty. I know a truly beautiful girl who lives near my home in Trowbridge. She is tall and slender with masses of shining black hair, rosy cheeks, and eyes the color of sapphires."

He shrugged. "I, too, know a woman who looks like that. Have done for a good portion of my life, for that matter, but I cannot say she suits my notion of what is beautiful. She is married, which might account for it, though now that I come to think of it, I never thought her beautiful when we were younger either. A madcap she was then. Sobered up a bit since she married Sydney and saddled them both with a pair of high-spirited children. He is also a friend of mine, Sydney Saint-Denis. They live at Bathwick Hill House."

"I have heard of him," Nell said, flushing when she remembered the context of that particular conversation.

Manningford glanced at her. "Have you, now? And what might you have heard that turns your cheeks the color of ripe cherries, if I may be so bold as to ask?"

Flustered, Nell said quickly, "My great-aunt merely mentioned his Chinese servant . . . that he . . . Oh, dear, you will think me very odd, to be sure, if I do not explain, but it was all so silly. She was talking about mysterious things . . ."

"Aye, Ching Ho might appear to an elderly English lady to be something of a mystery, I suppose," Manningford said, smiling.

He had a delightful smile. The thought startled her and she blurted out, "It was not that precisely. Aunt Flavia was talking about Oriental poisons . . . that is to say, how to lay one's hands upon them, and she thought—"

"Poisons!" Manningford threw his head back and laughed, inadvertently shaking his reins, giving his horses to understand that he desired them to go faster. But his hands were instantly quick and calming. "Here, lads, easy now," he said, struggling to achieve the same control over his voice. "Ching Ho and poisons! That's a good one. Easy, lads."

Nell waited for him to regain control over the team before she said, "It sounds ridiculous, put that way, but she was merely saying that she didn't believe in the mysterious Oriental poisons one reads about in romantic novels and—" She broke off when the laughter disappeared from his face, replaced at once by a grimace of disapproval. "Why, whatever have I said, sir? Oh, heed where we are!" she cried before he had had time to reply, for she had noted that they were passing the fountain in Laura Place, heading into Argyle Street. "That is her house there!"

In response he slowed, but she quickly realized that he did so only because Argyle Street was so much narrower than Great Pulteney Street and because there were other vehicles.

"Is Aunt Flavia not at home, then?" Nell demanded.

"That's it," he said brusquely. "Be still now while we go across the bridge. I cannot think what the designer was about to have made it so narrow. Even in those days, they must have wanted to drive vehicles across it in both directions at once, so why he had to put shops on both sides is a good question, don't you agree? To believe anyone can actually have intended this bridge to be part of his main route to London must be lunacy."

"Is that why Great Pulteney Street is so wide?" Nell asked, diverted. "I wondered about that, since it does not go anywhere in particular. There are those odd side streets too."

"Aye, none longer than about fifty feet. The money ran out before the project could be completed. Good thing, too, if you ask me. This bridge would never have accommodated more traffic than there is now, and all those elegant houses in Laura Place and Sydney Place would have been sneered at by the very folk expected to purchase them, if they had thought they would have to put up with the racket of turnpike traffic all day. Let me concentrate now. It won't do to lock wheels with someone else."

She watched anxiously for a moment, not wanting an accident to delay her in reaching Lady Flavia, but she soon saw that there was no cause for misgiving. As her brother, Nigel, would have put the matter, Manningford drove to an inch. He seemed to do so effortlessly, too, so that she could not imagine why he had expressed concern about other vehicles.

On the other side, they rolled swiftly along Bridge Street and, turning away from the abbey spires into North Gate Street, soon passed a tall church and a bustling marketplace without slowing any more than was necessary once or twice to avert disaster. When they had passed the Paragon Buildings, Nell said anxiously, "Are you certain you are going the right way, Mr. Manningford? My aunt said nothing to me about going out, you know, and while she might have stepped down the street or even so far as one of the shops on Pulteney Bridge without thinking to mention it, I cannot believe she would have come so far as this without telling me she meant to do so. Where are you taking me?"

He glanced at her in a measuring way before he turned his attention back to his horses and said casually, "Well, the fact of the matter is, Miss Bradbourne, that I am abducting you."

Nell gazed at his excellent profile in silence for a long moment before she said calmly, "I see." She shifted her reticule more securely into her lap, fiddling a little with the brightly colored strings that held it shut, saying nothing more.

He glanced at her again, clearly surprised by her calm. "I must say, I expected rather more of a reaction than that."

"I am displeased, certainly," Nell said in a matter-of-fact way, "but not so much as to have lost control of my temper, which is fortunate, since I have been told that one should remain calm in the presence of persons whose senses are clearly disordered."

"I see." To her surprise, there was amusement in his voice. "I am perfectly sane, Miss Bradbourne."

"You will have to pardon me, sir, if I take leave to doubt that statement. I shall not scream, however."

"Be a damned good thing if you don't. That offside wheeler is a mite ticklish, and I'm having all I can do, as it is, to keep his mind on his business. If you scream, we'll most likely have him plunging over the traces. And this sort of carriage, you know, is notoriously unstable."

"I should not wish to court disaster," she agreed. "Indeed, I shall even keep to myself my opinion of a man who would hitch an unsteady team to such a notoriously unstable carriage."

"Wise of you." He shot her an enigmatic look. "I am truly grateful. Particularly since this is not my team, and if even one of these damned brutes is injured, my brother-in-law will doubtless have my head served up to him on a platter the moment he returns from France. He's a marquess, you see, so I don't doubt he'd know instantly how to arrange it."

"Am I to assume," she asked reasonably, "that your brother-in-law would otherwise approve of the use to which you have put this team?"

She saw his lips twitch briefly before they tightened into a thin line and he said, "You're mighty cool for a wench who's just been told she's been abducted. I expected tears and recriminations at the very least. Most young ladies of my acquaintance would show rather more sensibility, I believe."

Nell gave the matter some consideration before she said, "I daresay I am not, in general, a woman of great sensibility, sir, but on the other hand, I must tell you that you are not precisely my notion of an abductor either."

His mobile eyebrows lifted comically. "I hope that does not mean you believe I shall set you down again before my purpose is fulfilled, ma'am, for you are bound to be disappointed."

"Am I? I suppose we shall find that out in good time. Is it permitted that I ask why you have abducted me, sir?"

He glanced at her again, at a loss to understand her. "Why does any man abduct a female?"

"Do you mean to ravish me, then?"

"Good Lord, no! Whatever gave you such a cockeyed notion as that? Do I look like a ravisher?"

"I have already said that you do not even look like an abductor," she reminded him. "It was you who implied that you were doing it for the usual reasons."

"I meant for money," he said harshly. "Your virtue is quite safe, Miss Bradbourne."

"You relieve my mind considerably," she said.

"Well, you don't sound relieved," he retorted. "I take leave to tell you, Miss Bradbourne, that I have known some odd females in my time—'"

"I do not doubt you, sir."

"—and," he continued firmly, "even the oddest of them would have either treated me to a fit of the vapors or lost her temper with me the minute I said I was abducting her. Why, Carolyn Saint-Denis would have tried to scratch my eyes out, or worse, and my sister, Sybilla, would probably have taken her horsewhip to me. But you don't turn a hair."

Nell cocked her head a little to one side, watching him, her right hand still fiddling in an absent way with her reticule. "Perhaps 'tis because they know you better than I do, sir. I have no cause at this present to claw your eyes out and every reason while you attempt to control a mettlesome team in traffic not to do so. As to taking a whip to you, why, you hold the only whip within reach, you know, and I daresay you would not hand it over without some reluctance."

"No, I wouldn't hand it over at all."

"How much is your wager?"

He flicked her another glance. "What makes you think there is a wager?"

"There must be. You said you would get money."

He said in a grim tone through his teeth, "One abducts an heiress in order to marry her, Miss Bradbourne, in order to control her fortune."

Nell was silent.

"Tongue get trapped behind your teeth, ma'am?"

She looked directly at him then and discovered that his eyes were an unusual shade of greenish hazel, set deep beneath his brows. Suddenly more disconcerted than she wished him to know, she turned away again, lifted her chin, and said with forced calm, "I believe that abducting heiresses is an indiscretion upon which persons of refinement do not look lightly, sir. Perhaps it is still done in some circles, but surely here in Bath—"

"An indiscretion, Miss Bradbourne?" Again there was that note of near-laughter in his voice. "You would label such an act as this a mere indiscretion?"

"I think you cannot have thought the matter out clearly," she said. She was thinking rapidly, having dismissed her first inclination, which had been to inform him as quickly as possible that he had much mistaken the matter, that she was no heiress, and then to insist that he restore her to her great-aunt at once. She had barely opened her mouth, however, when she realized she could not so easily betray Lady Flavia. After all, she knew nothing about Mr. Manningford and certainly had no cause to trust him. She would have to deal with him in a less diplomatic way.

They had turned onto the London Road, and his attention was fully claimed at that moment by his team. She waited until he had passed a coach laden with passengers before saying calmly, "I regret that I cannot go any further, Mr. Manningford. My aunt will begin to fret if I do not return to Laura Place soon, so I must request that you take me back there at once."

"Request all you like," he said cheerfully without taking

his eyes from the road. The speed at which they were traveling made her grateful that he was not one of those young bucks who drove in a careless neck-or-nothing fashion; nevertheless, she had no intention of allowing him to carry her another mile.

"Mr. Manningford, you are making a mistake."

"It will not be the first time."

"No doubt, but abduction is a serious crime, and I am not without protection, you know. You surely cannot believe you will succeed in forcing me to marry you."

"Do you think I could not? I doubt your family would welcome the sort of scandal that would arise from trying to set such a marriage aside, and they certainly won't prosecute once the knot is tied. No one would wish to raise that much dust."

"Rein in your horses, Mr. Manningford." Nell's voice was ice cold, her words crystal clear.

Manningford glanced at her and froze. "Where the devil did that come from?" he demanded, staring at the serviceable little pistol she held pointed at him in a perfectly steady hand.

"All that need concern you," Nell said, still in that calm frostbitten tone, "is that I know how to use it and have no qualms about doing so. Rein in your team."

A low growl from the hound at her feet drew Manningford's attention. "Good lad," he said. "I will keep him from harming you, Miss Bradbourne, if you will hand that gun to me at once."

The pistol moved in Nell's hand, stopping his hand the instant he began to shift his reins to reach for it. "The dog will not harm me, sir. Not, at all events, before I have put a hole in your shoulder or in your thigh. I have not decided which it is to be yet, though I am told that either can be very painful."

"Yes, by God, it can," he retorted. "I have had experience with gunshot wounds, and I have no desire to test your mettle, but how do you know the dog won't harm you? I don't even know that he won't."

"Dogs like me," Nell said simply.

"He growled."

"No doubt because you disturbed him when I startled you with my pistol. He has put his head down again, as you can see."

Manningford sighed and began to rein his team to the side of the road. "Very well, but don't wave that damned thing about. That stage we passed will most likely be along in a few moments, and I'd as lief not have to explain any of this to the driver or to his guard, if he's got one."

"You will take me back to Laura Place."

The phaeton drew to a halt. "As to that," he said, eyeing her pistol, "I should perhaps explain a thing or two to you."

"Do not try to make me believe that I ought to go anywhere else with you, sir. I am not such a ninnyhammer."

"I never said you were one," he said, "but the fact is that I have not been precisely factual in my explanation. I am not a marrying man, I fear, nor did I intend to become one."

"Goodness," Nell said, watching him even more narrowly than he watched her, "then you did mean to ravish me."

"No, I swear I did not."

"Mr. Manningford, it is perfectly plain to me—no, sir, do not move—that my first estimation of your character was the correct one. Your senses are clearly disordered. No doubt your family has persons out scouring the countryside to find you, to place you under restraint. I will thus be doing them a favor by restoring you to their loving bosom, to be well cared for."

"Well, there you're out, my girl, there is no loving bosom. My siblings all have families of their own, and my father is a damned odd fellow whom I've only just met and don't care if I never see again."

"Only just met?" A memory stirred in her mind.

"Yes, but don't let that distress you. And hide that popgun of yours. Here comes the stage."

Obediently Nell slipped the pistol under her skirt until the stage had passed, feeling no urge to draw the attention of passengers or driver. Manningford waved, then heaved a sigh of relief when no one showed any particular interest in them.

"So now you would cry off, would you?" Nell said with

a chuckle. But then, when he looked truly horrified, she added hastily, "What had my being an heiress to do with it, then?"

He still watched her narrowly. "Only that a friend of mine laid me a wager, saying I couldn't abduct you."

"I see. I must tell you, sir, that I do not approve of idiotish wagers. You ought to have told him you would not."

"I did. In point of fact, I said I'd be damned if I would do any such thing."

"Very proper. So then, why?"

"Circumstances changed. I require a certain amount of money to see me through a quarter-day. I asked my esteemed father for it, but instead of complying with my request, he chose to treat me as though I were a marionette to which he held the strings, so here I am."

"But you might ask someone else to lend you the money instead, might you not?"

"Is that an offer?" He grinned at her. "I thank you, but I have never in my life borrowed money from a woman, except of course from my sister, who does not count. I couldn't."

"I couldn't either," Nell said, stifling a laugh, "but pray do not take offense, sir. I mean that precisely the way I said it. I cannot possibly. I have no money."

"None? None at all?"

"Not a farthing. In fact, I came to Bath hoping to find some sort of respectable employment for myself."

Manningford stared at her for a long moment; then his lips began to twitch and his eyes to twinkle. When he burst into laughter, Nell watched him doubtfully, not certain even yet that she had not fallen into the clutches of a Bedlamite.

# 4

When Manningford's fit of laughter showed signs of abating, Nell said coolly, "I do not find the situation humorous, sir, but perhaps I am taking too narrow a view of it."

Instead of replying directly, he looked over his shoulder and lifted his whip to snap it high above his leaders' heads. The pace he set was considerably slower than it had been, but that fact alone was not sufficient to keep Nell silent.

"You are going the wrong way," she said, reaching under her skirt for the pistol.

"No, I am not," he said, "and keep that pistol of yours hidden, if you please. We are approaching the Snow Hill turnpike, and I'd as lief the keeper didn't see that thing."

"Well, he will see it," Nell said flatly. "I do not wish to go any farther. I thought I had made that plain."

"You did, but the case is altered now that I know you are not really an heiress."

"And what gave you any such notion as that?" she demanded, feeling warmth flood her cheeks. "I said only that I have no money, sir, not that I have no expectations."

He shot her a sharp glance. "Keep a still tongue in your head through the turnpike, my girl, and I'll tell you how I know. And don't start ripping up at me now," he added when she opened her mouth to protest. "There's another pike at Grosvenor Place, less than a mile from here. You can make your stand there if you still have a desire to do so."

They had slowed for the pike, and Nell gritted her teeth, leaving the pistol where it was, wondering what it was about the gentleman beside her that made her do as he had asked. Any sensible female, she told herself, would instantly demand assistance from the pike keeper, a burly fellow who looked as though he'd stand no nonsense from anyone.

"Good girl," Manningford said when they had passed through.

"Yes, you may well think so, sir, but I think I am a fool. I should like to know how you thought you would get me through these turnpikes, had I not been willing."

He shrugged. "I really didn't think about it, but there are ways to avoid the pikes altogether if one knows them. I do."

"I suppose you do, at that," she said. "Why did you suggest that I am not an heiress?"

"It was not a suggestion. No heiress would speak so off-handly about a need to seek employment."

"She might if she had nothing to live on but her expectations."

"Fustian. That great-aunt of yours, who is supposed to be the source of those expectations, would be preparing to take you about to all the parties she can find to launch you in style and find you a proper husband. Since she is apparently doing no such thing and expects you to find work—"

"Finding work is my own idea and one which my great-aunt strongly opposes," Nell said, trying to maintain the calm dignity that had served her so well before. "It has no doubt escaped your notice, Mr. Manningford, that I am wearing half-mourning. My father died seven months ago."

Manningford looked at her sharply, his countenance evincing brief confusion before his brow cleared and, to Nell's chagrin, he muttered, "Bradbourne! I thought that name sounded familiar, but assumed it was because of your being an heiress. Your father was Lord Bradbourne, then, the gamester who brought an abbey to a grange before he killed hims . . . That is . . ." He broke off again, stricken. "Oh, look here, I never ought to have said that."

"There is no need to apologize, Mr. Manningford," Nell said coldly. "Nor is there need for you to risk being seen any longer in my company, though it is no more than you deserve for having subjected me to this nonsensical abduction of yours."

"Risk? What are you talking about?"

Having no wish to discuss the matter an instant longer, she stared straight ahead, willing him to draw in to the side of the road again so that she might take leave of him with at least a modicum of her dignity intact. But when, without a word, he did slow the team and, a moment afterward, drew up in a narrow side road, she had a sudden quite inexplicable urge to burst into tears.

His voice was gentle. "Miss Bradbourne, I am profoundly sorry to have distressed you, although, since you deny that I had cause to apologize, I cannot think what I said exactly to have done so, and I cannot imagine, in any event, why you think that my being seen in your company will do me the least harm. 'Tis rather the other way round, as you must know perfectly well."

"I did think so," Nell said, "but that was before I knew that our dreadful scandal had flown beyond Trowbridge. If everyone in Bath already knows my appalling history, then I expect I shall have to leave, for I cannot subject Aunt Flavia to the burden of my company under such a circumstance."

"It is not so bad as that," he said. "I, too, associate with gamesters, you see, and I did not hear of it in Bath."

"I think perhaps it is a pity, anyway," she said with a sigh, "that your abducting me was not on account of a wager."

He had been watching her narrowly, but his eyes widened now, and the note of amusement returned to his voice when he said, "Why is that, precisely?"

"Well, it has occurred to me that if such a wager were large enough, we might . . . that is . . ." Unable to finish the thought, she looked at him with a rueful twinkle in her eyes. "It was a dreadful notion, sir, and not one to which you would have agreed, even had the circumstances been different. I cannot think what can have come over me. Pray, forget that I spoke."

He chuckled. "Miss Bradbourne, I begin to believe you show promise. The fact that you could contemplate even for a moment the thought of defrauding Halstead of his four thousand pounds makes me think quite differently about you."

"Halstead? Four thousand! I do not understand you, sir."

"Well, I understood you well enough, and if I thought for a moment that we could carry off such a hoax, I should be delighted to divide the spoils with you, but I don't suppose we could."

"I am afraid that that is precisely what I was thinking, more shame to me." When she remembered what else he had said, Nell sighed again. "There was a wager, then. Four thousand?"

He grinned at her wistful tone. "You sound just like a friend of mine," he said. "No doubt you will also agree with him that the wager was mad-brained from the start."

Nell straightened, giving herself a shake. "All wagers are mad-brained, Mr. Manningford, as I have good reason to know, but in point of fact, I have heard of others a great deal more preposterous than abducting an heiress for four thousand pounds, albeit not necessarily more stupid or more dangerous."

He ignored her last point, pinning his attention on an earlier one. "I don't doubt you've heard some crazy ones. Is it true your father once staked a team of horses against a brewery that one flower in his garden would bloom before another?"

Nell smiled reminiscently. "That was one of his more absurd wagers with his uncle Reginald. He won that time, and Reginald had the Crosshill brewery dismantled, board by board and stone by stone, and rebuilt at Highgate. Two years later, it was all done again, when Papa put the brewery up against a brace of Reginald's east-lawn peacocks and lost."

"Peacocks! I take it this brewery didn't make much money."

"On the contrary, people for miles around purchased their ale and beer from us, so it turned an excellent profit."

"Now, see here, Miss Bradbourne, I have a certain reputation of my own for making mad wagers, but I should never be so mad as to wager something of no worth against something of great worth."

Nell smiled again. "You had to know them," she said. "Half their fun lay in making their wagers ridiculous. You see, it had been a source of amusement for them since their

childhood. That is why . . ." But here she stopped, smoothed
a crease from her skirt with a conscious air, and focused her
attention upon the post-and-rail fence at the side of the road
where two blackbirds were playing tag with each other. When
Manningford made no attempt to press her to finish her
sentence, she said a moment later in a more cheerful way,
"We must be getting back to Laura Place, sir, before my
great-aunt has begun to fret about my long absence."

"Very well," he said, gathering the reins again, "but we
ought perhaps to go to Grosvenor Place and collect that friend
of mine first. I told him I would do so if it was at all possible,
and he will be wondering what has become of me. Do you
mind?"

"No, of course not," Nell said, thinking at the same time
that it was extremely odd to have been having such a
conversation with a would-be abductor, and thinking at the
same time that she must be daft to be thinking that she would
like to know him better. A moment later, back on the London
Road, she kept her hands firmly folded in her lap and her
eyes steadily on the road ahead, wondering what sort of
friend Mr. Manningford had who would so patiently await
his arrival with the young lady he had abducted.

They were held up briefly at the turnpike while Manningford persuaded the keeper that he intended to go more than
a few yards beyond to Grosvenor Place to pick up a friend
who was awaiting him, and that they would then return. The
rules regarding this sort of thing were quite clear, but the
keeper was by no means prepared to accept the word of a
young buck driving a carriage clearly intended to carry no
more than two people, and a fast carriage at that. Only when
Manningford pointed out that his friend was the gentleman
dressed in the height of fashion now approaching them on
the pavement directly opposite Grosvenor Place did the
keeper give way and allow them to pass, though he kept a
sharp eye on them as he attended to the two vehicles
following closely behind the phaeton.

Manningford drew up beside Mr. Lasenby, who had lifted
his gold-rimmed quizzing glass to his right eye, the better
to examine Miss Bradbourne. "Good morning, ma'am," he

said politely, letting the glass fall before casting an inquiring look at Manningford. "Going to introduce me, my lad?"

"Never mind doing the polite, Seppi," Manningford told him. "Just hop up here, quick as you can, before that turnpike keeper begins to think we're tipping him the double."

"What, didn't you get a proper ticket?" Mr. Lasenby demanded, climbing up to squeeze in beside Nell, who in shifting to make room for him found herself sitting awkwardly on her pistol. "Dashed fool thing to forget," he added. "And you such a knowing one! But you might introduce me to the lady all the same, you know, particularly if we're going to be driving along the high road squashed together like geese in a drove."

"Geese in a flock, Sep; sheep in a drove." Manningford smiled at Nell. "Mr. Lasenby, Miss Bradbourne, little though he recommends himself to you with his foolish chatter."

"Well, I like that," Mr. Lasenby said indignantly. "I am not the one who insisted upon driving to Reading in a dashed uncomfortable high flier, am I? Dashed right I'm not! And— Here, Bran, what are you doing turning full about in the middle of the London Road? You'll have us over or in a tangle with another carriage. Watch that fellow on the right, will you!"

"Hold your nash, Seppi. I've never overturned you yet, have I?" Manningford waved thanks to the gentleman who had halted his own carriage in rather a hurry to allow him to turn his around. "We are taking Miss Bradbourne back to Laura Place."

"Taking her back!" Mr. Lasenby looked from one to the other, then uttered a weak laugh. "I wonder what nonsense you can be speaking, Bran. Miss Bradbourne, I daresay you do not know what he is talking about. Pay him no heed, I beg you."

Nell looked straight ahead, biting her lower lip to keep the bubble of laughter she felt rising in her throat from bursting forth, and grateful that her short stay in Bath made it unlikely that any of her great-aunt's friends, or anyone else, would recognize her in her present position.

Manningford, shooting a glance at her, said nothing until he had negotiated the turnpike again, but once they were through, he said to Mr. Lasenby, "She knows the whole, Sep, and she objects to being abducted, so I am taking her home immediately."

"She knows?" Mr. Lasenby tugged at his highly starched neckcloth, evidently finding it suddenly a trifle too tight. "I say, Miss Bradbourne, I hope Bran's little indiscretion—"

But here he was interrupted by a crack of laughter from Manningford. "You sound just like her, Sep! 'Indiscretion' is precisely the word she employed to describe what I tried to do. Oh, and, Miss Bradbourne," he added in lower voice, "if you have not already done so, I beg you will put that pistol back where you found it before we reach Laura Place, and without waving it about, if you please, for all and sundry to see."

"Pistol!" Mr. Lasenby choked the word out. "She's got a pistol?" Watching in fascinated dismay as Nell gratefully removed it from beneath her hip and returned it to her reticule, he said as she did so, "Now, look here, Bran, I said the whole notion was mad-brained, and if you had not let your father get your temper up like you did, you'd have seen as much from the outset. For I'll tell you to your head, my lad, you have not managed this business with a jot of your usual finesse, and that's a fact."

Manningford chuckled, glancing again at Nell, who refused to look at him for the simple reason that she was still having difficulty, both in containing her laughter and in believing that any of what was happening was real. She was quite certain that at any moment she would awaken and find herself in her own bed, where she would be able to laugh without restraint for as long as she wished to do so, and without anyone's believing she ought to be clapped instantly into Bedlam.

"Sep is right, Miss Bradbourne," Manningford said ruefully. "I lost my temper last night, drank too much port afterward, and acted this morning without allowing myself so much as a moment to think. A single moment's reflection must have shown me the idiocy of succumbing to an impulse born out of temper.''

''Ought to have taken the post chaise instead of this rackety phaeton, for starters,'' Mr. Lasenby muttered.

Manningford chuckled again. ''With you acting as postilion, I suppose. Or do you imagine that fellow we had from Westbury yesterday would have obliged us by going on to Reading with Miss Bradbourne as our captive? If he had, Sep, I'd have had to leave you behind, since the chaise barely had room enough for the two of us. It would never accommodate a third.''

''It did accommodate a third,'' Mr. Lasenby said testily, ''just as this vehicle is accommodating a fourth, or had you forgotten King Ethelred, who, as I plainly see, is still taking up more than his fair share of the floor space?''

''King Ethelred?'' Nell said, looking down at the hound's head, which was all she could see of that noble animal, since the rest was well back under the seat. ''Is that what you call him?''

''It is what Sep calls him,'' Manningford said. ''He thinks him unready. He maligns him, I believe.''

''Well, what do you call him?'' she asked reasonably.

''Dog,'' he said.

''But that will not do at all,'' she said, looking again at the hound. ''He is rather regal, but not much like an Ethelred, more like the Emperor Maximilian, I think.''

''Max he shall be, then,'' Manningford said.

She grinned at him. ''Just like that, sir?''

''Just like that,'' he replied, smiling back at her.

Nell looked away and said quickly, ''I cannot imagine why you have never given him a proper name before now.''

''I only just acquired him,'' he said, and went on to explain.

When he had finished, she said, ''That is one wager my father never dreamed of. Did every card truly land facedown?''

''Every one. Was not your father the one who set out to lay jackstraws end to end along the road from Frome to

Beckington before some other fellow could twice walk the same distance?''

"The very same. He lost that wager, though. A heavy wind came up and blew half the straws away before he'd finished. He was most put out, because it had taken him nearly a month to collect enough straws to do the trick in the first place.''

Mr. Lasenby had been watching them, and listening, and this casual cordiality was too much for him. He said sharply, "Here, now, what goes on? Bran, you say she knows you meant to abduct her for a wager, yet here she is discussing dog's names and absurd wagers with you just as if you was both at a rout party, when she ought by rights to be laying charges against you.''

Manningford's eyebrows shot up. "I hadn't thought of that. Do you mean to lay charges, Miss Bradbourne?''

A gurgle of laughter escaped before she could stop it. "I do not think I should care to do that, sir,'' she said. When he regarded her with twinkling humor in his eyes, she shook her head and said, "Any competent magistrate would stare at such a tale as I might relate. 'A gentleman took me up in Sydney Gardens,' I'd tell him, 'and drove me to Grosvenor Place, where he took up another gentleman before returning me to Laura Place.' In point of fact, sir, there is no crime that I can see.''

"But, look here,'' Mr. Lasenby said, "he must have spun you some Banbury tale or other to get you into the phaeton, and he wasn't meaning to take you only so far as Grosvenor Place. In actual point of fact, ma'am, if you had not had that pistol—though why a lady residing in Bath should carry a pistol in her reticule is more than I can say. Why do you do so, ma'am?''

"I had no maid or footman to accompany me, Mr. Lasenby, and I have not always resided in Bath,'' Nell said.

"But surely—''

"Peace, Sep,'' Manningford said, and to Nell's surprise, since Mr. Lasenby seemed something of an amiable rattle-pate, he said not another word. There was a long moment of silence before Manningford said thoughtfully, "You know, Miss Bradbourne, I cannot help but feel that somehow

I ought to repay you for taking so sanguine an attitude to my outrageous behavior.''

"Well, I do not know how you might do that, sir, unless you know of someone in need of a companion, or perhaps a governess.''

He shook his head. "No one." He glanced at her. "I do not think anyone will hire you for a governess.''

"But I have been well-educated, sir, and the only other thing I do well is housekeeping, for I served my father in that capacity from the time I turned sixteen.''

"Well, you cannot go for a housekeeper. What else can you do? There must be something.''

"Nothing,'' she said firmly, "unless you consider my passion for reading or my foolish scribbles.''

"You write?'' He looked at her sharply.

"Well, not really. That is, nothing but nonsensical stuff for my own amusement. I daresay I should enjoy reading to an invalid or making up tales to amuse children, but I do not think I should make enough in either case to keep myself, do you?''

"No,'' he agreed. He fell silent again, but after a moment he said slowly, "I believe we must have a serious talk, Miss Bradbourne. Can you extend your complaisance to allow us to accompany you inside when we reach your great-aunt's house?''

Nell stared at him. "Mr. Manningford, you are not still thinking that I shall assist you to deceive the gentleman with whom you made your outrageous bet. Even though I myself might have suggested such a thing . . .'' Words failed her.

Mr. Lasenby stared. "*You* did, ma'am?''

"Be still, Seppi,'' Manningford commanded. "She did no such thing. Nor am I suggesting such a course. I do possess a certain amount of integrity, Miss Bradbourne, though I realize you have no cause to believe me when I say so.''

Relaxing, Nell smiled at him. "I have every cause, sir. Oh, yes,'' she insisted when he regarded her skeptically. "Just as I know beauty through having been acquainted with one, I know villainy, and you are no villain, sir. Mr. Lasenby chooses to think that you were merely careless, but I have talked with you a good deal this morning and have seen no indication of stupidity. Yet, despite what you claim to know about alternative routes, avoiding turnpike keepers, and other such obstacles as might have been encountered, I cannot believe you truly intended to abduct me. Not in a high perch phaeton, not all the way to Reading. I do believe you lost your temper, from some cause or other, and acted impulsively, but that is all I believe.''

Manningford opened his mouth and shut it again. After a moment's thought he said, ''No doubt you have the right of it. Sep is certainly correct in saying that I lost my wits. We must hope that had I not wakened with a sore head and my temper still in an uproar, I should more rapidly have recovered them.'' He reined in his team. ''Here we are now. Do we all go in, Miss Bradbourne? I believe I can safely promise it will result in your benefit, though not by so much as four thousand. Indeed, I do not know what amount I can offer, but if we put our heads together, perhaps we can find a solution to suit us both.''

Nell made up her mind quickly. ''Yes, do come in, the both of you. Only, there is no one about to hold your horses, Mr. Manningford. Shall you have to tether them to the area fence? Or perhaps the wrought-iron fence round the fountain will do. It looks strong enough, does it not?''

''Your porter will see to them, I expect,'' Manningford said comfortably. ''Go knock the fellow up, Sep, and then help Miss Bradbourne to alight. I cannot trust these fellows to stand.''

Mr. Lasenby jumped down obediently, smoothed his coat, and ran a finger quickly around the edge of his neckcloth as if to be sure it was properly in place before ascending the three steps to rap authoritatively on the door.

Nell waited with bated breath to see if any servant would appear. One never knew whether Sudbury, the butler, would be in the hall or down in the kitchen, since, except for a daily housemaid and Lady Flavia's devoted dresser, Botten, he and his wife were the only two servants she had seen since her arrival. However, after a moment's delay the door opened, and Sudbury, looking as stately as though he served a ducal mansion, looked down his long nose at Mr. Lasenby, then past him at Nell.

Mr. Lasenby spoke quickly, and the butler nodded without losing a jot of his dignity and then shut the door, leaving Mr. Lasenby to stand staring at it. A moment later it opened again, and at the same time, a thin, gangly boy of twelve of thirteen, in nankeen breeches and cap, shrugging on a well-worn coat, came running up the area steps from the basement kitchen and hurried to the leaders' head.

Manningford looked at the youth with misgiving. "Think you can hold them?" he asked.

"Aye, guv. Bang-up bits o' flesh 'n bone, they be. Bit resty, but I'll run 'em round yon fountain 'n they gits uppity."

Nodding, Manningford wrapped the slack of his reins around the brake handle and swung down, holding up his hands to assist Nell, since Mr. Lasenby had forgotten her in his stupefaction at having been left standing on the doorstep. Nell placed her hands on Manningford's broad shoulders, felt his strong hands at her waist, and wondered why such a common action as being helped down from a carriage should leave her feeling breathless. But with her feet solidly on the pavement she took her cue from Sudbury, turned to Mr. Lasenby, and said with as much dignity as the butler himself might have assumed, "Shall we go in, sir?"

She could see that Mr. Lasenby was dying to ask her why on earth the butler had not summoned one footman to hold the horses while another went to fetch the boy, but she had seen enough of him to be certain his manners were too good to allow him to ask such a question. Walking past him across the black-and-white-checked hall floor toward the graceful, swooping stairs, and trying to ignore a burst of outraged barking from outside, she said casually over her shoulder, "Is my aunt at home, Sudbury?"

"Yes, Miss Nell," the butler replied. "Her ladyship is in the drawing room. Shall I bring refreshment?"

Fearing there might be no suitable refreshment to offer, Nell opened her mouth to deny that they wanted anything so early in the day, but Mr. Lasenby spoke first, saying gratefully, "I'd not refuse a glass of wine, and that's a fact."

"Very good, sir," Sudbury said, "and whom shall I announce to her ladyship, if you please?"

They told him, and as the butler took Manningford's cape and Nell's pelisse and laid them carefully across the porter's chair, just as though he expected an underling to collect them, Manningford shot her a look that made her color to her eyebrows, certain he had guessed there were no other servants. He looked slimmer without the cape, and was dressed with a careless elegance that put her forcibly in mind of her brother. She had begun to think there was little to choose between the pair of them, and decided it was precisely that familiarity that made her feel as if she had known Mr. Manningford for years instead of an hour.

With a stately nod Sudbury preceded them up the stairs to the drawing room, opening the double doors and announcing their names in majestic tones. The frantic barking continued below, but was muted now, and no one chose to acknowledge it.

Lady Flavia, wearing a mauve silk morning dress, the style of which had been fashionable some years before, and seated in her favorite chair near the fire, her feet on the tapestry footstool, set aside her tambour frame and said with a welcoming nod, "You must be Rackton's younger grandson, Mr. Lasenby. I knew your grandpapa in my girlhood. Very autocratic, he was."

"Still is, ma'am," he said. "Devilish old tyrant."

"I read of your recent betrothal and must offer you my felicitations. Miss Wembly is a most excellent choice."

"His choice," Mr. Lasenby said with a sigh. "Wench has an income of fifteen thousand a year, and the tipstaffs were after me. Betrothal set that right, of course, but fear felicitations may be premature. Got a lamentable memory, you see. Forgot some dashed silly dress party, and she took a pet."

Manningford said, "Can't blame her, Sep, not when the party was held chiefly to make you known to her relatives, and she has not cried off, precisely, just said you must improve. You won't forget her ball in Brighton, however, for I'll remind you."

Mr. Lasenby nodded doubtfully, and Lady Flavia turned to Manningford with a decided twinkle in her eyes. "You are Sir Mortimer's younger son, are you not?" she asked.

"I have that honor, ma'am," Manningford said evenly. He glanced toward the window. The barking continued.

Nell stared at him. "That is why your name sounded familiar to me," she exclaimed, feeling another of those odd urges to laugh and realizing that she had felt them more in one day than in the previous seven months. "Aunt Flavia mentioned your father earlier. She said . . . Oh, dear, I am persuaded I ought not to repeat this, but she called *him* eccentric." The laughter that had threatened to overwhelm her more than once that morning would no longer be denied, and she sat down on the nearest chair and laughed until tears streamed down her face. Both her aunt and Mr. Lasenby stared at her as though they feared she had lost her mind, but Manningford, with a wry twist of his lips, pulled a large snowy handkerchief from his waistcoat pocket and pushed it into one of her hands. The barking outside suddenly ceased.

"Sudbury, no doubt," Lady Flavia said with a satisfied nod. "Nell, dear, compose yourself. I must tell you, I had not the least notion that you were acquainted with any young men in Bath. Indeed, I had been racking my brain trying to recall if there *were* any young gentlemen in town at this season and had quite decided there were none at all and we would have to make do with the older ones, and here you are with two splendid young ones in your train. 'Tis quite providential."

Recovering her equanimity at last, Nell shook her head, mopped her eyes and cheeks with the handkerchief, and said, "Not precisely providential, ma'am. I became acquainted with them only this morning when, apparently believing me to be on the brink of inheriting your vast wealth, Mr. Manningford attempted to abduct me in order to win a wager."

"On the brink!" Lady Flavia exclaimed, ignoring the rest and favoring Manningford with a basilisk glare. "On the brink! Do you dare to think me decrepit, young man? Do you expect me to pop off just to oblige you or any other young chub? I'll thank you to know that I am but three-and-seventy, *and* in excellent curl. Why, I expect to live a score of years and more yet!''

"Indeed, I hope you do, ma'am," Manningford said with a grin, taking a seat near her and signing to Mr. Lasenby to do likewise. "I had no such notion, you know, but only of winning four thousand pounds. That is reprehensible enough, however, so if you still want to ring a peal over me, I shall not object."

Lady Flavia stared at her. "Four thousand?" When he nodded, she said, "Do you hear that, Nell? Four thousand pounds, merely for a wager. Did you ever hear the like?"

"Well, in actual fact, Aunt—"

"Oh, well, of course you have heard the like, but four thousand, Nell! Perhaps . . . But no, it would not do, more's the pity. Unless . . . I say, Mr. Manningford, will the fact that you have not abducted my grandniece after all mean that you will have to pay out the four thousand?"

There was a moment's stunned silence before, with a look of comical chagrin, Manningford said slowly, "No, ma'am, I shan't, because in point of fact, there was no wager." He looked at Mr. Lasenby. "I did tell Halstead that I'd be da . . ." He broke off, glanced at Lady Flavia, then continued smoothly, " . . . that I should never think of abducting Miss Bradbourne. Did I not, Seppi?"

"You did," Mr. Lasenby agreed. "Might have refused to pay if you'd shown up with her after that, come to think on it. Fool thing to do, Bran, without making all clear with him first."

Another chuckle from Nell, albeit immediately stifled, drew Manningford's attention, and with a rueful grin he said to her, "Go ahead and laugh. I can't think when I last made such a fantastic mull of anything as I did of this, but I cannot say I am altogether sorry I made the attempt."

Sudbury, entering just then with a tray bearing a decanter and glasses, went first to Mr. Lasenby. "Your wine, sir. A very fine mountain sherry." Turning next to Manningford, he said, "I took the liberty of giving your dog a marrow bone, sir."

"An excellent notion. Thank you."

Nell had been thinking, and once Sudbury had ascertained that nothing further was wanted, and departed, she said calmly, "Mr. Manningford, there was something you wished to discuss."

He glanced at Lady Flavia, gazing at him now with open curiosity. "This is perhaps not the best time, Miss Bradbourne. You said that your great-aunt had objected . . . That is . . ." He broke off, at a loss for words.

With dignity Lady Flavia pushed the little stool aside with one foot and got up, reaching for the cane that rested beside her chair but showing no sign of leaning upon it. "I believe I shall speak to Botten, Nell. She was to have visited her sister today, but her nephew is occupied for some time yet and cannot accompany her, so she might as well have a look at my pomona-green crepe. I intend to wear it when we call upon Maria Prudham today."

"Aunt Flavia, do sit down," Nell said. "Surely you do not mean to leave me alone with two gentlelmen!"

"Pish tush, my dear. You are one-and-twenty, which ought to be quite old enough to look after yourself."

"Yes," Nell agreed, "and to make my own decisions too, but I do not mean to keep secrets from you, so you might as well hear the whole for yourself firsthand. I shall only have to repeat it to you later if you do not."

Lady Flavia plumped down again in her chair. "Well, what is it, then?" she demanded, gray eyes asparkle. "I adore secrets."

# 5

Nell smiled at Lady Flavia, then turned to Manningford and said calmly, "Since my great-aunt has
objected only to my desire to seek employment, I
collect from your comment that you might know of a situation
to suit me. There can be no good reason not to discuss that
subject immediately."

Mr. Lasenby sat up and gazed around the elegant room
in confusion. "Employment! You cannot be serious, Miss
Bradbourne. No one in such circumstances as these seeks
employment."

"My circumstances are not what they appear to be, sir,"
Nell said with an apologetic look at Lady Flavia. "My great-
aunt is in no way responsible for me."

"Now, Nell," that lady said tartly. "I will not have you
giving people the notion that you are not welcome here for
as long as you like to stay. You know perfectly well that
you are."

"Yes, Aunt Flavia, I do know, but I have already given
the facts to Mr. Manningford—inadvertently, I promise you.
He rather leapt from one small fact to the grand whole, I'm
afraid."

"The whole?" She regarded Manningford fixedly. "What
is this whole that you think you know, young man?"

He flicked a glance at Mr. Lasenby, who still looked
confused, Nell thought, as well he might. Taking pity on him,
she said to her aunt, "I fear that Mr. Lasenby does not know
what any of us is talking about, ma'am. He was not present
during my conversation with Mr. Manningford, you see. Do
tell me, Mr. Lasenby," she added abruptly, "why it is that
Mr. Manningford addresses you as Sep. I believe Sudbury
announced you as Joseph Lasenby, did he not?"

Lasenby looked at Manningford and said, " 'Twas all Bran's doing. Eton together, don't you know, and his sisters had an Italian governess at the time. Had the notion of calling me Guiseppe—the Italian form of Joseph, that is—and has done ever since. 'Sep' for short. But look here. No cause for pointless diversion, you know. Want to talk about private matters, I'll just step outside and have a look at that fountain, or step into another room inside, for all that.''

"No, don't do that!" Nell said quickly as he got to his feet. "I mean, do sit down, Mr. Lasenby. The matter of my seeking employment is truly not so private as all that.''

"Yes, but dash it, ma'am, you haven't explained why the deuce you must needs consider such a thing.''

Manningford said bluntly, "Her father was the late Lord Bradbourne, Sep.''

"He was? Well, fancy that. Daresay I didn't know him, you know." Mr. Lasenby frowned. "But wait! Wasn't he . . .?" Breaking off, he flushed deeply, looked from Nell to Manningford and back again, then said manfully, "I do remember, and I'm deuced sorry, Miss Bradbourne. Expect that explains your need, right enough.''

Manningford shook his head. "No, it does not. At least, if he was completely run off his legs, I didn't hear about it. At all events, though his manner of death might explain why she won't wish to make a stir here in Bath, it cannot explain why she is no longer an heiress." He looked at Lady Flavia.

Returning his look, she said firmly, "She is still heiress to all I have, young man." When he remained silent, watching her, she sighed at last and said, "There might not be so much as people think, of course. Still, I simply will not hear of her visiting a registry office or otherwise letting it be known that she seeks employment!''

He nodded. "I think I understand you, ma'am, and I promise that you have nothing to fear from me. Indeed, I mean to make you privy to a secret that, as yet, only two other persons in the world know, so you will see that it is as much to my benefit as to your own that I keep your secret. And though Sep appears to be a sad rattlepate, he is as close as an oyster when it matters. I'd trust him with my life.''

Mr. Lasenby shifted uncomfortably in his chair and grimaced, as if Manningford had accused him of doing something shocking.

Manningford didn't wait for comments. He said bluntly, ''The fact is that my father has been hiding away on the top floor of the Royal Crescent all these years, penning gothic romances and calling himself 'a Gentlewoman of Quality, Residing in Bath.' ''

''Goodness,'' said Nell, awed. ''I have read some of those books. But surely to goodness he hasn't written all the ones that are so inscribed! Why, there must be dozens of them that claim to have been penned by a Gentlewoman Residing in Bath!''

''He probably did write them all,'' Manningford said gloomily. ''Unfortunately, he has recently had an apoplectic fit of some sort, in which his vision and right arm were affected. He can still see but he cannot write, and before it happened he had already begun a book that is bespoken to be finished by mid-August. He insists that it must be finished. By me.''

Nell bit her lower lip, trying to imagine the reckless, unpredictable Manningford writing any book. ''Do you think you can do such a thing, sir?''

''No, I do not.''

''By Jove,'' Mr. Lasenby said, ''I should rather think not! Why, no one could. That is to say, I suppose your father really did write those others if he claims to have done, but—''

''He wrote them, all right,'' Manningford said, ''but worse than that is that they have attracted royal attention. According to what he let fall in the course of his ranting yesterday, his fit was caused by a letter from his publisher informing him that the Prince Regent has condescended to grant permission for this next book to be dedicated to his royal self. Not that permission was invited, of course, but 'tis as good as a command, and thus one can understand my father's insistence that the book be finished.''

Nell looked confused. ''But his publisher must know his identity if he writes to him. Can you not simply write and tell him that your father is too ill to continue?''

"My father insists that because of the Regent's interest the novel must be finished, and in any case, his publisher knows nothing about him. Letters from the Gentlewoman of Quality are addressed to a Miss Clarissa Harlowe, care of the receiving office. My father's man collects them for him there."

Lady Flavia frowned. "That name sounds familiar, but I cannot think why it should do so."

"He told me it comes from a novel by Samuel Richardson that was written all in letters, although I must tell you that had he not chosen it years and years ago I should more likely believe it amused him to think how much my brother's wife, Clarissa, would dislike having her name used in such a fashion. No doubt the choice was made just as he said it was, however."

Lady Flavia chuckled. "No doubt."

Nell looked at the tips of her fingernails and said, "I think I can imagine where this conversation is leading us, sir, but I cannot possibly pretend to be any kind of authoress."

"Oh, you needn't be one. 'Tis merely his right eye and hand that refuse to obey him. He can still talk and think well enough. What I had in mind was that you might, for a proper fee, act as his scribe. Since you do not want it widely known that you seek employment and he does not wish any of this known, you ought to suit each other down to the ground, don't you agree?"

"I should think he would prefer to engage a proper secretary," Nell said. "I have no experience in such matters."

"He will not want a secretary," Manningford said. "In fact, I expect to have the devil's own time convincing him that he wants anyone." He looked uncomfortable for a moment, then said, "The plain truth is that he threatened to cut me off with no more than the proverbial shilling if I do not see the fool thing through, and I mean to offer him your services as a compromise. He must know I cannot write such a novel myself."

"But if he accepts the notion of a scribe, will he not insist that you take that role, sir?"

"Not," Manningford said with the smile of a mischievous

boy, "when it is pointed out to him that no one has ever been able to decipher my lamentable scrawl."

"Fact," agreed Mr. Lasenby, nodding judicially. "Can't read it at all myself."

Manningford grinned at him, saying, "I assume your education included learning a creditable copperplate, Miss Bradbourne."

Nell nodded, her thoughts awhirl, but Lady Flavia said, "Nell's hand is particularly elegant, Mr. Manningford; however, I daresay Sir Mortimer will not agree to having her in his house. In any event, one could not approve such a plan as seemly."

"Wait, Aunt Flavia," Nell said quickly. " 'Twill answer well enough, I think, if we consider carefully. I cannot stay here, of course, nor can I go every day to Royal Crescent as Miss Nell Bradbourne, but I daresay we can think of a way to get by that, you know. As to the rest, if he will allow me to do so, I should be pleased to help Sir Mortimer. I know I can get on well with elderly gentlemen, for several were accustomed to visit Papa, so the only difficulty will be to convince him to accept my help."

Mr. Lasenby said succinctly, "Dash it, must do so if he wants his book written. Bran won't do it."

Manningford smiled at Lady Flavia. "I should like to take your grandniece at once to make my father's acquaintance, ma'am. Will you agree to accompany her, for propriety's sake?"

"Propriety?" Lady Flavia shook her head. "There is little enough of that in any of what you have suggested, young man, but I cannot think it any more proper for two gentlewomen to visit a bachelor establishment than for one to do so."

Mischievously Nell said, "I daresay my aunt would enjoy a ride in your phaeton, Mr. Manningford."

That was too much for Mr. Lasenby. "Now, see here, Bran, you can't take the Lady Flavia up in that rig! Not the thing, dear boy. Not the thing at all. Not enough room, for one thing. That dashed dog of yours, for another. Must hire a chair. I shall walk beside it, if you like."

The rueful look returned to Manningford's eyes. "I am not generally known to rush my fences this way, Miss Bradbourne. You must forgive me. 'Tis only that I think I see an answer to my problem, if only I can clear away the obstacles."

"Yes, and so do I see it, sir, but not if Aunt Flavia is to attempt to play propriety. She is too well known, and even if she were to agree to adopt a disguise, it would not answer. I think I know the way, unless . . . But surely your father has at least one or two female servants in the house."

"Cook is still there," he told her. "The others have gone, but Borland—my father's manservant—has promised to hire more. The difficulty is that my father frequently sacks them; however, he has said he means to turn such affairs over to my management, so I ought to prevent any future fits of such capriciousness."

"Then the answer is not so difficult. I shall simply become one of your new servants. No, no, Aunt," she said, laughing. "Such a ruse will answer perfectly, for I am persuaded, Mr. Manningford, that your maids do not live on the premises."

"No, they come to the house daily, and have done since my elder sister married and went to live in London."

"Excellent. I shall simply arrive each morning at the same time the maids do and leave when they leave."

"Nell," exclaimed Lady Flavia, "you cannot think of doing such a thing! Why, how will you get there? Royal Crescent is clear the other side of town!"

"Fiddle," Nell said. "Even at that, it cannot be more than a mile from here. I am country bred, ma'am, so such a distance is as nothing to me."

"The crescent's atop a mighty steep hill," Mr. Lasenby informed her anxiously.

"I can manage a hill," she told him. Then, looking at Manningford, she lifted her eyebrows. "Will it answer, sir?"

"No."

"No? But I thought—"

"The maidservants arrive very early, Miss Bradbourne." Nell smiled at him. "Do you think me a layabout, sir?"

"No, but I do think you ought not to be out at such an

hour, and certainly not alone. I shall send a carriage for you.''

''Nonsense. Even in my short time here, I have seen that practically no one takes a carriage. You would draw too much attention to me if one were sent to collect me each day.''

Lady Flavia had been listening with more than usual patience to this dialogue and now said thoughtfully, ''You could take my chair, Nell. Of course, there must be chairmen, but I daresay Sudbury will know a pair of lads glad to make an extra shilling or two and who will keep still tongues in their heads. You might then find use for them during the day, Mr. Manningford, or they can simply return for her each afternoon.''

''But that will be almost as bad, ma'am,'' Nell protested. ''It will be much better if I walk than if a chair is seen—''

''It needn't be seen,'' Manningford said abruptly. ''The stables are in Julian Street, behind the crescent. Your people can take you there, and you will enter the house through the garden. Our people will know who you are, though, and as for the proprieties, Lady Flavia, I can arrange for a maid-servant—once we have some—to remain on the upper-floor landing the whole time Miss Bradbourne is with my father. Will that satisfy you?''

Lady Flavia smiled at him. ''As to that, young man, I am more concerned with the appearance than with the reality, for I daresay Nell can look after herself. However, if she is truly going to insist upon this dreadful course, your plan is certainly more acceptable to me than any she has suggested.''

Mr. Lasenby murmured, ''Dash it, take her pistol. Safe as houses then, I daresay.''

Lady Flavia looked surprised. ''You have a pistol, Nell?''

''Yes, ma'am. Does that shock you?''

''Not at all, my dear. I should have fretted less about your walking alone in the gardens, had I known you had it. 'Tis rather odd, of course, but I daresay your father taught you.''

''No, Nigel did. He was bored one day. But I believe that we are now agreed, Mr. Manningford, are we not?''

He nodded and said, ''But I do think I ought to take you

now to meet my father. You'll not want to ride three in the phaeton again, so we'll get some men to carry your chair, then meet you in Julian Street to show you the way from there. 'Tis better, even now, I daresay, that you avoid the front of the house.''

She consented, agreeing with a perfectly straight face that for her to be driven in a sporting carriage through the most fashionable streets of Bath would be unsuitable. Mr. Lasenby, in complete accord with the judgment, volunteered to walk by her chair, but Manningford, with a sardonic glint in his eyes, vetoed the notion, suggesting that it might be as well if neither of them were seen in her company just yet. Sudbury, called in to confer, said he would arrange at once for the men, and suggested that if Manningford was on the point of leaving, he might tell the lad holding his horses that Sudbury had need of him.

"Oh, dear," Lady Flavia said with a frown. "That means Botten will be further delayed in getting to her sister's house, which certainly means she will be cast into the sullens. But Nell's needs must come first. Good day, gentlemen.''

When they were gone, Nell turned a laughing face to her great-aunt and said, ''Is it not the most ridiculous coil, ma'am? Imagine me working for an author of such books. They are so silly and unbelievable, but everyone reads them, even when they claim they do not. Only think of the Regent's reading them!''

"Oh, I believe some of the newer tales are quite superior, my dear. I had one out of Baldwin's Circulating Library that I found to be quite amusing. You may read it before I return it. Much of the tale takes place right here in Bath.''

Agreeing that she would enjoy such a book, Nell excused herself to change her plain gray stuff gown for something more suitable to visit an invalid. Passing her great-aunt's room some minutes later, she opened the door to find Botten within, stitching the pale green crepe.

The dresser, a woman of some fifty summers, with faded blond hair and a soft complexion, professed herself glad to help Nell with her change, and Nell was soon ready to depart, looking very becoming in a dove-gray half-dress with white thread-lace trim, and a simple gray bonnet that set off her flaming curls to admiration. Donning her black gloves, she picked up her gray knit reticule, lighter now than earlier, and went downstairs.

Lady Flavia's chair being kept beneath the swooping stair in the front hall, the two muscular chairmen who had been hailed in and given the direction by Sudbury waited until that worthy had assisted Nell to enter it, then picked it up with ease and bore her out into the street. She had never ridden in such state before, and found it an unusual, albeit generally pleasant, way of traveling, once she became accustomed to the sensation of tilting forward, caused by the fact that the taller of the two men had taken the rear of the chair. That sensation ended abruptly once they began to climb, however, and since the streets were not crowded, the men made good time, arriving in Julian Street twenty minutes later, to find Manningford waiting alone, except for the dog, like a toffee-colored shadow at his side. He helped her out of the chair.

"Where is Mr. Lasenby?" she asked, shaking out her skirt and adjusting the light shawl she wore draped across her elbows.

"Inside, writing to tell his grandfather he means to remain for a time in Bath," Manningford said, firmly shutting the door of her chair before telling the chairmen to carry it into the nearby stable and wait there until they were needed again.

Placing a firm hand beneath Nell's left elbow, he guided her toward a tall iron-and-wood gate, pushing it open to reveal a large shaggy garden ablaze with the colors of late spring.

"Oh, how lovely!" Nell exclaimed. "But why has no one trimmed those hedges or removed the dead flowers and leaves?"

Manningford glanced around as though seeing the garden for the first time, shrugged and said, "My father undoubtedly sacked the gardeners as well."

"Well, that will not do," Nell said with a minatory look. "It would be one thing if there were no money, but since you assure me there is plenty, this is but simple neglect."

"Tell him so," Manningford recommended, reaching past her to open a door into the house.

She lifted her chin. "I am not so impertinent, sir."

He grinned at her. "Are you not, Miss Bradbourne? I should have thought you equal to anything. There are times when you put me forcibly in mind of my sister."

"I doubt that that is a compliment," she said thoughtfully, "for I must tell you, sir, that whatever you have put me in mind of my brother, it has not been because of anything particularly admirable in your behavior."

"Then shall we consign our relatives to perdition? Talking of one's family can only be boring to anyone else."

"But families are important, sir."

"Are they?" He smiled at her. "I cannot agree, but in any case, I did mean what I said to you for a compliment."

She could not resist returning his smile, wishing she were worthy of such praise. It must, she thought, be an excellent thing to be equal to all the challenges one encountered. She had already discovered, however, that quite frequently she was not.

They passed along a narrow whitewashed corridor to a door leading into the stair hall, and there Nell paused to gaze about her, astonished by the faux-marble walls and the would-be stone steps. The house was very quiet.

"Are there truly no servants, sir?"

"Only the cook and a scullery maid. Shall I send for one of them? Are you nervous, ma'am?"

"No, not at all. I was not raised to be missish, you know. My mother died when I was quite young, and my father went through a flock of housekeepers before I took the reins myself. For some reason, any number of them seemed to think he might marry them. I could never understand such misplaced optimism."

"Could you not?" he asked.

His tone was cynical again, and she laughed. "If you mean to imply that he gave them cause to believe such a thing, you really ought not to say such things to me."

"I made a point of not saying any such thing to you."

"Well, yes, but . . ." She chuckled again. "You are quite abominable, sir. In point of fact, although I have no good reason to believe that my father's actions raised false hopes in his housekeepers' breasts, the possibility does exist. Still, they must have been daft if they believed him.''

''No doubt, but people do believe the oddest things.''

She agreed, gazing at the pictures on the stair wall, where hunting scenes and sketches of Bath hung cheek by jowl with ponderous family portraits. It was as if someone had simply stuck every picture in the house up there without order or reason. Oddly, the effect was both interesting and decorative.

Manningford was watching her. ''My sister Sybilla decided that the stair hall was tiresome, and since my father never sees it, she saw no reason not to alter it. I like the result. We go up this second flight now. His rooms are on the top floor.'' He paused on the landing and looked at her searchingly. ''I hope you are not having second thoughts, Miss Bradbourne. He will not be grateful to you, nor pleased to see you, I might add.''

She smiled at him. ''He will not frighten me, sir.''

He looked long at her, then said slowly, ''No, I begin to think nothing does frighten you, though I cannot help but think that one or two events in your past might well have frightened a person of less resolution.''

''Goodness, sir,'' Nell said, striving for a lightness in her tone that she could not feel, ''you will put me to the blush.''

''You must forgive me.'' He gestured for her to precede him, adding gently, ''When one has racketed about as much as I have, ma'am, one learns to pay as much heed to the things people don't say as to those they do. You flout convention by walking alone in a public garden, but you carry a pistol in your reticule. You behave like a lady of quality, yet you agree without a blush to a scheme that would mortify many other young women. You laugh easily, yet I sense sadness and tension beneath the laughter.''

There was nothing Nell wished to say to that, least of all to tell him that she had hardly laughed at all for months before meeting him, so she held her tongue and gave her attention to the narrow wooden stairs. At the top she paused, waiting for him to come up beside her, wondering if he would say any more.

He did not. He smiled at her again and gestured toward a door just inside the corridor leading off the landing. ''That is his bedchamber,'' he said. "I should like to spring you on him before he has a chance to say he won't see you, but I daresay that would only send him off into another fit. I don't mind if he has one, of course—''

"Sir!" Nell exclaimed, truly shocked.

Manningford drew a deep breath and let it out again before he said, "Look here, Miss Bradbourne, you might as well know from the outset that I don't care a damn for my father. He has never given me the least cause even to feel that ordinary consideration one feels for the common man in the street. He has ignored me all my life, exerting himself only to forbid me to do anything of which he does not approve, frequently threatening to cut off my allowance when word of any outrageous behaviour reached his ears, but consistently forbidding me to seek gentlemanly occupation.''

"But surely,'' Nell said, looking at the closed door ahead of them, "there must have been something you could have done. Perhaps your brother would have helped you.''

The glint of sardonic amusement in Manningford's eyes deepened and he shrugged. "My brother makes few decisions on his own, ma'am, and his wife does not approve of me. To her credit, I must point out that I am just as irresponsible, selfish, and heedless as ever she has accused me of being. Indeed, my myriad faults have been described to me by many others in addition to Clarissa, and with equal regularity. So many who say so very much the same thing must certainly be right.''

"Goodness," Nell said, shaking her head with an expression of extreme sympathy on her lively face, "you poor, poor man.''

The look in his eyes sharpened, then relaxed, and his lips began to twitch. He said in a carefully even tone, "Someone recently told me that you are never impertinent, Miss Bradbourne. I wonder who that can have been.''

"Why, sir," she said with wide-eyed innocence, "it was I who told you, but no doubt such adversity has impaired your memory.''

Taking her arm in a firm grip, he drew her to a padded bench against the wall on the landing and plumped her down upon it. "You deserve that I should take you straight in,'' he said, "but I have at least some notion of civility left to me. Moreover, Borland is as likely as my father to have a fit if I simply open the door and present you to their notice. I'd not miss my father, but the entire household would sink without Borland, so you will await me here." He went to the door of the bedchamber and scratched softly.

The door opened at once, and Borland stood there, his sharp gaze flying from Manningford to Nell, whereupon his eyes widened and he looked back in dismay at Manningford. "Master Brandon," he protested in his raspy voice, "you cannot—"

"I can, Borland, so it is of no use to tell me that I cannot. I have honored my father's wishes for eight-and-twenty years, but that was before he demanded more than I can give. I quite understand that the wretched novel must be written—oh, don't look so no-account," he added when the manservant gasped and stared wretchedly at Nell. "She knows the whole of it, and you may tell him for me that if he does not agree at once to see the pair of us, I shall shout the truth from the rooftops of Bath. It is naught to me if people know his secret. Certainly no one will think for a minute that I had a hand in it, so if they laugh, they will laugh only at him."

There was a heavy silence that lasted a full minute before Borland turned and looked back into the bedchamber, his expression as he did so showing clearly that he would not have been surprised to discover that his master had suffered another seizure and died on the spot. What he saw apparently startled him nearly as much, however, for he turned back with a look of amazement on his face and said, "Bring her in, Master Brandon."

"What, at once?"

The response came from within the room, in a gruff but surprisingly firm voice. "Aye, you damned self-centered knave, at once! I can scarcely be expected to change my attire for the occasion, but damme, I'm still your father, and if you try such threats with me again, I'll see you suffer for it."

Exchanging a speaking look with Borland, Manningford turned and gestured to Nell.

She arose, stepped forward, and without a thought put her hand in his, not knowing whether she sought to give or take comfort, certain only that she was glad to find his hand, warm and strong, gripping hers.

He drew her forward, and Borland stepped aside uncertainly to allow the pair of them to enter. "Shall I come in, Master Brandon, or . . ."

"Wait here," Manningford said quietly, and shut the door, turning toward the man in the bed, who had leaned forward, away from the many pillows against which he had been propped, his expression showing both impatience and alarm. Manningford said hastily, "Father, this is Miss Bradbourne. She—"

"Good God, you're Flavia Bradbourne's niece, ain't you?" Sir Mortimer demanded harshly, falling against his pillows again but not taking his gaze from her.

"I am her grandniece, sir," Nell replied, making her curtsy. Noting his pallor and thinking he must be in pain, she added gently, "I apologize for disturbing you, but Mr. Manningford believed the matter was of some urgency to you."

"It is, it is! But never mind about that. Tell me about Flavia. Damme, but she must be an old woman by now!"

"She'd not thank you for calling her so," Nell said with a grin. "More likely, she'd threaten to dust you with her cane."

"Hasn't changed then," he said with satisfaction. "She can give me a few years, of course, though you mightn't think it to look at me now. Little scrap of a thing, she was, like yourself, though her hair was gold as a guinea. A beauty, a real beauty."

Manningford said, "Miss Bradbourne has certain claims to beauty too, sir, if I might be so bold as to say so."

"Oh, certainly, certainly. No need to take offense!"

Nell's eyes twinkled. "I thank you for the compliment, both of you, but I can never claim to be such a beauty as Great-aunt Flavia was in her day. Why, she was a diamond of the first-water."

Sir Mortimer said, "I'll not contradict you, Miss Bradbourne." He fell silent for a moment, then added, "Do I take it that my idiot son thinks you can write a novel?"

Nell was dismayed but replied calmly, "Oh, no, sir, Mr. Manningford had it in mind only that I should act as your scribe, because no one can read his hand. You see, I need the . . ." Remembering that he knew her great-aunt gave her pause, but she gathered herself and finished firmly, "I need the money."

"So Flavia has run herself to a standstill, has she? Can't say it surprises me to hear it. Extravagant little puss."

"She did not," Nell said quickly. "That is, it was not extravagance but the fact that her jointure remained the same when prices increased. It is really too bad."

Sir Mortimer shrugged, and for the first time she was able to see that his ability to move had been impaired, for only his left shoulder went up. She noticed, too, that his face appeared to sag a little on the right side, and that his right eye seemed somehow different from his left.

"Will you allow me to assist you, sir?"

"I seem to have no choice," he said grimly, glancing at his son, but his expression, in Nell's opinion, showed respect rather than vexation, though his voice was still gruff as he added, "Don't you think to go haring off now, young man. This is your doing, and you'll stay to see it through, damme if you won't!"

"I will," Manningford said, but he said it to Nell.

# 6

For a fortnight their plan succeeded well enough, the only occurrence to upset Nell's composure during that time being the arrival of a letter from her father's cousin, who chose to treat her flight with dignity. Suggesting that, as a Bradbourne, she ought to have traveled post rather than by the common stage, Jarvis wrote that he had no objection to her journey and added that she ought to have applied to him for money rather than be obligated to Lady Flavia. But since he enclosed a draft on a Bath bank (for which, as an enclosure, she was obliged to pay sixpence), though she might wish he had not guessed so quickly where she was, the most she could complain of in his letter was that good manners compelled her to write and thank him for it.

In Royal Crescent, Manningford had taken the reins more firmly in hand than anyone had expected him to do, and Nell believed he was rather enjoying the experience. Not only had he found he could deal very well with his father's man of affairs (who was delighted to be able to do business face-to-face rather than by post, as had been the habit for many years), but also he had succeeded all by himself in convincing the Hammersmyths, his father's late butler and housekeeper, to return.

Quarter-day had passed, but he had seemed to take no notice of it, other than to send Max down to Westerleigh to his brother, with a recommendation to see what sort of a gun dog he might make. His mood remained light, and if he seemed to be busy in his father's study whenever Nell sat with Sir Mortimer, and ready to escort her to her chair when they had finished, she certainly had no objection to make to that. She liked him and had rapidly come to accept him as a friend, though she still found it disconcerting that he frequently understood her thoughts before she spoke them aloud.

For the first few days, until Mr. Lasenby departed in response to a curt summons from his grandfather, a maid-servant sat on the padded bench outside the bedchamber door, but with Lasenby gone, Nell had deemed her presence there unnecessary and suggested she find other duties. By the time Lasenby returned, complaining of his grandfather's despotism (but ruefully admitting that he had forgotten to visit Miss Wembly in London prior to her family's departure for the south coast), no one thought about asking the maid to resume her place on the landing.

Nell found it hard to believe that Sir Mortimer had been a determined recluse for so many years, for he seemed, now that he had accepted her visits, to look forward to them. Sadly, by the end of the second week she had begun to notice that rather than gaining strength, he was weakening, and that he was simply too ill to work at the pace that would see his book finished when the publisher expected it to be. Not only was he not accustomed to telling his tales aloud, but he frequently had difficulty thinking of the words he wanted to use, and even more difficulty keeping track of his story. She thought the result worse than any tale she had ever read and was certain that even she, with her lack of experience, could have done a better job of writing it.

She had been going early each morning to the Royal Crescent and returning late in the afternoon to Laura Place, and as far as either she or Lady Flavia could tell, no one suspected that she was doing anything out of the way. Thus, she would have been content to continue as they were, hoping that with Sir Mortimer's experience, he would somehow manage to create gold out of dross, but suddenly one afternoon he lost what little patience he had.

"Damme, but I don't know what's come over me," he muttered as he fumbled for a word. "That's the fourth time in less than a quarter-hour that I have lost the thread! This will not do, Miss Bradbourne. It won't do at all."

"I wish you would call me Nell, sir," she told him for what she thought must be the hundredth time.

" 'Tain't proper," he muttered, clearly still searching his mind for the word he wanted. "Pretty young woman like you oughtn't to be spending all her time with an old man, wearing her fingers to the bone with nonsensical scribbling. Ought to be going out to parties and the like."

"Well, I cannot do that, in any event," she reminded him. "I am in mourning, as you know full well."

"Must be nearly over and done b' now," he retorted. "Royal family's nigh well given up mourning the queen, after all, and Bradbourne did himself in about the same time, did he not?"

"Just afterward," she said coolly, wondering how this old man, cooped up as he was on the top floor of a house in Bath, could know so much of what went on elsewhere in the world.

"Fool thing to do, to kill himself." He stirred in obvious discomfort, and Borland, who had been sitting out of the way in a chair by the window, got up at once and moved to straighten his pillows. Sir Mortimer ignored him. "Why did he do it?"

Nell swallowed the emotions stirred by his question, determined to maintain her composure. She had quickly learned that it did her no good to reveal her sensibilities to this man, that it was better to give as good as she got. She said flatly, "I should prefer not to discuss that subject, if you please."

"Well, I don't please. I want to know what would drive a seemingly robust man to blow his brains out."

Her expression wooden, she said, "He found that he had been ruined through his own foolishness, sir, and he was disappointed in his son. And now, if you please—"

"Disappointed, was he? Can't blame him for that when his son's a damned young scoundrel who didn't even bother to attend his funeral. On the Continent, by what I hear, and likely to remain." He shifted painfully, adding, "In my day, that would have meant pistols at dawn as the cause, but these mealymouthed times, it can't have been any such thing. Only such affair I've heard about in years was some loose fish shot right here in Bath, and that was no affair of honor. Take that damned stuff away, Borland!" This last was in reference to the glass the manservant was just then attempting to press to his master's lips.

Borland said gently, "The doctor insists you take your tonic regularly, sir, so it won't do to be forgetting it." He tilted the glass, and since he had prudently placed his large hand behind Sir Mortimer's head to steady it, the old man could not move away and was compelled to drink the stuff. He did so, screwing up his face at the taste of it.

Grateful for the timely respite, Nell struggled to compose herself and wondered how he could know so much. Deducing that his admittedly large correspondence must provide the bulk of his information, and hoping he would say no more to her if he thought she was reading, she began to skim through the material she had taken down that day, noting only that the work was unimpressive, both in quantity and in quality. When Borland moved back to his seat by the window, she looked up again to find the old man's eyes quizzing her, and was able now to perceive in them pain of a quite different nature.

"Pretty awful stuff, ain't it?" he said miserably.

She was silent for a moment, then said, "You know, sir, I think perhaps Elizabeth ought not to run away from school. One reads that sort of thing so frequently that one begins to wonder if there are any young ladies still residing in their boarding schools. And to hire herself out as an abigail to a lady meaning to depart at once for a distant exotic country seems a trifle implausible too. Perhaps if she were older from the outset and simply left school because her time had come to do so—"

"Now, damme, Miss Bradbourne, don't you get to thinking you know more about writing this stuff than I do," he growled. "Been at it thirty years and more, don't you know."

"Whatever made you begin, sir?" Nell asked, adding quickly, lest he take offense, "I mean, 'tis not an occupation one expects to attract a gentleman." She managed to avoid adding "like yourself," but she saw from his expression that he knew what she was thinking. She had seen that same expression on Manningford's face more than once, and found it just as disconcerting now.

Sir Mortimer had no objection to answering her question.

"Shortly before Brandon was born, two friends and I were riding through a village in the 'Shires one day—too hot for hunting, it was—and we chanced to encounter some villagers in a market square, squabbling over a broken-down gig. We rode on, of course—no concern of ours—but soon found ourselves proposing possible grounds for the dispute. We ended by deciding that each of us should write a tale, just for a lark, including such events as we might imagine to have led up to it. The exercise amused me more than I expected, and my little fantasy developed into a work called *Cymbeline Sheridan.* I expect you have heard of it."

"Goodness," Nell said, "of course I have heard of it! Why, everyone has, for I daresay it is as much a classic in its own way as *The Monk,* and I know for a fact that it was my mother's favorite book. Did you really write it, sir?"

"Well, of course I did," he retorted testily, "or I should not say so. Never thought anything would come of it, but I sent it to John Murray, a London publisher, when my friends dared me to do so, and then, after my poor wife died and I found I didn't care at all for the company of others, I turned back to the writing instead. Never wanted my name bandied about, of course, and since the common taste runs to the likes of Ann Radcliffe and Madame d'Arblay—Fanny Burney, she was then—I chose to be an anonymous Gentlewoman of Quality."

"I do know your books now," she said, "for 'tis noted that they are written by the author of *Cymbeline Sheridan.*"

"Aye, so now you must agree that I know what I'm talking about when I tell you young ladies don't want to be reading about a heroine past her prime. They want a young woman, innocent in the ways of the world, to be saved by a properly virtuous hero from an utterly wicked villain. They want ghosts and Gypsies, princes and dukes, gloomy castles, dark woods, snow-white horses, and magic potions. Damme, if they don't!"

"But none of those are real," Nell protested. "I must tell you, sir, that I have been reading a most amusing tale lent to me by Aunt Flavia, called *Emma,* about ordinary people doing ordinary things. The author, a Miss Austen, writes about the sort of people she sees each day, doing things they really do, and her skill is such that she makes the reader laugh at their foibles right along with her.''

"Yes, yes, I know the muck you mean," he said impatiently, "though she's been dead now nigh onto two years, so I expect you think I ought to speak kindly. But I can tell you, her work won't last. Think about it! Pokes fun at persons of rank, she does, the very ones most likely to pay out good coin for the books. Oh, folks read them, but their interest will pass, and you'll do well to remember, miss, that my books—nearly all of them about lovely young heroines marching innocently from one peril to the next—are vastly more successful than hers. Why, if she made even a third as much money in all her life as I've made on *Cymbeline Sheridan* alone, I shall own myself astonished!''

"Well," Nell said, stirred by his arrogant tone to argue the point, "I think her story more interesting than this, sir." She tapped the stack of paper in her lap, adding frankly, "Aside from disbelieving the existence of such absurdities as magic potions and dark, gloomy castles, I tell you to your head that in this day and age, any girl who sits waiting for a virtuous prince on a white horse to ride to her rescue will most likely end her days as a decaying spinster.''

"And how old are you, Miss Bradbourne?''

There was a silence before Nell said grimly, "Old enough to know when someone is attempting to divert me from my point, sir, but such a tactic will not serve. You have hired me—at a very good wage, I might add—to help you get this story written.''

"But not to write it," he snapped, his face turning an alarming shade of red as he struggled to sit up straight in the bed. "I agreed to attempt this idiotic plan, but I shall end it instantly if you mean to insinuate your own simpleminded ideas into *my* story, miss.''

Appalled as much by the way she had allowed herself to speak to him as by a reaction that could not in any way benefit his health, Nell ruthlessly stifled indignation to say, "You are quite right to remind me that I have no experience in such matters, sir, and that it is not my business to be telling you what I think. I must apologize and hope you can forgive me.''

"Poppycock!" His blue eyes blazed. "You don't fool me! No woman with a head of hair like yours ever spoke mealy-mouthed inanities with any sincerity whatever, and that's plain fact. If you've got something to say, say it, but don't prattle rubbishing apologies to me. I won't believe a word of 'em!''

"But I do apologize, and most sincerely, for causing you distress, sir.'' She glanced at Borland to see that he was poised on the edge of his chair, and forced a calmer note into her voice when she added, "I often speak before I think, which is a sad fault in me and one I have frequently struggled to overcome.''

" 'Tis something, I suppose, that you don't declare yourself proud to speak your mind,'' he said, and she was glad to see the manservant settle back again. "Can't abide folks who call it a virtue whenever they speak the first thought that comes into their heads. Never met one yet who appreciated that same virtue in anyone else. Daresay I never will, human nature being what it is. I'll wager that if you were to speak the truth to me now, you'd say you don't think this work is near as good as *Cymbeline Sheridan.*''

"No, sir,'' Nell said quietly. When he did not reply, when it seemed, in fact, that he had lapsed into a silence of despair, she roused herself to add, "Since you have written many wonderful books, sir—so wonderful that his highness, the Regent, wants you to dedicate this one to him—I cannot believe you would thank me if I were to continue merely to write down what you tell me, when I know that you are not happy with the result. Nevertheless, I have no right to speak my mind if you dislike it, and certainly I never meant to say as much as I did.''

"You're a damned impertinent young woman,'' he muttered. "I don't want to see your face again today.'' He sounded tired. As he turned his face to the wall, he added curtly, "Get her out of here, Borland.''

Rising with dignity to her feet, Nell said, "I am perfectly

capable of removing myself, sir. Is it your intention to give notice that my services are no longer required?''

There was no answer.

She glanced at Borland, whose eyes rolled up toward the ceiling as though he hoped to gain assistance from above. When his glance met hers again, she smiled ruefully, and he got to his feet, shaking his head. He made no move to approach the bed.

Placing her notebook in the satchel she used to carry her things, she shook her skirt out with her free hand and turned to leave the room, moving with care so that the figure in the bed should not know how much his reaction had discomposed her. But once she was safely on the other side of the door, she expelled a long breath and let her body sag against the wall, closing her eyes and wishing she could as easily shut out the lingering echoes of her hasty tongue and his angry response. She stood like that for a long moment before straightening, then turned toward the stair and walked straight into Manningford.

His strong hands grasped her upper arms to steady her, and his breath stirred the curls beneath her flimsy lace cap when he said quietly, ''A bad day, Nell?''

She felt warmth flooding her cheeks at the thought of the picture she must present to him. Straightening quickly and attempting without success to step away from him, she forced her gaze to meet his, realizing that he must have been in the study with the door open, and crossed the carpet on silent feet, for she had heard nothing to warn her of his approach.

She had no wish to speak to him there, lest their voices be overheard to the further distress of Sir Mortimer, in the room behind her; yet she found it impossible to move away from him as long as he continued to hold her, and he seemed not to realize that she wished to move. The warmth of his hands on her arms was disconcerting, his nearness more so. It was not, of course, the first time she had stood so near a gentleman, or been so near to him, for she had been seeing him every day for nearly three weeks without becoming shy in his presence, so why his nearness now should disorder her senses was a mystery. Nonetheless, she could seem to find neither her tongue nor the strength to disengage herself from his embrace.

"Perhaps we should step into the study," he said.

"No!" Glancing at the door behind her, she looked back at him in mute appeal, grateful beyond measure when he took her meaning swiftly, stood aside, and let her precede him to the stairway. By the time they had reached the floor below, Nell had regained her customary composure and was able to accompany him into the library without another distressing thought.

The room had become a favorite retreat for her. Its windows, draped in peach-colored velvet a shade darker than the walls and several shades lighter than the carpet, looked out over the crescent and the magnificent panorama beyond. A Chippendale bureau bookcase that filled the wall opposite the fireplace, and a pair of secretary bookcases that flanked its white marble mantel, were loaded with books of the sort she most enjoyed reading, books that Manningford had told her from the first day she might take away to read if she liked. She had spent a number of hours here while Sir Mortimer napped, which he did at least once a day, for now that there were servants in the house again, there was always a cheerful fire to welcome her, and no one disturbed her unless she rang the bell.

The chamber was comfortably furnished and elegant as well, although it was a rather decayed elegance, for Nell would have staked her best gown on the likelihood that it had not been refurbished in a decade. Noting that Manningford had prudently left the door ajar, she moved to one of a pair of wing chairs facing the fireplace and took a seat there, looking into the fire and letting her body relax.

"What happened?" he asked. "I collect that he is in one of his twittier moods today."

She looked at him ruefully. "It was entirely my fault, sir. I spoke out of turn, and he became very angry with me. I am sure it can have done him no good."

"Well, if we are to fret every time he loses his temper, we shall all of us soon be fit for Bedlam. I'll wager he's lost it at least once a week these past twenty years and more, for he has never been noted for his even temperament.''

That drew a smile from her. "No," she said, "but the doctor insists that he must not be distressed, and I . . .''

"You distressed him?" Manningford said flatly. "What did you say?''

"All that I ought not to have said, I fear. I had the temerity to criticize his writing. You ought to have told me that he wrote *Cymbeline Sheridan,* sir. I had no idea!''

"Nor did I," Manningford said. "Did he indeed write it? I am scarcely bookish, but I have certainly heard of that one.''

"Well, I should think you must have done," she said. "A person must have been raised in a monastery not to have done so, and I collect that you went to a perfectly ordinary school.''

"I doubt the lads at Eton would appreciate your description, but I'll not quibble over it.''

She shot him a saucy look. "My brother went to Harrow, sir, so you will not be surprised that I have long been given to look upon Eton as a vastly inferior sort of school.''

"We don't think much of Harrow either. You said once that he and I are alike. Tell me about him.''

"Oh, you are not really so much alike as I first thought," she said, adding quickly, "He is presently in France, in any case, and you once said that to talk of one's family is boring, did you not?" Biting her lip, she added, "I ought never to have criticized your father, sir. It was badly done of me.''

"Nonsense," he said, adding, "My sister and her husband are in France too, in Paris, to be exact. If your brother is doing the fancy, 'tis likely he will encounter them there.''

"I shouldn't think so. Nigel prefers gaming to dancing.'' She didn't add that she thought he would be apt to stay away from anyone likely to know his history, but she was aware of a certain amount of strain in her voice, and she was not surprised when she looked up at Manningford to see that his eyes had narrowed. He did not press her, however, and after a brief silence merely suggested that she might like some refreshment.

"A pot of tea, perhaps?''

"Only if you want something yourself, sir. I ought to go home. Sir Mortimer said he will not need me again today."

"I heard what he said," Manningford said. "I'll ring, shall I? I wouldn't turn down a glass of the old man's Madeira."

When he had turned away to tug the bell cord, she said in a small voice, "You heard him?"

"Just the bit when he told Borland to get you out of there." He moved to the second wing chair and stood beside it, his right hand lightly resting on the chair back as he looked down at her. "He must have been speaking more loudly than usual, or directly at the wall between the two rooms. Generally, you know, one hears only a murmur of voices in the study. I think you'd better tell me the whole, don't you? You cannot fear that I'd take you to task, after all."

"I have told you," she said, not thinking it necessary to assure him that she did not fear him in the least. "Oh, not the details, but the important part, that the writing is difficult for him and that he has no respect for my opinion. There is no reason that he should have, of course. I have no skills to speak of—certainly my scribbles are nothing great—but I have read any number of books, for there was frequently nothing else to do at home." She smiled at him. "I don't know why I tell you this, you know, for it has nothing to do with the problem at hand. I merely told your papa that I thought he ought to make a change or two in his story, and he became out of reason cross. I cannot blame him. I must have seemed intolerably impertinent."

One of the two footmen who had been engaged entered just then, and Manningford turned toward him and gave the order for tea and wine to be served to them, saying nothing further until the man had gone away again. Then, sitting down in the wing chair, he said gently, "How bad is it, this book of his?"

Nell hesitated, then gathered her courage and looked him straight in the eye. "If I were to tell you that I know I could write a better one, would that tell you how dreadful it is?"

He did not answer her at once, and when he did, his words were not what she had expected them to be. "Do it," he said.

"I beg your pardon."

"You heard me. How long would it take you to write out a fair copy of what there is so far, altering it to suit yourself?"

"Why, I cannot say. I have thought about it, you know, ever since I read over what he had done before I began to help. It is disjointed and rough, but the plot is sound and the comical bits delightfully amusing, so I found myself wanting to alter first one thing, then another. I daresay, in such a case, one always believes one's own way is superior. Of course, I know nothing about writing for publication, so your father will undoubtedly suffer another fit if I should even attempt such a thing."

"Then we shan't tell him."

"Pray, do not be absurd, sir. How can we not?"

After a moment's thought, he said, "Does he think the work he has done so far is up to his usual standard?"

"No," she replied. "Indeed, he has said as much to me. His weakness and his inability to make his mind behave as he wants it to, both seem to distress him very much."

"Then it is our duty to help him." He turned when the footman reentered the room carrying a tray and followed by a young parlormaid. "Set the tray on the table by the hearth. We will serve ourselves."

Shooting a curious glance at Nell, the maid lowered her eyes and set about helping the footman adjust the items on the tray, but the glance served as a sharp reminder that there were many who would not approve of her presence in Sir Mortimer's house, even without the presence of his handsome son. The thought brought a flush to her cheeks, and she had all she could do not to look conscious of wrongdoing, so she was rather relieved when Mr. Lasenby chose that moment to enter the room.

"Here you are!" He strolled into the room with the assurance of one in no doubt of his welcome, and although Manningford frowned, since his friend's attention was riveted on the tray, he did not notice. "Here, I say," Lasenby exclaimed when the footman and maid turned to leave, "pour me out a glass of that wine before you go, and I'll have a plate of those sweet biscuits as well. Can't think why the pair of you are in such a rush to be off."

Manningford said, "I told them we'd serve ourselves, Sep."

"Well, I can't think why we would wish to do that when you've finally got proper servants in the house. I'll tell you what it is, Bran, you folks here in Bath treat your servants in a dashed odd fashion, and that's the truth of the matter. Never seen such a place! Hope you don't expect me to get accustomed to it, for I never shall. Not brought up to it, don't you know. Not brought up to it at all." He seemed at last to sense something unusual in the atmosphere of the room, for with a glance at Manningford and another at Nell he added, "I say, I hope I ain't intruding. Thought you'd be glad of the company, but I'll play least in sight if you don't want me."

"Oh, no," Nell exclaimed at the same time that Manningford said, "No need for you to go anywhere, Sep. We can as easily have our conversation later."

"Now, dash it, Bran—"

An involuntary ripple of laughter escaped Nell's lips at the indignation in his voice. "Oh, do stay, Mr. Lasenby. There was nothing particularly private in what we are discussing. Not where you are concerned, at all events," she added, remembering the servants. When they departed a moment later, she looked at Manningford. "Truly, sir, he already knows as much as we do, and while I am certainly ready to take your advice as to what it is best for us to do, I cannot help but think that a third head will prove beneficial to our cause."

"Not if the third head is Sep's," Manningford retorted. "He's got nothing on his mind just now but what old Rackton will next have to say about his trying to make mice feet of his betrothal."

"Daresay I'll find out soon enough," Lasenby said, "for I distinctly recall that there is some affair or other I am supposed to remember."

"Brighton," Manningford said helpfully. "Wembly ball."

"Ah, yes, but I say, Bran, did you know there's a race-track right here in Bath? I could scarcely credit it, but it's a fact. Landsdowne Course—they say it's the highest flat course in England. We must take a look, dear boy."

"Not just now, Sep."

"Right, you were wanting to talk about your tangle here, were you not? Fact is, you ain't as accustomed as I am to being riveted to the family nest, so daresay, if things get too bothersome, you'll soon be champing at the bit." He glanced at Nell, adding hastily, "Assure you, ma'am, if he does take it into his head to bolt to Newmarket or the-Lord-knows-where, you can count on your humble servant to try to talk him out of it."

"I am sure that I may," Nell said, glancing at Manningford and adding when she saw that he was frowning, "but I am persuaded that Mr. Manningford will not leave me in the lurch, sir."

"Good God, no, ma'am," Mr. Lasenby said, his eyes widening. "Bran's a gentleman, ain't he? Would never do such a thing. Just meant that he must feel a trifle tied by the heels here, don't you know. He—" Manningford having cleared his throat, he glanced at him and said, "Well, dash it, Bran, no need to take a pet. You've already stayed longer than you intended, or anyone else might have expected. You don't even like the old gentleman. Stands to reason you can't like dancing to his tune."

"Be quiet, Sep."

"Yes, by Jove, of course. I say, have you tried these short biscuits? Best I ever tasted. Give you my word. May I serve you some, Miss Bradbourne?"

"Yes, certainly," Nell said, "and then do sit down, Mr. Lasenby, and give us the benefit of your opinion. Mr. Manningford has suggested that I might alter Sir Mortimer's work, but I am by no means certain that anything I write would be an improvement."

"No reason it wouldn't be," he said. "Thing is, are you sure you ought? He mightn't like it, you know."

"You don't understand," Manningford said. "Miss Bradbourne informs me that he is having grave difficulties with this novel of his, and I have suggested that she do what she can to improve upon his labors. That is all. But if such a thing is to be done at all, I should prefer it to be done at once."

Mr. Lasenby shook his head. "Now I think on it, I don't believe the old gentleman will like it a bit," he said.

"No," Nell said, "nor do I. He as good as gave me my notice today, merely for daring to voice my opinion to him."

Mr. Lasenby nodded. "I should think that settles it, then."

"No, it doesn't," Manningford said. "It is nonsensical to pander to his wishes when this weakness of his distresses him so. It cannot be good for him."

"Well, I should think it would be worse for him to snuff it in a towering rage," Mr. Lasenby said.

"No need to concern ourselves with that possibility until we discover whether Miss Bradbourne can do the thing," Manningford pointed out.

"But, dash it, Bran, how will we know? I don't know anything about such stuff, and I'll wager you don't either."

"We'll find someone who does," Manningford said.

Nell gasped. "You want me to let someone read what I write even before Sir Mortimer sees it? I couldn't! Why, I cannot even imagine doing such a thing."

Manningford looked at her. "If my plan succeeds, a good many people will be reading your work, for my father informed me at the outset of this venture that nearly everyone who is anyone in the *beau monde* subscribes for his books the moment Murray makes it known that they are available for publication. What I suggest is that you take what you've got home with you and see what you can do to improve it. It will do my father no harm to forgo the pleasure of your company for a few days. Perhaps he will then think twice before indulging his temper again."

"Perhaps, sir," she said doubtfully.

Manningford smiled. "I may well be overstating the case. Now, if you have finished your tea, I'll see you on your way, and we'll begin fresh again on Monday morning."

# 7

When Nell returned to Laura Place, Sudbury, behaving with a stateliness beyond even his usual measure, opened the chair door for her and, once she had emerged, directed the men to take the chair to its usual place beneath the sweeping stairway. Then, when the men had departed, he said quickly when she turned toward the stairway, "Her ladyship is not alone, Miss Nell."

She looked back. "Company, Sudbury? Who is it?"

Something in his very lack of expression warned her before he said, "Mr. Jarvis Bradbourne, miss. He has been sitting with her ladyship this past hour and more. I regret to say that he did not so much as await an invitation before informing her ladyship that he intended to dine with her. Such behavior is not what we are accustomed to in this house."

She had stiffened at the mention of their visitor's name, and it took effort to keep her voice calm when she asked, "Does Mr. Jarvis know where I have been, Sudbury?"

"No, Miss Nell. He assumed from the outset, I might say, that you were staying in the house, and not having had orders to the contrary, I did not attempt to deny the fact. I did, however, refrain from indicating any awareness whatever of your immediate whereabouts, and her ladyship told him, in my hearing, only that you were spending the day with friends."

"I see." She glanced up the stairs at the drawing-room door, shut at the moment, then back at the butler. "I daresay I ought to go straight up to her."

"As to that, Miss Nell, I am persuaded that there is no great need to do so if you do not wish it. Her ladyship will not be expecting you as early as this, after all, so there is sufficient time to be changing your dress if you should be desirous of doing so.''

She was sorely tempted to accept his suggestion, but she shook her head. ''Her ladyship has already sustained more of Mr. Jarvis' conversation than she ought to have had to, Sudbury, and I am woefully conscious of the fact that it is my presence in this house that has brought him down upon her. Oh, and that reminds me,'' she added, plunging her hand into the pocket of her cloak and withdrawing a small drawstring pouch. ''Mr. Manningford was kind enough to pay me my week's wages before I left. Will you be so kind as to give the money to Mrs. Sudbury? I expect she will be wanting to purchase some extra items for dinner.''

''Thank you, miss,'' the butler said, pocketing the pouch. ''Things have been more comfortable these past weeks, I must say, but she was in a bit of a fret as to how she was to put a proper spread before Mr. Jarvis this evening, knowing from experience that he is not what we should call a delicate trencherman.''

''No, Jarvis does like his dinner,'' Nell said with a grimace. ''When one is wondering if he is even human, one does remember that. I shall just go up and tidy my hair, Sudbury, and then you may announce me. I think a little extraordinary formality is called for, don't you? It will perhaps impress him enough to keep him from trying to call the tune here.''

''That is what her ladyship thought as well, Miss Nell.''

Hastening upstairs to her bedchamber, Nell wasted no time indulging in fripperies, though she was sorely tempted to linger, having no desire to face Jarvis Bradbourne even with her great-aunt stoutly behind her. It took little time to wash her hands and face and coax her curls into order, however, and with a last glance in the glass to assure herself that her appearance would give him no cause to suspect that she had anything to hide from him, she went down to the drawing room, pausing one last moment at the door to inhale a long steadying breath and release it slowly before nodding to Sudbury to open the door.

Inside the room, Lady Flavia, seated in her usual chair

near the low-burning fire, greeted her arrival with seeming composure, but Nell was quick to note the look of relief in her eyes when she said, "You are before your time, my dear. How very pleasant, to be sure. And you see that I have a surprise for you." She indicated, seated in the chair opposite her own, a stocky man in his thirties exquisitely attired in biscuit-colored pantaloons and a dark-blue wide-shouldered frock coat, his brown locks fashionably disordered, his shirt points stiff enough and high enough to impede the motion of his head and force him to turn his entire torso toward Nell as her ladyship added, "Jarvis informs me that he means to remain in Bath for at least a week or more. Will that not be delightful?"

Fixing a smile upon her face, Nell agreed that the news was delightful indeed, and stepped forward with her hand outstretched to greet her cousin. A glint in his chilly gray eyes as he rose to make an exceedingly graceful leg to her gave her to know that he was not in the least deceived by her welcome.

Jarvis Bradbourne might easily have passed for a man ten years older, a fact due as much to his foppish affectation of constant weariness as to a life spent—as Nell was certain it had been—in dissipation. Straightening, he raised his gold-rimmed quizzing glass to his right eye and peered at her through it, looking her up and down with a sorrowful expression on his round sallow face before allowing the glass to drop, swinging it gently back and forth on its narrow black-velvet ribbon.

"Still in mourning, my dear? By my oath, I commend your fortitude, but do you not think it a trifle gauche to continue to draw attention to the events surrounding your parent's demise?"

Nell's eyes flashed fire, but before she could snap out the retort that leapt to her tongue, Lady Flavia said briskly, "I see that your manners have not improved, Jarvis, try as you will to pretend to civility. One would think that a man with so fine a regard for his name and appearance would take a little more care lest his tongue betray his true character when he least wishes it to do so. Pray recall where you are and attempt to behave like a gentleman. You may turn that log on the grate, if you will, and then sit down again and tell me more about the new paintings you have acquired at Crosshill. You will be interested to know, my dear Nell," she continued, just as though she had been speaking mere commonplace to the red-faced Bradbourne, "that Jarvis has acquired an amusing work he believes to have been painted by Mr. Holbein, the man who painted that famous portrait of King Henry the Eighth. He was just telling me about it before you came in. Are you going to attend to that log, Jarvis, or are you not?"

"I am not," he said, moving to pull the bell cord. "I fear that I am not in the habit of attending to such tiresome details as that myself, and will be more likely to snuff your fire or have the coals out onto the carpet if I attempt such a thing. I will be happy to order a footman to attend to it, however."

Exchanging a look with Lady Flavia, Nell turned quickly to look out the window, lest Jarvis glance her way and note her dismay, for despite the fact of her wages from Royal Crescent and the bank draft from Jarvis, Lady Flavia had seen no good reason to hire more servants, other than a scullery maid to assist Mrs. Sudbury. The view of the fountain's spray calmed her as it always did, however, and she was able to tell herself that Sudbury would cope easily enough with her cousin's demands.

"Nell, my dear," Jarvis drawled behind her, "no doubt you have failed to observe that I am kept standing by your reluctance to sit." Then, when she only looked at him, he added in the same tone, "Too wearing, my dear, for one of my fragile constitution, a constitution, I might add, that has been sadly overtaxed, as you must know, from the moment the intelligence was brought to me of your precipitate departure from Highgate. You cannot have known what a blow your flight would deal to my self-esteem, my dear, or I am persuaded that you would never have gone off in such a scrambling way. By my oath, you must tell me why you found it necessary to do so just as I had begun to think matters were in a fair way to being settled between us."

Lady Flavia's eyebrows shot upward. "Settled? Dear me, Nell, surely you did not tell me as much."

Nell sat down on the settee near the window, thus forcing Jarvis to turn his chair if he would continue to look at her, and said in a detached way, "I believe I told you that he had desired us to wed, ma'am, and that I had refused him. I had hoped that the notion had not fixed itself so firmly in his mind as it seems to have done, however, and I assure you that he has been given no cause whatever to believe that my mind is similarly affected."

"Come, come, my dear," Jarvis murmured gently, "surely you know that the offer was born of my fondness for you as well as my awareness that your life was sadly altered by the unfortunate events of last December. By my oath, I had not thought of marrying again after my previous sad experiences with that state, and if your dear father were still alive or your beloved brother in a position to support you, I could acknowledge that there were other prospects open to you. But in view of the reality, I could do no less than make what must be thought a generous offer."

He looked at Lady Flavia. "You must agree, ma'am, that she does herself no good by this stubborn disinclination to see where her fortune lies. I could not reconcile it with my conscience merely to allow her to dwindle into one of those poor women forced to batten on their more fortunate relations. Only think of her pride! Instead, to continue to be one of the Bradbournes of Highgate . . . well, what could be better? Of course, we must all wish to see young Nigel restored to his honors, but in the event that that cannot be—as I very much fear will prove to be the case—we must do what we can to see that Highgate does not suffer, or dearest Nell, either; for by my oath, no one believes that her father or her brother can have intended to ruin her prospects by their selfish actions." He dabbed gently at his lips with a lace handkerchief and added dulcetly, "You will both forgive me, I know, if I speak frankly on that subject."

"I wonder," Nell said, remembering one of Sir Mortimer's more caustic comments, "if you will appreciate equal frankness, sir, when I tell you to your head that never did you receive the slightest encouragement to believe that I would accept your suit, nor even that I considered it to be as obliging an offer as you seem to believe. If I have been ruined by my father's or Nigel's act, so be it. I cannot imagine why you should wish to marry someone who bears such an aversion to you as I do.''

"Perhaps," he replied, still in that gentle tone, "because, being older and wiser than you are, my dear, I see more clearly than you do what perils lie ahead of one in your position, and care enough for you to wish to help you avoid them.''

"Nonsense," said Lady Flavia with her customary crispness of manner. "No young woman with Nell's expectations can be thought to have ruined herself.''

Nell cast her a warning look, but she was oblivious to it, having fixed her imperious gaze upon Mr. Bradbourne, challenging him to deny her words.

He did not hesitate to do so. "You will find that you are mistaken, ma'am," he said. "Once the *beau monde* discovers the entire truth about Cousin Jasper's death, by which I mean to say the lurid details of dear Nigel's overly impulsive act—''

"Those persons who believe your version of it, you mean," Nell snapped. "My brother did not fire his pistol before time!''

He lifted one eyebrow. "As you wish, my dear. I should not dream of contradicting you, though I fear you will discover all too soon—if those facts should become known—that no family of rank will ally itself with one of such singular disrepute, even though the name be Bradbourne. Bad blood will out, you know.''

Nell could not mistake his meaning. If the whole truth about Nigel's duel was not yet known—and she had certainly gleaned no hint of scandal here in Bath—it was because Jarvis himself had hushed it up, and he was telling her now that what he had done he could undo. She looked at her great-aunt.

"Poppycock," declared Lady Flavia with asperity. "If the presence of bad blood made it impossible for one distinguished family to ally with another, there would soon be no member of the *beau monde* left who could form an eligible connection. Only think of that Marlborough lot, for goodness' sake, or the Jerseys, or indeed the royal family itself. At least Nigel is not suspected of having secretly married his mistress before ever he married his wife, as the Regent is.''

What Jarvis' response to this might have been they were never to know, for at that moment the drawing-room door opened, and to Nell's astonishment, a stiff young man in livery at least two sizes too large for him stepped in and in stentorian, even lofty, accents demanded, ''What be ye wantin', mum?''

Lady Flavia said calmly, ''Tend to the fire, Amos. It has nearly burned itself out, I fear.''

''Right y' are, mum,'' the lad said, whereupon Nell recognized him as Botten's nephew, the youth who had held Manningford's horses for him in the square. He moved with a swiftness unseen in any seasoned footman, knelt by the fire, and dealt with the problem with dispatch, then straightened, turned to Lady Flavia, and said cheerfully, ''Right, now, mum, what else be ye a-wantin'? That is,'' he added hastily, his cheeks flushing red, ''will there be aught else, m'lady?''

''No, thank you,'' she replied tranquilly, ''that will be all. You may inform Sudbury that he is to announce dinner as soon as Mrs. Sudbury desires him to do so. We do not keep town hours, Jarvis, as you know,'' she added for that gentleman's benefit as the lad bowed himself awkwardly out of the room.

Jarvis was watching him through his quizzing glass, his expression one of disbelief, and when the door had shut again, he turned back to Lady Flavia. ''By my oath, ma'am, what on earth was that?''

''A footman, Jarvis,'' she replied, ''only a footman.''

''I should never have known it. Surely you do not parade that specimen before your lady friends.''

''Pray, do not be absurd, Jarvis. Amos is a perfectly respectable young man, a connection of my dresser's, in fact.

After all, Botten has been with me for many years now, and footmen must train somewhere.''

"Yes, as boots or pages!" Bradbourne grimaced. "It is to be hoped that he does not spill the soup on one of us at table.''

If Nell or Lady Flavia harbored a different hope, they were disappointed, for Amos, though he had none of the attributes of a proper footman, acquitted himself well. Sudbury actually served them, a fact that Lady Flavia explained casually was no doubt due to his fearing much the same thing that Jarvis did. She took advantage of her years when the servants had left them alone and the meal was drawing to a close by informing him that since she seldom entertained gentlemen and had not been expecting him, there was no decent port in the house over which he might linger.

"You will be wishing to get straight back to the inn, at all events, I daresay," she said. "The York House, is it not? I trust they are treating you well there.''

"Very well, ma'am, thank you." Fastidiously he blotted his lips with his napkin and placed it on the table, but showed no sign of being in any haste to depart. Smiling at Nell, he said, "I hope you will not object if I call upon you again, my dear. We really must decide what is to be done about your future, but in the meantime I will arrange for you to receive a proper allowance while you are here.''

"I do not want your money, Jarvis.''

"Nonsense, 'tis none of mine, but from the Highgate rents, for things are running in more proper train there now, and you will not be pretending to despise a proper allowance from that source, I hope!''

With commendable calm, considering the state of her nerves by then, Nell said, "I shan't take it if you intend to use the Highgate purse as a weapon, sir. In any case, there is no reason for you to put yourself out on my behalf. I am of age now and may be trusted to look out for myself. Indeed, I was accustomed to do so in many ways long before my father passed away.''

"Well, we shan't quarrel now," he said. "I shall remain here to see to some matters of business, so we will talk again.

I should tell you, however, that I have encountered certain difficulties regarding Highgate affairs. Have you perhaps had any word from your brother, containing his direction?''

"No," Nell said, adding tersely, "I wish I had."

"If we do not hear from him soon," Jarvis said with a sigh that did not fool her in the slightest, "I fear I shall have to present the fact of that wager before a chancery court. It is a course most repugnant to me, because one does not like admitting that one's father and cousin treated such an estate so lightly, but if I can see no other course open to me to protect the estate, you must admit, I will have no choice.''

Lady Flavia said hastily, before Nell could speak, "Surely we will hear from Nigel soon, Jarvis, and everything will be arranged as it should be. He must be grateful to you for your help that fatal night, and for your forbearance, as well, regarding that wicked wager.''

He looked gratified. "I wondered if Nell had told you the truth of the matter, ma'am, since her father insisted that he had never meant to stake the estate at all, that it was an error in the wording. No need to concern yourself that I will take advantage, whether that was the case or not, unless it becomes utterly necessary. I cannot agree with Nell that an error was made, however, for my father and Cousin Jasper were always making idiotic wagers with one another, were they not, and I know that my father, before his death, expected to win Highgate, not merely a stupid hatchment. But since there has been even a suggestion that the thing was inscribed incorrectly in the betting book . . . well, I for one would hate to come into the property in such a way, and that is what I told Nell after her father so imprudently put a period to his life. Ah, forgive me," he added, glancing at Nell's expressive face. "I have been tactless again. But really, my love, even you cannot think your dear father acted with prudence, then or before.''

Since the only thought in Nell's mind just then was that Jarvis' head would look rather fetching served up on a platter to a pack of wild dogs, it was just as well that, once again, Lady Flavia was the one to respond, telling him, in exactly the same tone that she might have used had he not spoken a word out of the way, that she was sure it would all come right in the end and that she and Nell would leave him now. "Sudbury will show you out, sir. Nell, darling, bid your cousin good night." And with those words and a swish of her wide skirts, she arose and stepped toward the door. Nell hastened to open it for her, leaving Jarvis half out of his chair.

In the drawing room with the door safely shut behind them, Lady Flavia took her customary seat and said matter-of-factly when Nell did not follow suit, "What is it, my dear?"

"What if he takes it into his head to wander about the house?" Nell demanded.

"Sudbury will see that he does not. Do you fetch me my knitting from that chair yonder, my dear, and perhaps you will be so kind as to assist me to wind that new skein of pale blue yarn into a ball. Yes, that is the one. You may sit on my stool if you like. There is room." Obligingly she moved her feet to one end, and Nell sat down before her, obediently taking the skein and arranging it on her hands so that Lady Flavia might wind her ball. "You ought not to show your hackles so easily, my dear," the old lady said a moment later.

"I know, but he infuriates me. I am certain that he is not what he pretends to be. He is too smooth, and one always senses a threat beneath his words."

"One does, of course. Also, one begins to believe that whatever took place that night was not as he described it."

They were silent after that until Sudbury came in to inform them that Jarvis had taken his leave, but when Nell moved the other wing chair up near the fire and sat down again, Lady Flavia remembered her early return to Laura Place that afternoon and demanded to know the reason for it.

When this had been explained to her, she tut-tutted over Sir Mortimer's volatile temper and agreed that it could not be good for him so often to be losing it, and when Nell hesitantly revealed Manningford's suggestion that she ought to attempt to smooth over the rough places in Sir Mortimer's story, to her surprise, her great-aunt agreed with enthusiasm that it was the very thing that she should do.

"For one must own, my dear, that you have the skills necessary for such a task. Why, your letters have always been most amusing to read, you know, which encourages one to believe that you can make as good a job of it as that Miss Austen, who wrote *Emma*. 'Tis the very thing for you, and only think if one could actually make money by writing amusing little tales for others to read! One would be most astonished, I should think.''

''Well, I should certainly be astonished,'' Nell declared roundly. ''I have never thought of such a thing in all my life, ma'am, and I cannot believe for one moment that Sir Mortimer would approve of my taking any such liberty with his work.''

''Oh, piffle. He ought to be grateful, if what you say of his work is true, and I have no reason to doubt you, for I doubt he can ever have written anything worth the reading.''

''Well, you will not say so when I tell you he wrote *Cymbeline Sheridan*,'' Nell told her.

The reaction was all she might have hoped. ''Good gracious! Sir Mortimer wrote that? I should never have believed it if anyone but you had told me so. To think of it! But that settles it, my dear,'' she added earnestly. ''You must do your very best, for it will not do at all for the Prince Regent to be honored in a book that is not up to the standard he expects.''

''But I am not asked to write a book, only to alter one, and indeed, ma'am, even that might well be beyond my powers!''

''Nonsense, my dear. Anyone could write a book, I expect, if one but took the time to try. Why, what can be so difficult? 'Tis but a trifling business of putting words on a page.''

Nell did not attempt to debate the matter, but she had a notion of her own that it would not prove to be so easy as that. Bidding her aunt good night soon thereafter, she took herself to her bedchamber, where she got out the pages Sir Mortimer had written before she had begun to work for him and those she had written for him, sat down at the little table that served her for a dressing table, cleared a space, and began to work.

Several hours later, her back aching from sitting on the little stool that was all that had been provided with the table, she flung down her pen in frustration, wondering how anyone ever managed to write a novel. Though she had altered a good deal of Sir Mortimer's work, she was by no means either finished or satisfied with her alterations, but she knew she would be sorry if she sat much longer without a better chair. Morever, her standish was nearly empty, which seemed to her to be an excellent reason for stopping and going to bed. Deciding that she would try again in the morning, she straightened her pages and prepared for bed, unable to entertain the tiniest hope that Sir Mortimer or anyone else would approve of what she had done.

The following day, when Lady Flavia demanded to know how it had gone, Nell was diffident, and when her ladyship demanded to have the revision read aloud to her while she knitted, her first reaction was near-terror. Knowing, however, that if the project were to succeed, she must accustom herself to others reading what she wrote, she agreed at last to fetch her work. But she insisted that Lady Flavia must read it for herself.

"I could not bear it, ma'am, to be reading and wondering at the same time if what I am reading is making you ill."

"I am sure it will do no such thing," Lady Flavia assured her staunchly. She received the pages with enthusiasm and began reading at once, muttering a little to herself from time to time in a way that made Nell want to leave the room and never return. But at last she raised her eyes from the pages and said, "You frequently write well, child, just as one would expect you to do, and some bits are most amusing, but do you not think you would do better to write about what you know and less of this fantastic stuff about foreign dukes and princes? I know nothing about such things, of course, so I cannot know that you are wrong in any of your details, but I must own that what makes Miss Austen's tales so amusing is the fact that she knows her characters well enough to point out their absurdities without making them any less human." She sighed. " 'Tis an art, after all, one supposes."

Nell agreed. "I am afraid that the bits you like best are Sir Mortimer's, ma'am, and I cannot pretend to write as well as he does, or Miss Austen either. I have tried to write it as he would wish me to, only to smooth it out and bring some sense to the whole. I thought the result rather awful, though.''

''Oh, no,'' Lady Flavia declared hastily, returning the pages to her. ''One merely thought to suggest . . . But there, I shall say no more. It must be for Mr. Manningford to decide if you are to show it to his father, after all. And you will not be seeing him until Monday, so you can work on it for two whole days, and no doubt you will be better pleased by then with the result.''

Nell had already decided that she would have to do a great deal more work before she dared show it to Manningford, for the thought that he might despise it was nearly more than she could bear. It was odd, though, she thought, how she had such a strong desire to fix Sir Mortimer's ridiculous story, as though she had caught some peculiar disease, for now that she had begun, though frustrated, she did not want to stop. As soon as Lady Flavia was settled with her knitting, she took a seat at the elegantly carved escritoire near one tall narrow window, discovered to her satisfaction that it contained a proper standish and an adequate supply of writing paper, nibs, and ink, and set to her work.

It was slow going, but she forced herself to concentrate, and several hours later, when Sudbury interrupted her to inform her that Manningford was in the hall requesting speech with her, she found to her astonishment that Lady Flavia was no longer in the room. Rising at once from her chair, she clapped a hand to the small of her back, wincing. ''I must have a good chair, Sudbury. Do you see if you can find me one, if you please, and show Mr. Manningford in. Where is her ladyship?''

''In her bedchamber, dressing to go out, Miss Nell. Since Mr. Manningford desired speech with you, I did not disturb her.'' Sudbury paused, a twinkle entering his eyes before he added, ''Perhaps you would care to tidy your hair a bit and smooth your skirt before I show him in.'' He nodded toward the pier glass above the mantelpiece, and Nell turned toward it, standing on tiptoe so that she could see her head and shoulders.

She gasped. Her curls were standing on end, as though

she had pushed a rake through them, and there were two spots of ink on her right cheek. Glancing at her hands, she saw that her fingers were also smudged. "Ask Mr. Manningford to wait five minutes," she told the butler as she snatched a handkerchief from beneath her sash and, waiting only until he had gone, damped it with the tip of her tongue and proceeded to tidy herself, leaving red marks in place of the ink stains on her face. The state of her hair made her long for one of the lace caps she wore when she visited Sir Mortimer, but after a brief struggle to force the riot of curls into order, she gave it up and moved quickly to sit down when she heard Sudbury's hand once again on the latch.

Manningford, striding into the room with a harassed look on his face, did not appear to notice her untidiness. His manner was blunter than she was accustomed to see in him. "Good day, Miss Bradbourne, I am sorry to trouble you. I came to discover if you have had time yet to work on that fair copy."

Bristling at his tone, she said, "Indeed, sir, I have, but surely you might have waited until Monday morning, when I return to Royal Crescent, to ask me."

"The problem is more urgent than that," he said. "My father has had another attack."

"Another attack!" Nell's hands flew to her mouth. "It must have been my fault for speaking to him as I did! Oh, will I never learn to control my wretched temper?"

"I daresay you will," he retorted in damping tones, "if you will take care not to fall into a distempered freak whenever anyone brings you bad news. It was not your fault. Indeed, if anyone is to blame, it is I." He turned abruptly and looked out the window for a moment before he added, "I told him after you left yesterday what I thought of his behavior toward you, and I reminded him that he had no choice but to accept your services or let his secret be known. But now, if that accursed book is to be done, you must do it alone, for according to Borland, this time I nearly sent the old man to his grave."

"Oh, dear," Nell said, collecting herself in a sudden desire to soothe him, "but I am sure you did no such thing, sir.

Your father has been extremely ill, after all, and we ought never to have allowed him to exert himself so unwisely over his novel.''

"No," he said, turning, "and that is why I must know if you can do the thing, for from what you tell me, the entire work requires alteration. I cannot do it—that has already been established—but I intend to see the matter through, one way or another. May I see the portion you have modified? Though I do not pretend to know much about it, I believe I can tell if you have produced anything worth showing to someone who does.''

Nell was reluctant. "I cannot claim to have done anything noteworthy, sir. Indeed, I found the work most difficult. Oh, but here is my great-aunt," she added on a note of relief when Lady Flavia entered the room just then. "She has read the whole and must be accounted something of a judge. She will tell you that the task you require is not one for me to accomplish.''

Lady Flavia, smiling and holding out her small hand, said calmly, "I shall say no such thing, sir, you may be sure, but perhaps we had better all sit down and discuss this task.''

The matter was quickly explained to her, and once she had exclaimed her dismay over Sir Mortimer's second attack, she said, "But you are fretting yourself to flinders over finishing this novel of his, sir, and you need not be, for although my dearest Nell sets her achievements low, one is convinced that, given her head, she could do the thing for you, and very well indeed.''

"Excellent," Manningford declared. "Just what I wanted to hear! Show me at once what you have done, Miss Bradbourne.''

# 8

Reluctantly Nell indicated the papers on the escritoire and Manningford moved to the chair there and began to read.

The two ladies watched him anxiously, and the instant he looked up, Lady Flavia said, " 'Tis mighty promising, sir, do not you agree?"

"I think it damned foolish," he replied with a grimace.

Nell gasped. "Well, thank you very much, I am sure, but you have already said you know nothing of such things, and I never claimed you would like it!"

"Don't fly into the boughs," he retorted. "I don't pretend for an instant to know anything about such stuff." He looked at Lady Flavia. "Do you truly think it up to snuff, ma'am?"

"Certainly, sir," Lady Flavia said stoutly. "A trifle fantastic, perhaps, but then—"

"Just as I thought," he said, pouncing on this mild criticism. "There are bits I truly enjoyed, where the writer exhibited a turn for description or for bringing a certain character to life before plunging the reader back into stilted nonsense about wicked dukes, foreign princes, and the like. Nobody of sense could swallow such stuff as that, though."

"Just what one has said, oneself," Lady Flavia admitted with a sigh. "Do you not agree that if Nell is to take responsibility for the whole, she would do better to alter it so as to write about things she knows? The best bit, to my mind, is when she describes Elizabeth's loneliness just before that young woman accepts the arrangement with Lady Dashing to accompany her to that odd country, the name of which I shall not even attempt to pronounce. I suspect that that is just how Nell herself felt at Highgate before coming to Bath, and for the most part, you know, the tale could as

easily take place here, for I am sure Bath has its own fair
share of villains and innocent young women, though not, to
be sure, of dashing young heroes.''

Nell, whose reaction to even the complimentary part of
Lady Flavia's comment had been a feeling of acute discomfort, said tartly, ''I cannot change Sir Mortimer's story
so much, and for that matter, I can scarcely be held to know
anything about Bath, having spent so little time to any
purpose here.''

Lady Flavia, with a gleam of intent in her eyes, said gently,
''But surely, my dear, Mr. Manningford could take you
about, to show you the city, you know.''

He gave a sharp nod, saying, ''And in any case, you must
know Bath better than you know that fantastic land on the
Continent that you and my father betwixt you have created.''

She flushed. ''At least I know what your father wants, sir,
and the novel is his, after all.''

''What he wants is a finished work that can be dedicated
to his royal highness,'' Manningford said. ''Unfortunately,
he can no longer dictate his own tale to you, for after this
last attack he could not speak at all for a time, and though
his ability to do so has recovered somewhat, his doctor insists
that he must avoid unnecessary exertion. That is why, since
the old man only wants the wretched thing done without his
being unmasked as the author, I had hoped we might oblige
him.''

''By having me write the tale.'' Nell's tone was bitter, but
Manningford did not appear to notice.

''Just so.''

''Well, I cannot do it on those grounds,'' she said flatly.
He stared at her. ''I thought you had already agreed.''

''Then you deluded yourself, sir, for the situation is greatly
altered now, as I am sure you must see for yourself if you
will only take the trouble to do so. When all I was doing
was writing down Sir Mortimer's words, there was nothing
for anyone to cavil at. Even when I agreed to revise parts
of his story, I did so with his plot, characters, and setting
firmly in my mind. What you are now asking me to do is
to discard the bulk of his work and submit my own tale to

Mr. Murray as that of an author whose work he knows and admires. I cannot do it.''

There was a heavy silence. Even Lady Flavia seemed to have nothing to say, for she turned her face to the fire and sat staring at the crackling flames. At last Manningford sighed and said, ''You are right, of course. I failed to perceive as much before, because I was concerned only with meeting my father's demands without submitting him to further anxiety. I see now that that cannot be done.'' He slumped in the chair, looking defeated and very tired.

Nell's temper subsided instantly. She had a strong urge to run to him and put her arms around him, to comfort him—just as, she told herself firmly, she would comfort her brother in a like circumstance—but she resisted it, and although she could think of nothing to say that might cheer him, her mind began to grapple with the problem he faced. Only a moment's reflection was needed to tell her she could do what he wanted; she was not by any means certain she could do it without compromising her principles.

He was watching her. ''What is it?''

She met his look. ''Merely a fantasy, sir, and nothing to stir your hopes.'' When he continued to look at her, she sighed, adding, ''I cannot deny that I should like nothing better than to do as you wish. Moreover, I can see that it might be possible to make more extensive revision than I have without altering the main portion of Sir Mortimer's story. What has presented the greatest difficulty, after all, is my effort to keep the setting and characters as he would want them without knowing exactly what was in his mind when he created them; therefore, had I the freedom to alter those where necessary—even, perhaps, to use Bath, not as a brand-new setting but as a model for things I wish to add to his setting—I believe I could do what you ask of me. The style of writing is and would remain his, of course, since, having listened to him as much as I have, it is no great thing for me to imitate it.'' Noting the spark of hope that leapt to his eyes, she added quickly, ''But it is of no use to be thinking I shall do any such thing, sir, for I could not make the attempt without his leave, and he will never permit it.''

Manningford frowned and said, "Do I understand you to say, then, that if left to your own devices, you could transform his work into an acceptable novel?"

"By no means," she retorted. "I am saying only that if I can do so in good conscience, I should like very much to try. I have no reason to be certain the attempt would succeed, and I would need both his blessing and his help."

He looked at her for a moment before he said more gently than she had expected, "There may be a way to accomplish the deed without compromising either your scruples or his. Will you see what you can achieve in the next few days if I will promise faithfully to explain matters to him in the meantime, to tell him frankly what you are attempting to do on his behalf, and discover what his wishes might be?"

Nell's first impulse was to refuse, but a look of near-desperation in Manningford's eyes stopped her. At first she had assumed that his only reason for having anything to do with the novel was his apprehension that Sir Mortimer would otherwise refuse him money he required. Despite that assumption, however, and Mr. Lasenby's hints that he must be longing to get away from Bath, she had seen no sign of either resentment or restlessness. That seeing Sir Mortimer's book completed had become a personal matter with him was as clear to her now as though the information had been printed upon his countenance. She said quietly, "I will do as you request, sir, but—forgive me—do you think it wise to speak to him so soon after . . . ?" Delicately she allowed her voice to face into silence.

He smiled at her ruefully. "I do not know the best course, ma'am, but although Borland did not spare me, the doctor said it was more likely the old man's having attempted to get out of bed that caused his fit, an opinion that would seem to be supported by the fact that the attack did not occur until some hours after either you or I spoke to him. In the event, I will promise you to keep my temper in check, and if it appears that my proposal is distressing him unduly, I will abandon it. Will that suit you?"

Nell had little confidence in his ability to control his temper if Sir Mortimer, as seemed only too likely, were to lose his, but she could not resist the pleading look in his eyes, and she nodded.

He sighed in relief, arose from his chair, and said briskly, "I'll leave you now to get on with it, for Sep means to depart for Brighton in an hour, and I promised I'd see him on his way. To remind him to go, actually," he added, smiling wryly at Nell. "Oh, and you need not continue your daily visits to the crescent now. No doubt your great-aunt has been unhappy about them and will be glad to see them curtailed." He bowed to Lady Flavia.

"As to that, sir," she said, "Nell is quite her own mistress, and will do as she pleases, and one supposes oneself old enough to cease to heed what the quizzes may say. Do you pull that bell, if you will, and Sudbury will show you out."

When he had gone, Nell said, "You know, ma'am, I cannot help thinking we are making a grave mistake by fancying I can improve upon Sir Mortimer's work. I am but the veriest amateur."

"Nonsense, my dear," Lady Flavia replied comfortably. "You have only to pretend that Sir Mortimer's characters are people to whom he has introduced you, and then improve upon their natures as you will. I declare, it would make one feel quite powerful, would it not? But all any novel is, after all, is a few good characters, an interesting setting, and some sort of plot. Only the last bit, surely, can be at all difficult."

Nell remembered the discussion she had had with Sir Mortimer on the subject of plots. "An innocent heroine," she murmured, only half-aloud, "saved by a properly virtuous hero from an utterly wicked villain."

"What's that you say?" Lady Flavia demanded. "Speak up, child. You young people mumble so, and one is not hard of hearing, whatever ill-natured persons might say to the contrary!"

"No, ma'am, certainly not. I was just remembering something Sir Mortimer told me, and my imagination began to stir. If you will excuse me," she added, gathering the manuscript pages, "I shall go to my bedchamber and see what I can contrive."

"No, no, stay here. 'Tis far more comfortable for you,

and I was, after all, on the point of going out to pay calls when that handsome young man arrived. I had thought to invite you to accompany me, because someone is likely to invite us to dine, but I quite understand that you want to see what you can accomplish before Monday. No doubt Mr. Manningford will be all agog to see the result.''

Nell agreed vaguely, but her imagination was stirring so that she scarcely paid any heed, other than to bid Lady Flavia to enjoy herself, before sitting back down at the escritoire. For a few moments she sat there staring into space, thinking. Then, turning to the first page of the manuscript, she began to read and to make notes to herself. A quarter-hour passed, then another, and the longer she worked, the more excited she became, until she could not bear it any longer but simply had to begin again at the beginning, with a fresh sheet of paper.

From the moment her nib touched the paper, the pen seemed to take on a life of its own and fairly flew along, with scarcely more than a second's pause each time she had to dip it into the ink. For the most part she was copying the original, but she found herself adding and deleting words, then altering scenes and characters—some slightly, others more drastically. The writing was no longer frustrating or difficult. Nor was it a matter of simple self-amusement. It flowed now from a sense of urgency to get the words down on the paper before they faded from her mind. The hours passed swiftly, and she had not even looked up when Sudbury opened the drawing-room door and looked in to see if she wanted anything.

The butler, noting her abstraction, shut the door softly and went away. The next time it opened, it was to admit Lady Flavia.

''Gracious me, child, are you still at it?'' she demanded, startling Nell and causing her to splatter her work.

Reaching automatically for silver sand to sprinkle on the blots, she looked over her shoulder in surprise. ''Back so soon, ma'am? I thought you'd be gone for hours.''

''And so I have been,'' Lady Flavia declared, shutting the door behind her and going to sit in her chair. ''I even stayed longer than usual, for Maria Prudham has been telling me she was set upon by footpads last evening, at the top of Avon Street! If one is not safe in the center of Bath, one is not safe anywhere.''

''How dreadful! Was she hurt?''

''No, for they only took her money, but she was sadly frightened, for she was in her chair and the bearers ran away, which, as you may guess, they are not supposed to do. But do not tell me you have been writing all the while I have been away!''

Noting the time on the mantel clock, Nell exclaimed, ''Good gracious, I can scarcely credit it myself, ma'am, but I have not stirred since you left. I feel as though I have been sitting only a few minutes, however, and there is more that I should like to write down before it goes out of my head. Will you be vexed if I continue?''

Lady Flavia looked interested. ''I shall endeavor to stay as quiet as a mouse, my dear, if you will allow me to glance through what you have written today.''

Nell hesitated. ''I have not read it yet myself, ma'am.''

''Oh, I shall not expect perfection, you know,'' Lady Flavia said. ''I just thought I might amuse myself so that you could continue with your work.''

Making no further objection, Nell handed her the finished pages and turned back to her work.

If Lady Flavia was surprised, after Nell had watched her so anxiously before as she read, that she did not seem to be paying any heed to her now, she did not say so, and soon the only sounds in the room were the scratch of Nell's pen, the turning of pages, and the occasional crack of a spark on the hearth, where coals from the morning fire lay dying for lack of attention. In the next hour these sounds were augmented several times by a gasp or a chuckle from her ladyship, and once by a choke of laughter, but Nell did not hear these, so absorbed was she in her work. And when Sudbury entered to announced dinner, she was startled again, and laid her pen aside with obvious reluctance.

Smiling ruefully at her great-aunt, she said, '' 'Tis the oddest thing, ma'am, for when I tried to keep everything as I thought Sir Mortimer would want it, I struggled with every word. Now the pen just flies! All at once I knew how I ought to do the thing, and after that the hours passed like minutes and a great number of pages got written. Oh, dear,'' she added with a look of dismay when her gaze came to light upon the pile of pages by her great-aunt's chair, "I quite forgot you had been reading.''

Lady Flavia's eyes twinkled. "You will no doubt be wanting to make a few more alterations, I believe.''

Nell's face fell. "Is it quite horrid?''

"Not at all, but one fears that some of your characters have grown rather more recognizable than you will desire them to be.''

Bewildered, Nell said, "Recognizable? But how can that be, ma'am? They are entirely fictional. Indeed, they are Sir Mortimer's own characters, for although, thanks to the example set by our Regent, I have no great opinion of princes and have changed the hero into a more ordinary gentleman, I have kept Elizabeth and the duke as they were. He is related to her now, certainly, but he is still very wicked and she is still perfectly innocent, so there has been no extraordinary change.''

"Oh, my dear, do you not know what you have described here?''

"Well, of course I do,'' Nell said, but her voice lacked conviction, for she realized as she said the words that she had small memory of what, precisely, she had written. "I cannot repeat all of it, of course, for I daresay I am a little tired now, but surely I cannot have put anyone I actually know into the story. Indeed, I do not know any dukes or princes, and Elizabeth is quite unlike anyone I have ever met.''

"One is not surprised to hear you say so,'' Lady Flavia said with unaccustomed gentleness in her tone. "Do not tax yourself over the matter now, my dear, but come and eat your dinner. Then no doubt you will wish to look over what you have written today. On the whole, I must tell you, the tale is more amusing now, and one is all agog to learn how it will end.''

Nell went along obediently but feared she was not good

company at the table, for her mind seemed to occupy itself with her story, making it difficult to attend to Lady Flavia's gentle flow of polite conversation. The meal was over soon enough, however, and they returned to the drawing room, where she had made haste to gather her pages together. Then, lighting a pair of tall working candles, for the light in the room had begun to dim, she sat down and began to read what she had written.

Though she made a few corrections, she found little to explain Lady Flavia's comment until she had read for some time. Lady Flavia knitted placidly, permitting herself no more than an occasional glance at the reader, until suddenly Nell gasped and looked up with an expression of mingled shock and embarrassment and exclaimed, "The duke! How can I not have recognized him?"

"An excellent caricature of Jarvis," Lady Flavia said with a chuckle. "One particularly enjoyed his grace's arrival with all the servants scurrying to attend to him, fluttering in fear, though he smiled and nodded. Just what Jarvis would like, one expects. 'Tis overdone, of course. Even Jarvis would not dare, one hopes, to kick a footman from his path or to strangle a valet who scorched a cravat. Indeed, one doubts he would exert himself to such an extent. But one has seen him stand, just so, waiting while his cloak is placed about his shoulders and his gloves or cane put into his hand, not to mention the duke's habit of exclaiming, 'By my oath,' just as Jarvis does. And you certainly ought not to leave in that bit about his being a gentleman only by reason of his birth, since it sounds exactly like something you might have said to his face upon at least one occasion."

"I have," Nell admitted. "More than once, in fact."

"And the scene you added at the beginning about the wager and the duel at the gentlemen's club, my dear. Truly—"

"Oh, 'tis trite, I know, but there is nothing in that, ma'am, for I am sure I have read such stuff myself in any number of books. There can be nothing for anyone else to recognize."

Lady Flavia looked unconvinced, but she made no further effort to discuss the matter, and Nell returned her attention at once to her manuscript. She made a few more changes, frowning over some of them, but when she had attended to these, her pen began to fly again, and though she murmured a reply when Lady Flavia announced that she was retiring, she scarcely took her eyes from her work until one of her candles guttered and went out. Then, glancing up, she was bewildered at first to find herself alone in the room, until she looked at the clock and discovered that it was after eleven.

Taking her work upstairs, she prepared for bed, falling asleep the moment her head touched the pillow, and when she awoke, she found that although her right arm ached a bit, she wanted to begin writing at once. It was Sunday, however, and her conscience stirred her to dress for church instead and join her great-aunt in the sunny, rather barren little morning room, where they were accustomed to break their fast.

Later they walked the short distance to the Laura Chapel to attend the morning service, lingered afterward to chat with several of Lady Flavia's friends, and accepted an invitation from one of these to accompany her home for a light luncheon. Lady Flavia, who had changed few of her habits despite Jarvis' contribution or Nell's wages, plainly believed the invitation to be a boon. Nell chafed to be back at her work.

It was midafternoon when they returned, and she was wondering if she might simply excuse herself to her work again, when Lady Flavia declared that she thought she should enjoy a comfortable nap in her bedchamber. "Just to settle one's meal, you understand," she added airily.

Nell suspected that her great-aunt knew perfectly well that she was aching to write, and desired her to enjoy the comfort of the drawing room, so she did not reveal her awareness that Lady Flavia rarely napped during the day, but only smiled gratefully and bade her enjoy her rest.

For an hour the writing went well, but then suddenly it was as if she had lost whatever magic it was that had kept her pen speeding along. She found herself dipping the nib into the inkwell, then sitting and staring at the page until the ink had dried on her pen. She read over bits she had already written, searching for inspiration, but none came. She made little sketches in her margins, and though it was fun to imagine them the faces of her characters, the exercise did nothing to take her work forward. At last she gave it up, throwing down her pen just as Lady Flavia entered the room.

The old lady stopped on the threshold. "What is it, my dear? Do I intrude?"

"Certainly not, ma'am," Nell said as she stood up, stretching her arms in a most unladylike fashion. "Forgive me, but my limbs seem to have turned to sticks, and my fountain of inspiration has dried up at the source. I cannot think why, but the writing has come to a complete stand."

"There must be a cause," Lady Flavia said practically. "Of what are you writing?"

" 'Tis no great thing. Merely that Elizabeth has made one of a party with Sir Percy to attend a public ball at the town's assembly rooms. The duke intends to abduct her from there, you see, to force her to marry him. I don't doubt that the words will begin to flow again once he does so, but the bit about the ball seems out of reason difficult."

"I see what it is, of course," Lady Flavia said with a wise look. "You have never been to the Bath Assembly Rooms."

"But that cannot signify, ma'am, for I have never been to a gentlemen's club either, and I can assure you that, after all I have heard from Papa and Nigel, I experienced no difficulty whatever in imagining what one must be like when I wrote of the villainous wager between Sir Percy and the duke."

"Ah, but you know that while most of your readers will never have set foot in such a club, any number of them will actually have attended a public ball or concert. You must visit the upper rooms, of course. Once you have seen them and know how things go on there, the words will flow again."

"But I am in mourning, ma'am. I cannot attend a ball."

"Oh, piffle, I daresay no one would think a thing about it. You need not dance, after all, but only watch to see what is done. And if you are of a mind to be particular," she added hastily, seeing the mulish look on Nell's face, "there is nothing to be said against attending a concert, for you are no longer in deep mourning, my dear. And unless there is good reason for Elizabeth to dance, she too can merely attend a concert.''

''I did hope she might dance with Sir Percy,'' Nell said with a sigh. ''Will there be a concert soon, do you think?''

''Oh, yes, certainly, for although the Season here no longer lasts nine full months, as it was used to do, there are concerts and balls from midsummer through Christmas. We must send young Amos to purchase a newspaper, but I daresay there will be a concert Thursday, and if there is not, there will be an assembly Wednesday evening. I am persuaded that Mr. Manningford will accompany us if we ask him to do so. You needn't dance, truly, my dear, but only see what occurs,'' she added when Nell still seemed reluctant, ''and now, if you are not going to write any more tonight, perhaps you would care to take a hand of cribbage.''

Nell agreed and managed to turn her mind from her work for an agreeable hour, but as she prepared for bed that night, she found herself wondering how difficult it would be simply to skip the part about the ball and go on writing from the point of the abduction. She wondered why she had not thought to do that before, and began to look forward at once to the morning. She fell asleep instantly, and there were no abductions in her dreams. Instead she dreamed she was dancing with Manningford. As they danced, he held her in his arms in a delightful but most unseemly way, gazing down into her eyes so steadily that she knew he wanted to kiss her. She waited, gazing provocatively back at him, encouraging him far more than any lady ought to. He did not do as she expected, however, and when the music changed abruptly and he looked away, she reached up and grabbed hold of both his ears, kissed him soundly on the mouth, and woke up laughing.

She had scarcely sat down at the escritoire the next day when Sudbury entered to announce that Manningford and Mr. Lasenby were in the hall requesting an interview with her. Rising to meet them, she suddenly remembered her dream and, feeling warmth flood her cheeks, turned quickly from Manningford to greet Mr. Lasenby with rather more enthusiasm than he might have expected.

"I thought you had gone to Brighton, sir," she said, giving him her hand.

He bowed over it, saying with a twinkle, "Had to return, ma'am. Knew Bran must be finding things in the deuce of a pucker, what with the old gentleman so ill again and all."

"The truth is," Manningford said with a grin that made Nell instantly remember the first day they had met, "that the stupid fellow claims to have forgotten where he was bound. If he could forget that, I suspect we ought to be grateful he remembered where he had been."

"Didn't have to," Lasenby retorted. "Just told the lads to turn round and go back where they came from."

Shaking her head at him as she gestured for both gentlemen to sit down, Nell said, "But you cannot have forgotten about Miss Wembly's ball, sir. You promised her you would not."

He grimaced. "Can scarcely believe it myself, ma'am, but I did. Bran tore a strip off me, of course, and m' grandfather will set up a devil of a screech. I'm only a younger son, you see, so one can't blame the old fellow for doing his possible to see me wedded to a girl who's inherited a fortune. M' memory's clearly failing, though. 'Tis the oddest thing."

"But didn't the postilions know where you were going?"

" 'Course they did," he admitted, "but the fools only knew to take me to Brighton, and much good that did me when I couldn't think why I was wanting to go there, so I did the best thing I could think of and told them to put me back where they found me."

"Well, you must write to Miss Wembly and explain the circumstances. I daresay that if you make your apologies with suitable eloquence, she will forgive you."

"Do you think so?" He seemed extremely doubtful, but when he showed a marked inclination to discuss the matter more fully, Manningford cut him short, asking bluntly if Nell had attempted to do as he had asked.

"Yes, sir," she replied, gesturing toward the manuscript on the escritoire. "You will not want to read it now, of course—"

"The devil I won't," he said, getting to his feet and striding across the room to sit down at the desk. "You just talk to Sep and pay no heed to me. I want to see what you've done.''

Her stomach clenched as she watched him begin to read, and though she tried her best to attend to Mr. Lasenby's attempts to suggest possible reasons for his odd lapses of memory, she found it impossible to keep her attention from wandering. When Manningford chuckled, she glanced at him anxiously, but he did not so much as look up from the page, and a moment later Mr. Lasenby, who had stopped talking and was watching her, suggested that perhaps she would like to take a hand of piquet with him.

''Generous fellow, Bran is—as I've got reason to know— but he can be dashed rude when he's of a mind to be, and it ain't a particle of use to try to distract him if he don't want to be distracted. Dash it, ma'am, but it's a good thing I came along. You'd have been bored to oblivion otherwise, for I daresay your aunt is out paying calls at this hour.''

''Yes, she has gone to visit her friend Mrs. Prudham,'' Nell said, still watching Manningford. Though he was seated at the desk, he had turned his chair so that he might sit with one leg crossed negligently over the other, and she could see his expression change as he read. When he frowned, she instantly interrupted Lasenby, who had continued his flow of small talk, to demand to know what was amiss.

''This bit here about the gentlemen's club is all wrong,'' he said. '' 'Tis plain as a pikestaff you've never set foot in one.''

Before Nell could attempt to defend herself, Mr. Lasenby protested, ''But, dear fellow, of course she has not. Moreover, I can't think what difference it can make, for only girls read that sort of book, and none of them will know the difference.''

''Everyone reads my father's books,'' Manningford said curtly, ''and not only has she got maidservants tripping about when anyone must know there are none in such a place, but she's got this fool of a hero of hers wagering a straw against a pot of gold that he can ride a horse backward from Bath to Bristol in a day's time.''

''Well,'' Mr. Lasenby said reasonably, ''you have made

nearly that same wager yourself, Bran, only as I recall it, it was from Hampton Court to Richmond, rowing backward against the tide. Or was that the time—?''

"Never mind that," Manningford retorted. "I never wagered such a paltry sum in all my life. A straw! Give me patience. Why write of what you cannot know?" He glared at Nell. "Can you not keep your idiotish heroine down in a country house? Have her get off a stagecoach and into the wrong carriage by mistake; then your wicked duke can force her to marry himself or anyone he chooses, even a rogue at death's door, for pity's sake."

"That would make no sense at all," Nell protested. "No one could induce a young woman to marry a dying man."

"Well, 'twould make as much sense as this," he said, tapping the pages before him. "Your Elizabeth has allowed this duke to murder her father, not to mention his own, banish her brother, who is naturally the rightful heir, to some far-off foreign land, and take over her vast estate without so much as lifting a finger to stop him. She gets the wind up only when the fellow wants to marry her. Stands to reason, most readers would think her a fool to run off just when he wants to make an honest woman of her. You've got to change some of this."

"Well, I won't," Nell said hotly. "I take leave to tell you, sir, that your notion of a good tale is absurd. I daresay next you will be wanting me to make Elizabeth consort with free-traders, or Sir Percy tend a turnpike or train bears. Or perhaps you'd prefer Elizabeth to fall out of a window into his waiting arms and go off adventuring with him, or, even better, have her rescue him by shooting the wicked duke with an arrow from her trusty bow. This story of Sir Mortimer's and mine is real!"

"Fustian. It can be no such thing. There never lived a duke as wicked as yours."

"Perhaps not a duke," she snapped furiously, "but there are men as wicked right here in Bath at this very moment!"

Instead of taking up the gauntlet as she expected him to do, Manningford fell silent, looking at her now in a speculative way that made her flush to the roots of her hair.

Mr. Lasenby said diffidently, "Bran, dear fellow, I daresay Miss Bradbourne will make allowance for your distress over the old gentleman, but dash it, my lad, there ain't no cause to speak so objectionably to a lady."

Ignoring him, Manningford said gently, "Right here in Bath, Nell? Perhaps you would care to explain that statement to me."

"No, I shouldn't," Nell said hastily.

"Well, but I think perhaps you'd better. Sep, go for a walk or something, will you?"

Mr. Lasenby got obediently to his feet, but Nell said quickly, "No, no, there is no reason for him to leave."

"Yes, there is," Manningford insisted. "I have come to wonder about a number of things these past weeks, my girl. I mean to have this one explained to me."

"I am not your girl," Nell said. When he merely continued to look at her, she sighed. "Very well, I suppose there can be no good reason not to explain at least a little of it to you, but there is likewise no cause for Mr. Lasenby to leave."

"By Jove, I'm glad to hear that," that gentleman informed her with a lazy smile as he took his seat again. "My memory being what it is nowadays, I daresay I should forget how to get back here."

Manningford leaned back in his chair and glanced at him, murmuring, "Just so you forget whatever she tells us, Sep."

# 9

Nell caught her lower lip between her teeth, reluctant to speak, but both gentlemen remained silent, waiting, the one with well-bred patience, the other not patiently at all. "I don't know where to begin," she said at last.

"At the beginning," Manningford recommended.

Had he shown sympathy, she might not have been able to oblige him, for it was difficult to think back to the beginning without falling prey to her emotions. Since he did not make that error, however, she was able to say almost matter-of-factly, "That would be the wager, I expect."

"Ah, yes," he said, "you mentioned your father's penchant for odd wagers with his uncle. 'Tis from that you got the notion for the straw against the pot of gold, I suppose, but it will not serve. Their stakes cannot have been so uneven as that."

"Well, they were certainly as ridiculous, sir, for my father staked the Highgate hatchment against his uncle's brewery. You will recall that I told you about the brewery. At the time their disastrous wager was entered in the betting book, it was once again on Crosshill land and had been there for some years."

"Wait a bit," protested Mr. Lasenby. "Did you say he staked a hatchment against that brewery? A hatchment? The bits of black ribbon on a coat of arms that one puts above one's door when a member of the family cocks up his toes?"

"Just so, Mr. Lasenby. Papa's wager, made some time before her death, was that the queen would outlive the king. When his majesty became so ill last summer, Papa was in alt because he believed the income from the brewery would eliminate his most pressing debts."

"I can understand that," Mr. Lasenby said feelingly.

Nell smiled. "Then you will also understand his distress when the king survived. In any case, the wager was nearly forgotten—by Papa, at least—when Reginald was killed in a hunting accident in mid-November. Papa was deeply affected by his death, so you can imagine his shock when Jarvis arrived at Highgate the afternoon following the announcement of the queen's demise, a fortnight later, to declare that he had come to collect on the wager. What was even more shocking was his insistence that, according to Reginald, Papa had staked Highgate itself against the brewery, not merely the stupid hatchment."

"But surely the estate is entailed," Manningford protested.

"No, for Papa was heavily in debt when Nigel came of age, so the entail was broken then by mutual agreement in order that Papa might sell off a few acres. He intended to resettle, of course, as soon as he was able, only through one cause or another, he had not yet done so. But he would never have staked it in a wager! In fact, he knew he had done no such thing, and he said Reginald must have been joking, for he was a great jokesmith."

"Easy enough to prove," Manningford said. "You mentioned a betting book. One had only to journey to London to look at it."

"Oh, not even so far as that," Nell told him. "I ought to have mentioned that the bet was made here in Bath. Reginald and Papa were both members of a club known as the Bee Hive—at least, I believe that is what the place is called."

Manningford said, " 'Tis called many things, but I know the club you mean, for 'tis practically the only one of its kind still active in Bath. I am a member, and my father, as well. The club boasts a large membership, in fact, though there is rarely anyone there anymore. 'Twas formed in the middle of the last century to sidestep what were then the new gaming laws, and has successfully done so, except for a brief scuffle with the authorities just prior to the turn of the century, when the two men who owned it were charged with keeping a gaming house and placed under a distraint for failure to pay their fines. They sold out, and the place has remained respectable ever since. Its members call it the Bees. Their detractors, knowing that most of the younger set avoid the place, call it the Bees-waxers' Club.''

''Bees-waxers?''

Mr. Lasenby, who had settled back comfortably in his chair, chuckled sleepily. ''Means 'old bores,' ma'am, and 'tis an apt description, I believe. Bran and I looked in there one evening last week, thinking to find someone to oblige us with a game of cards or dice, don't you know, and I thought the card room was littered with corpses, for nearly every chair was occupied with an old stick slumped back with his eyes shut. Dead asleep, every one of them. Devil a game did we see!''

Manningford smiled. ''I remember that my brother-in-law Axbridge said much the same thing several years ago when he recorded a wager in the club's book. I was showing him where the Regent, as Prince of Wales, had once inscribed a bet. There are any number of notable names in the book, for 'tis the club's greatest claim to fame and well nigh a historical document. Prinny, you know, practically never comes to Bath—and Bygrave, the club secretary then, though he died last year . . . Why, what is it, Miss Bradbourne? You are as white as a sheet.''

''Mr. Bygrave was killed in a duel, I believe,'' Nell said in a tight voice.

''So he was, right there in the club, by a fellow who fired before the signal was given.'' He regarded her thoughtfully. ''The fellow disappeared, and as no one seemed to know who he was, the whole business came to nothing. I shouldn't have thought such a tale would have reached your ears, ma'am.''

''The fellow's name was Bradbourne, sir, but I can tell you that even in his cups, my brother would never have done such a dastardly thing as to cheat in a duel. Mr. Bygrave had recorded my father's wager with Reginald, you see, so it was logical that Nigel should seek him out to ask him to support Papa's claim. To Nigel's shock, however, Mr. Bygrave refused to do so, insisting that Highgate had been the stake all along, that my father was merely attempting to renege on his wager. Nigel flew into a passion, violent words were exchanged, and the result was a duel between the two. Had their tempers been given time to cool, that must have ended it, but Bygrave himself pressed Nigel to settle the matter at once, there in the club. It will not surprise you to hear that what few witnesses there were, were the worse either for sleep or for drink, except Jarvis, who insisted that Nigel had fired before the signal. Jarvis assured Papa and me that he had managed to get Nigel safely out of the country, but the shock of hearing such a dreadful tale so soon after Reginald's death and his own apparent loss of Highgate to Jarvis was too much for my father. He retired to his book-room and shot himself.''

"So it is your cousin who owns Highgate now.''

"No, for, most surprisingly, he did not claim the estate after Papa's death. To be sure, I thought he intended to do so, since that had seemed to be his purpose. But he was all concern, all sympathy, and said he would do naught to pursue the claim, that instead he would look after Highgate in Nigel's behalf until Nigel himself might dare to return. Now, however, he speaks of taking the wager before a court of chancery.''

Mr. Lasenby said casually, ''You know, ma'am, the wager must be what they said it was, for a betting book, you know, is quite sacred. Well, stands to reason, it must be when so much depends upon it. Still, shouldn't be at all surprised if, under such circumstances as you describe, your cousin might not find it difficult to find a court willing to uphold his claim. Dashed particular they are now about such things. Time was when a fellow could lose a fortune gaming and there was naught to do to reclaim it. But the law being what it is now— forbidding extravagant stakes and all—''

Manningford said, ''A gentleman still honors his debts, Sep, whatever they may be, and his heirs are bound to honor them.''

"To be sure,'' Lasenby said hastily, with a apologetic look at Nell. ''I was not intending to imply that either the late Lord Bradbourne or the present one must not have felt obligated to do so, but dash it, Bran, the whole business sounds havey-cavey.''

''It does, indeed,'' Manningford agreed.

''Perhaps so, but it is perfectly true,'' Nell told them, ''so surely, Mr. Manningford, you will no longer insist that this plot is absurd. To be sure, the facts are not identical, for Sir Mortimer knew nothing of the wager or the duel. I added those bits. Not that that signifies, since I doubt you will have induced him to accept any sort of meddling from me.''

''Well, you are out, ma'am, for he has agreed to reserve his opinion,'' Manningford informed her with a teasing look. ''He will judge what you have written, and if it meets with his approval, allow you to continue. I won't say I had an easy time of it, or that he did, but I did not lose my temper, nor did he.''

It took a moment for her to take in the full meaning of what he had said, and when she did, she didn't know whether to be glad or sorry. She said only, ''He wants me to read it to him?''

''He does. He pointed out that the book will, of necessity, be somewhat delayed, but there is no getting round that, so Borland is to write a letter purporting to come from the Lady of Quality and informing Mr. Murray of the fact.''

''I see,'' Nell said, her mind still awhirl. ''What if Sir Mortimer does not like what I have done?''

''Then we will put our heads together again. But aside from such irregular details as your description of a gentlemen's club, the tale seems entertaining enough so that I have no hesitation in asking you to read it to him. He can discuss with you—as well as he is able—such details of character and plot as he desires, and make whatever suggestions he is moved to make, so that the two of you can be comfortable with the fact of the book's being at least a collaboration between you. He must do no dictating, however, and you will see him only when it is necessary to do so. Can you agree to that arrangement?''

Nell frowned. ''I do not know, sir. I have no confidence in myself, you see, and 'tis of no help to learn that my description of the club is incorrect, for only last night I found myself unable to describe a simple ball. My aunt suggested that I attend some function at the Assembly Rooms—thinking, you know, that actually to see the setting would help me imagine what balls there must be like—but while that might answer well enough in one instance, I certainly cannot visit a gentlemen's club.''

"Sep or I can describe one to you well enough,'' he said with a smile. "In fact, you must make a list of any such places that have been included, since I daresay that living out of society as you have, you will not know much about them. And my father, you know, though he mixed enough when he was young, cannot know much about modern social functions. For both your sakes, I daresay you ought to get about more and see more sights, but we must do it rather quickly, because I received a letter in this morning's post from my sister Axbridge, who informs me that she and Ned will soon be with us. Borland wrote to her when my father first became ill, of course, but thanks to the vagaries of the mail once it gets beyond England, it was my letter, written later, that reached her first. I am to tell her friends she will be here only a few days, but knowing her formidable habit of taking command, I don't doubt that we may look to see her running things in the Royal Crescent for weeks to come, which will leave me with nothing more to do than to take myself off again, I suppose.''

He did not sound as though the idea appealed to him particularly, but Nell had to bite her tongue to keep from protesting against the very notion of his departure from Bath anytime in the near future. "When her ladyship arrives,'' she said hesitantly, "she will no doubt have her own notions about how to manage your father's novel.''

"No, she won't,'' Manningford said.

"But surely—''

He grimaced, saying, "My father forbids me to mention his books to her. Says they are none of her business.''

"Then how can you think of leaving, sir, when you have said you will see the thing through?''

He looked at her, and at first she thought he did not quite know what she meant, but then he smiled and said, "I cannot, of course. But first things first. You desire to visit the upper Assembly Rooms, so perhaps we ought to see about making up a party for the next ball to be held there."

"I cannot go to a ball, sir," Nell said firmly.

He looked at her, taking in her half-mourning. "Well, a ball is a ball, of course, and if you merely require to see the place . . ." He paused, watching her, and Nell, suddenly able to think of nothing to say, could feel the warmth creeping into her cheeks again. "Look here, you have been to a ball, haven't you?"

"Well, no," she confessed, "not a real ball. I have danced, of course, at country parties, but I have never properly come out, you see, for my mother was dead by the time I was old enough, and neither she nor my father had any sisters, and Papa didn't care a string for such stuff." She smiled at him, adding, "Nigel pointed out to him once that I might make a better marriage if I were offered on the Marriage Mart—the London Season, you know—but Papa said I should be just as likely to make an eligible connection in Wiltshire as in London, only, of course, one doesn't particularly if one has no fortune."

"But what of the Lady Flavia? Could she not have made a push to see the thing done?"

"Well, I confess I did wonder at the time why she did not, but of course I was too proud to ask her, and now I quite understand that . . . that it was beyond her power."

Mr. Lasenby said curiously, "Is she so decrepit, then? I don't mind telling you, I'd never have guessed it. Seems an energetic old lady, by and large, with a constitution of iron."

"Of course she is not decrepit," Nell said. "But it cannot have escaped your notice, sir, that she is not so rich as people believe her to be. There, I have put the thing plainly, have I not? There must be no more secrets between us."

"I agree," Manningford said, his tone firmer than she was accustomed to hear from him. "Did you think her wealthy when you came to Bath, Nell?"

"Well, yes, but if you are thinking I meant to hang upon her sleeve, it was no such thing."

"I didn't think that at all, so come down off your high

ropes. I did think you might have expected her to have such resources as would protect you from your father's cousin, if he is—as I begin to suspect—the real reason you came to Bath."

Nell bit her lip. "You see too much, sir. I suppose I did think that. I did not suppose, certainly, that he would never find me here."

"And has he done so? Is that the reason you said the wicked duke was in Bath?"

"You sound rather fierce," she said, "but indeed there is no cause. Jarvis is certainly wicked, for no one will convince me that he did not somehow arrange for everything to happen as it did—or if not everything, then a good part if it—but 'tis all done now, and I do not believe he would harm me."

"Are you so certain of that?"

"What could he hope to achieve?"

"I do not know. What does he want of you?"

Nell flushed bright red. "He desires to marry me, sir, and I remember perfectly well what you said about the wicked duke's wanting to marry Elizabeth—doing the honorable thing by her—so before you demand to know why that should be repugnant to me—"

"I'll demand no such thing."

"No," Mr. Lasenby said in surprise. "Dashed impertinent thing to do, ma'am. No one would ask such a question. Even if one should wish to know the answer," he added naively.

Nell smiled at him. " 'Tis simple enough, sir. I do not like him. Not only is he wicked, but he is too old for me. When I marry, as I have no doubt I will one day, it will be with a man much more nearly my own age."

"Then Mr. Bradbourne is elderly, ma'am?"

"No, not elderly, but he is nearly twelve years my senior, and I mean to wed a man more nearly my own age."

"Well, that's dished us," Mr. Lasenby said sorrowfully. "Eight-and-twenty, the pair of us, and Bran a year older than that, come December."

She chuckled. "Have I cast you into the dismals, sir? I do not believe it. And you must marry Miss Wembly, after all."

"Must I? Oh, dash it, of course I must. Believe I'll write her that letter, ma'am, and promise to mend my ways. Perhaps if I begin to jot things down, I shan't forget them so easily."

"What a very good idea! I am sure she will forgive you."

"Again," Manningford murmured.

Nell cast him a speaking look, but when he caught her gaze and held it, she found herself hoping he would not ask her any more questions about Jarvis Bradbourne. It was a forlorn hope.

"I collect that Bradbourne's desiring to marry you is not something you have deduced, but that he has actually asked you to do so," he said, still watching her.

"Yes."

"And you refused him."

"Yes."

"What made him think you might not refuse?"

"Wishful thinking, I expect," she retorted. "He can have had no other reason."

"Can he not?"

"No."

"He holds no sort of authority over you?"

Nell opened her mouth to deny that Jarvis held any power whatsoever, then shut it again. Manningford made no effort to press her, and Mr. Lasenby likewise said nothing. At last, frowning, she said, "I suppose he might have thought that I had no recourse other than to do as he bade me. There is only Aunt Flavia, and since she had never appeared to take particular notice of me, he would have had every reason to discount her. When he announced that he intended to move into the house at Highgate, there was no one to stop him, for Nigel, of course, was on the Continent. It is possible he expected me to marry him to avoid gossip about our living in the same house together."

"I should have thought he would want to avoid such gossip quite as much as you would," Manningford said.

"But his attitude was protective, you see, even avuncular, so the pressure would have been applied to me rather than to him. People tend to take him at his own valuation of himself, you see, and since no one at home perfectly understands what happened, or why my father took his life, they would be likely to think Jarvis rather noble for taking it upon himself to look after Highgate and me until Nigel returns. They might also think he was being rather big about it into the bargain—for you can be sure the wager and its result are well known in our county.''

"Had you no one to support you?''

"No. Some of our neighbors have been very kind, of course, but there was no one to whom I could turn but Aunt Flavia.''

"Well, the man appears to be an encroaching knave,'' Manningford said, relaxing, "but there is nothing in what you have said to prove wickedness or evil. Certainly not on a level with your duke,'' he added with a teasing smile.

She blushed. "I concede that the duke bears a slight resemblance to Jarvis. I gave him similar characteristics, which I have since, on my great-aunt's advice, attempted to disguise a little, but I must tell you, sir, that though I do not really believe Jarvis murdered his own father or mine, I do believe he is responsible for Papa's death and for Nigel's exile, and nothing that anyone can say will make me believe differently.''

"Then we must set about proving it,'' Manningford said.

Her eyes opened wide. "Proving it?''

"Yes, of course.''

Mr. Lasenby agreed. "Nothing else to do, ma'am. Can't expect a magistrate to know what the fellow's done if we can't show him, now, can we?''

"No, of course not, but I cannot think for a moment how we might prove such a thing. You may be sure that he has covered his tracks, if indeed there were any to cover.''

Manningford said thoughtfully, "I think Bygrave might be considered to have been a track, you know, and he is now covered by six feet of good English soil.''

Nell stared at him. "Mr. Bygrave?''

He nodded. "You say you are certain that your brother would not have fired his pistol before time.''

"Never.''

"Then the only alternative is that someone else fired that

shot. It would have been a relatively simple matter, you know, for everyone, as you say, was either three parts drunk or asleep, and, moreover, was expecting to hear a shot and to see someone fall. Half the difficulty of setting up a lark is to make people believe what you want them to believe. If they are predisposed to believe most of it before you begin, the rest is easy."

"But would not a second shot have been heard, even if people did not know precisely what had happened?"

"Good Lord, no," he said. "In closed quarters like a clubroom, reverberations of one shot might have sounded like half a dozen, and there is no saying but that both your brother's pistol and Bygrave's might have discharged when that first shot was fired. Reflex, you know, from just being startled. In fact, your brother's must have done so. Anyone, even ape-drunk, would have been bound to notice if his gun hadn't been fired at all. At all events, there would have been a vast amount of confusion."

"You sound as though you have had firsthand experience."

"He has," Mr. Lasenby informed her with a grin. "Never was used to be able to hit the broad side of a barn, don't you know, but that never stopped him, particularly. And in the past five or ten years he's become a crack shot. A friend of his—"

"Sydney Saint-Denis," Manningford said gently. "Always told me that if I was going to learn to do a thing at all, I ought to learn it thoroughly. People take Sydney for a fop, but there's a deal more to the man than meets the eye. He's damned competent with a pistol, for one thing, and he's got a few other tricks he learned the two years he lived in China that would curl your hair. He's taught me one or two of them, but I don't flatter myself that I'm anywhere near as clever as old Sydney is."

"Can shoot, though," Mr. Lasenby said loyally. "Sure as I stand here, Miss Bradbourne . . . well, sit here," he amended, "Bran can shoot the pips out of any playing card you'd care to name. Been challenged to two duels, too. In the first, he nicked a silver button off his opponent's coat.

Poor fellow promptly deloped. Never occurred to him Bran hadn't meant to do it.''

"And the second?" Nell prompted, darting a glance at Manningford, who appeared to have fallen into a brown study.

"Well, that wasn't so impressive," Mr. Lasenby admitted. "Fact was that Bran had stayed up all the night before, playing cards, and when he got to the ground before his opponent did, he just lay down under a tree and went to sleep. Fellow showed up, declared that if Bran was so calm about the whole thing that he could just doze off, waiting, he'd be damned if he'd fight him, so he woke him up and apologized for the whole.''

Nell chuckled, but Manningford did not appear to notice, so at last she said, "Have you fallen asleep again, sir?"

He started, looking surprised. "Fallen asleep? Of course not. I have been thinking what we must do next. Sep and I can look into that business at the Bees-waxers', but we must also arrange to meet this precious cousin of yours, and I haven't a notion how to do that without setting him to thinking. Is he a member of the club? Very often a man does join his father's clubs, and you said he was there the night in question.''

She frowned. "I have not the least notion. He is as much a gamester as his father was, for I remember that Papa and Nigel were used to wonder where either of them came by the amounts they claimed to have lost at the tables. We could only suppose that the rents at Crosshill were greater than one would suspect and that Reginald's steward there was something of a magician. But he was in Bath that night only because he accompanied Nigel to look at the betting book and talk to Bygrave. He rarely visits here, I think, for he prefers London, and though he says he is here now on business, anything relating to Crosshill or Highgate would be done in Salisbury or Trowbridge, so that must be a fudge, and he is here only to plague me.''

"Then you must introduce us," Manningford said. "I can judge better how to bring him into the open if I know him than if I must go by guess.''

"Well," Nell said thoughtfully, "if we are to attend a concert or some such thing in a party, I can arrange for Jarvis to accompany Aunt Flavia and me and you can ask your friend Mr. Saint-Denis and his wife. That way I can see the sights and you can meet Jarvis. I don't much care for encouraging his attention in such a way, but will that not answer, sir?"

"A casual meeting would be better," he said, smiling at her, "but we cannot expect him to cooperate, I suppose."

They might have discussed the point longer had Lady Flavia not entered the room just then, having returned from paying her calls. Delighted to see the gentlemen, she demanded to know what Manningford thought of Nell's latest work, and it was not long after that before she was in possession of all the facts of the recent discussion, and Nell found herself with an ally.

"It will not do for her to invite Jarvis to make one of a party," Lady Flavia said firmly, "and you must not think you will get to know him in only one meeting. If I know anything about him, he will be all pomp and ceremony, too concerned with making a good impression to let his true character show." She thought for a moment. "I believe you ought to set yourselves to show Nell about a bit. Seeing more of town life, even in Bath, will help her finish that novel, and it will encourage Jarvis to make a nuisance of himself at the same time. He will do so, mark my words, particularly if he comes to believe— as he surely will—that one of you is making Nell the object of your attention. I promise you, he won't like that notion at all."

Nell was not altogether certain how she felt about it either, for it was all too obvious that her great-aunt expected more to come of her plan than a simple chance to introduce the gentlemen to each other.

# 10

They put their plan into action at once when it was discovered that a concert was to be held that very night at the upper Assembly Rooms. These rooms were considered to be the finest in all Europe, and when they arrived, Nell found it easy to imagine the magnificent hundred-foot-long ballroom filled with dancers in place of the benches set out for the concert.

The performance itself was mediocre, and there had been no time to arrange a party, so neither she nor Lady Flavia objected when the two gentlemen suggested a walk to look at the two card rooms and the tearoom. Having fortified themselves in the latter with tea and sweet biscuits, they strolled on through the "corridors of scandal," those long halls surrounding the main suite of rooms, where ladies of an earlier era had retired from the ballroom to exchange tales and tattle. There were no such persons there now, only a few stragglers like themselves, and one latecomer emerging from a chair that had been carried inside.

They did not see Jarvis at the concert, but upon returning to Laura Place they were informed by Sudbury that he had called and had expressed disappointment at finding the ladies from home.

The following day Nell's interview with Sir Mortimer went more easily than she had expected. Instead of being angry that she had altered his book, as she had thought he might be, he actually seemed grateful that she had attempted to improve it. His appearance appalled her, however, for since she last had seen him, his condition had deteriorated so much that despite Manningford's having warned her what to expect, she had all she could do not to express her dismay at seeing his complexion so gray, his eyes so sunken, his face gaunt and drawn.

She greeted him as cheerfully as she was able, and as she removed the manuscript pages from her satchel, she added for lack of anything else to say, "I am told that your daughter is coming to visit you, sir. You will be pleased to have her home again."

His reply being no more than a grunt, she looked up to see that his gaze was fixed upon the pages in her hand. She sighed. "You want me to get on with reading, I suppose, but I must tell you, sir, I am terrified to hear what you will say. Pray do not let me read on and on if you detest what I have done, and I shall try not to be offended by any criticism you offer." She glanced at Borland, who had taken his customary place near the window, and was glad when he nodded and smiled at her encouragingly.

Sitting down at once, she began to read. She had a good reading voice and generally enjoyed reading aloud, but her throat felt tight and her voice had a tendency to quaver. When she had read for some minutes undisturbed, she looked up to see that Sir Mortimer was leaning back against his pillows with his eyes shut. Fearing that he had dozed off, she faltered, but when his eyes quickly opened again, she went on reading more confidently.

Not until she reached the part about the gentlemen's club did he attempt to interrupt her, groaning his protest, but by then she was able to look up and smile at him. "I know, sir. Mr. Manningford has already informed me that even an idiot would guess that I have never set foot in such a club; however, he has promised to describe one to me—the Bees-waxers' here in Bath, as a matter of fact—so that I can make the necessary alterations. We cannot call it the Bees-waxers' in your book, of course, but if we can discover how that name came to be, perhaps we can make up another name in a similar fashion. We could all it the Old Bores' Club, of course, though since you were used to be a member, I daresay you would not agree to that."

Sir Mortimer made some gravelly noises in his throat, and his shoulders began to shake, and although neither his mouth nor his voice seemed to wish to obey him, she realized he was laughing, and grinned at him. "I hope you are not laughing at me, sir, although I expect it is no such thing and you are only congratulating yourself on having had the good sense to avoid a club with such an infelicitous reputation."

His eyes atwinkle, he nodded. Then, after a long moment and a visible struggle with his disability, he mumbled, "'Ees."

"Yes," Nell said gently. "The Bees' Hive, or just the Bees, is the true name, Mr. Manningford told me. Very odd, I thought."

"'Nitials." Frustration clouded his face when he saw that she did not at once comprehend what he was attempting to tell her. He shifted awkwardly on the pillows and turned his head a little, then drew a heavy breath and repeated, "'Nitials."

"I . . ." Nell looked at Borland. "I do not understand him, Borland. Do you?"

"I believe he is attempting to inform you that the club you mention was not originally intended to be mistaken for an apiary, miss." When his master relaxed against the pillows again, he went on, "As I recall it, the place—more than twenty-five years ago, this would be—was known as the Avon Club, for the street it was on as well as for the river. But then the lower part of Avon Street became notorious as a back slum, and there was a scandal when it was found that the club was being run as a gaming hell, so the new owners—several of them, I believe there were—decided to change the name. As I recall it, there was dissension of some sort, and in the end they resorted to their initials. Perhaps the dispute had grown out of which name to put first, or perhaps they thought it better that their names not be widely known."

"Who were they?" Nell asked curiously.

"Now, that I cannot tell you," Borland said. "Members, possibly, for 'tis not unheard of for one or two to buy into such a club, though still not considered quite the thing, you know. And of course several of the names, at least, must have begun with the letter B. Many names begin so, of course—my own in fact," he added with a glint of humor, "though I assure you, miss, I should not lower myself to such a pitch. But it all happened so long ago, you see, and my memory, though competent, is not what it used to be. The master might remember more. A right wonderful memory he's got."

Sir Mortimer was watching Nell, and when she looked at him, he shook his head, but she did not care just then whether he could recall the names in question, for a notion had entered her mind the moment Borland had begun to explain the matter, and her imagination had begun to spin. A villain, she decided, might accomplish much if, with regard to some of his ventures at least, he were known only by his initials.

It was clear by then that Sir Mortimer meant to encourage her to continue with her work, but when she stood up to take her leave of him, suggesting that she need not return until she had a good deal more to read to him, he became rather agitated. With Borland's help she was soon given to understand that the old man wished to hear every day what she had altered the day before. Nell was a little dismayed by the request, for she knew she would get on faster if she did not have to make the trip to Royal Crescent on a daily basis, but he seemed so distressed when she told him so that she soon agreed to do as he wished.

"You know, Miss Nell," Borland said a few minutes later when he escorted her to the head of the stairs, " 'tis my belief the master's taken quite a liking to you. It ain't the tale he cares about so much as seeing your face, or he would have had me ask you to send pages over each day to be read to him. He might easily have trusted to me to understand his wishes and tell you what changes he wanted made, you know, instead of setting himself the difficulty, as he has, to communicating them to you himself."

"Well, it is my belief that he's bored," Nell said with a sigh. "How dreadful to be all alone as he is, Borland, with only you, kind though you are, to bear him company. It is to be hoped that when my Lady Axbridge arrives, he will admit her to his bedchamber and do what he may to become acquainted with her and all his family again."

"He won't do that, ma'am. He don't want to see them,

and only becomes agitated if he is pressed to do so. Master
Brandon visits him, as you know, but though Sir Mortimer
don't order me to throw him out, the lad don't stay to chat
with him beyond talking a bit of business, and nor does Sir
Mortimer want him to do so. Says he's done naught for the
lad before now and that to be making so many demands of
him now is a damned impudence.''

"But as Mr. Manningford's father, he has every right to
make demands, Borland, and in fact, I believe that Mr.
Manningford is enjoying the responsibility he has been given,
though it was perhaps not quite fair of Sir Mortimer to
threaten to cut him off with no more than a shilling if he
did not do as he was asked.''

" 'Twas a feather, not a club, that the master wielded in
that instance, Miss Nell.''

"Do you mean that there is no fortune?'' Nell's eyes
widened in dismay, but Borland shook his head.

"No such thing, miss.'' He said no more.

"I see,'' Nell said. "It is not so difficult to understand
you, I believe. I daresay the will is already written and will
not now be changed, but if that is true, why does he not tell
him so, so they can become better acquainted with one
another?''

"He don't see it that way, poor gentleman,'' Borland said,
making no attempt to dispute her interpretation, "for he don't
think Master Brandon would help him if he didn't hold some
sort of club. I tell you this only because the master is lonely
and I hope you'll not deny him your company. It were one
thing when he had his journals, his novels, and his reading
to occupy his hours. But now . . .'' He spread his hands
helplessly.

"Do you not read to him, Borland?''

"Aye, ma'am, I do, but I'm no hand at it. He said once
I'd a voice like a corn crake.''

"I see,'' Nell said, repressing a sudden quite unexpected
gurgle of laughter at so apt a description. "He is not very
conciliating, is he, Borland?''

"No, ma'am.''

Nell said farewell to him then and turned away, having

been given much food for thought. Manningford was waiting for her downstairs, and after she had assured him that Sir Mortimer had approved her work, and told him what the old man had said about the Bees-waxers', he escorted her to her chair, informing her as they passed through the sunlit back garden that he had decided that since there was nothing else offering entertainment that night, he and Mr. Lasenby would visit the club. "I want to see that betting book, and Sep can draw you a floor plan and discover some more of the history of the place. Then, I thought, tomorrow night we might attend the fireworks display in the Sydney Gardens. Lady Flavia will enjoy that, I expect, and I'll invite Sydney and Carolyn Saint-Denis to join us there. They will no doubt have ideas about other places you ought to see. You will like them both. I do."

"I shall look forward to meeting them, and to seeing the fireworks. What else have you got planned for my education?"

He suggested a visit to the abbey and Milsom Street the day after the fireworks display, and a ride on the downs above the town the day after that. "To give you an eagle's view of the place, you know," he added casually.

"And not merely because you are beginning to feel a bit caged, sir?" Her eyes twinkled, and he smiled back with the warmth she had begun to expect to see when she talked with him.

"You are coming to know me rather well, Miss Brad-bourne."

She agreed, grinning at him and conscious of a deepening sense of kinship with him, a feeling that was becoming more and more familiar, as though she had known him all her life. She had thought at first that it came to her because he was so much like her father and brother, interested only in gaming and dicing and kicking up larks, but she knew now that it was no such thing.

When she had first met him, she had not thought he would be kept long in Royal Crescent, for although he had said he remained because he needed money, she found it hard to believe, even before quarter-day had come and gone, that he would allow himself to be constrained for such a cause. In her experience, gentlemen in need of financial recuperation went to the horse races or to the gaming tables. And certainly no sense of obligation kept him. Other sons might have felt obligated to attend an ailing father, but he was not among them, and though she had at first thought him an unnatural son, she knew now that not even the highest stickler could cavil at his having so little regard for a man he scarcely knew.

Nor had it occurred to her at first that Manningford might have stayed out of consideration for her. His attitude toward her all along had been kind but careless, and even now, with all the encouragement he was receiving from her great-aunt to do so, she could not suspect him of dangling after her. He was no hero on a white charger, thundering to the rescue of an innocent heroine, but just her good friend. When she compared him to Sir Percy, the hero of Sir Mortimer's novel, the thought made her laugh. In fact, as she realized the following evening, the hero she and Sir Mortimer had created was, in many ways, much more like Sydney Saint-Denis than he was like Brandon Manningford.

The party for their outing to the gardens included Nell, Lady Flavia, Mr. Lasenby, Manningford, and Mr. and Mrs. Saint-Denis, and after strolling along the gravel paths for a time, they had taken their places in the box Manningford had hired for them, enjoyed a tasty supper, and then sat back to enjoy the colorful display. Nell had plenty of time to observe her new acquaintances, and decided she liked both of them very much.

Carolyn Saint-Denis, with her raven tresses, deep blue eyes, and rosy cheeks, was a beauty in the most fashionable sense of the word, looking much as Nell herself had often wished to look. But, apparently unconscious of her beauty, she was an animated, laughing creature, full of life and laughter, a perfect foil for her amiable, rather foppish, lazy husband. At one point, seeing friends in the distance, she had turned quickly to Mr. Saint-Denis and tugged at his sleeve to direct his attention to them.

Patting her hand as he carefully disengaged himself, he

said in a sleepy tone, "My dear Caro, a matron lady, even one with two painfully energetic children, does not bounce about in public or seize unsuspecting persons by their coat sleeves. Consider my vanity, if you please."

She smiled saucily at him. "I will consider it, dearest Sydney, if you insist, but I believe it only fair to warn you that you are becoming just a trifle stuffy again. I cast but a hint your way, you see, knowing that you will prefer to attend to the matter yourself, rather than leave it to me."

He looked at her for a long moment, the dawning twinkle in his gray eyes warming to something more than simple enjoyment, until Carolyn's cheeks grew quite pink with pleasure. It was just such a look, Nell decided, as she would like to be skilled enough to place in Sir Percy's eyes when he gazed upon Elizabeth. Indeed, if she could produce an intimacy between the pair of them that was anything like what she was rapidly coming to see between the Saint-Denises, she would be very pleased with her book.

Hearing her name spoken, she turned away from Carolyn and Sydney to find herself face-to-face with Jarvis Bradbourne, who had bent over the railing of the box in order to make himself heard above the cheers of the crowd when a fiery rocket exploded overhead. As the cheering died away, Jarvis said, "How delighted I am to find you enjoying a bit of gaiety again, Cousin."

Lady Flavia, hearing his voice, turned away from Mr. Lasenby, who had been speaking close to her ear, and said, "You here, Jarvis? What can you want now?"

"I called at the house to pay my respects, ma'am, and was so fortunate as to be told by the admirable Sudbury where I might find you. Since it was such a short distance, I took the liberty of paying out my sixpence to join you, but I see that your box is too full to accommodate me, so I will just take Nell for a short stroll, if I may. Walk with me, my dear."

She hesitated. There was no reason that she could think of to be rude to him, but neither did she want to go with him. She felt a sense of menace whenever he was near, and though she could not believe he would do anything so absurd as to try to force her to leave with him, and had never been given actual reason to believe he meant harm to her, she had no wish to listen to more of his persuasiveness.

When she did not speak, Manningford got to his feet and said calmly, "Sydney, Caro, care to join us for a walk?"

"I thought this indolence was too pleasant to last," Mr. Saint-Denis said, getting to his feet and helping his wife adjust the light scarf she wore over her shoulders as protection against the evening's light breeze. "Don't believe I know you, sir," he said to Jarvis. "Sydney Saint-Denis. This lady is my wife."

Nell said, "Forgive me, everyone. He is a cousin of mine, Jarvis Bradbourne, who is visiting Bath for a few days."

Jarvis made his leg, then said pointedly, "I've something of a rather private nature to say to you, Cousin."

"Well, this is hardly the place for it," she told him, "and if you must know, I don't wish to walk alone with you."

"You don't trust me," he said with a sigh. "By my oath, but that is foolish, my dear, for I wish to marry you, and thus have every reason to protect your good name. Certainly you need not fear to walk a little apart with me. I leave for London in the morning, and I would have speech with you before I go."

Glancing at Manningford, she said, "Very well, then, but only a little way. What is it?" she demanded, scarcely waiting until they had moved far enough along the torchlit path to be beyond earshot of the others.

"You've been avoiding me, my dear, and though I find that somewhat tedious, I have no doubt that you will soon come to your senses. Your friends are kind to you now, but should they chance to discover your entire history—that is to say, your brother's history—I doubt you would find them so amiable."

She looked up into his face. "Are you threatening me, sir? I confess, I did not expect such a thing from you."

"And you were not mistaken, my dear. Only think of how carefully I have used you, how tenderly I have nurtured Highgate on your impulsive brother's behalf. But in eight months we have traveled no farther forward. I have respected your megrims and your mourning, but now I see that you have put both behind you, and I cannot be expected to remain patient much longer without something to show for it. I wish to protect you and the Bradbourne name, my dear, but I would be a fool to continue along this path without some reward for my efforts.''

"You will marry me or you will ruin us both—is that it?''

"Such bluntness, Nell, does not become you. I quite agree that it would be a pity to use you so, and I should prefer that that particular tale never come out. I have been at some pains to prevent it, after all. But the note of hand Nigel bestowed upon me that fatal night is not sufficient to allow me to do all that needs doing, and as he does not seem to have sent anyone his direction, I have been unable to request broader authority from him. However, there is the wager, and even without it, since I am his heir apparent, I anticipate no difficulty in persuading a chancery court to grant me full power to act, if not complete title. It is for the purpose of looking into that matter that I am going to London in the morning.''

His tone was so confident that Nell longed to slap him, but she knew she dared not. Since his arrival in Bath she had been expecting him to take some such step as this, to press her to change her mind about marrying him. Since she knew now, if she had not before, that she could never do such a thing, every cell in her body ached for her to tell him that he didn't fool her, that she knew full well that taking Highgate from her family had been his intent all along. But she did not know his immediate intent, and she did not want to put him on his guard lest he do something horrid. Surely, she thought, if he believed himself safe, he would proceed with caution, slowly and meticulously. He had waited this long; he would not go headlong now without cause.

So it was that she said as calmly as she was able, "You will do what you believe necessary, I suppose. I cannot believe that a court will grant you title to land that is not yours, however, so perhaps you would do better to be content merely to be granted legal power to act on Nigel's behalf.''

"You wish to forget the wager," he said gently. "I quite

agree that it don't redound to our credit. By my oath," he added with ponderous humor, "the court is likely to think the whole family as crazy as loons when they hear of it."

"Then don't tell them. That the stakes were as you say they were can be contested, you know, and in the event, you might find that the law nowadays will not support such extravagant stakes."

An expression of annoyance crossed his face, and she knew she had struck a nerve. He had not expected her to know anything about gaming laws. She sent a silent thank-you to Mr. Lasenby for the information and waited to see what Jarvis would say next.

"My dear Nell," he said calmly, "that law pertains only to such matters as are placed in dispute, and there can be none in this case, since the wager is properly noted in a well-respected betting book, signed by both principals and a witness. Moreover Nigel is not present to dispute my claim, and you have no cause."

She believed him and, thus, could content herself only with the knowledge that, for a brief moment, she had put him out of countenance. She must trust to luck, not to the law, to find a means of stopping him before his plan could succeed. On the good side, matters of chancery, as she had heard often enough, were not concluded in a day or a week. There would be plenty of time to think of a rub to put in his way before the wheels of the law had begun to turn against Highgate.

When they returned to the others, a look brought Manningford to her side. "He is certainly a paltry fellow," he said quietly.

"Well, stop looking daggers at him," she said, drawing him a little away from the others. "You cannot want him for an enemy."

"By the look of him just now, it seems I shall be given no choice in the matter. Your cousin does not like me, my dear."

"Never mind about that; he is going to London to learn what he can expect from a court of chancery," she said, determined to keep to the point but undeniably warmed by the casual endearment.

Manningford frowned. "Is he? I confess, I found nothing at the club last night to stop him—that bet was recorded just as he said—but I should still think he was being a trifle premature if he truly has heard nothing yet from your brother."

"He still maintains that he has no wish to flaunt the wager before the public eye but says it may be necessary for him to do so, whether he likes it or not."

"In other words, he goes to test the water."

His tone was pensive, and Nell looked into his eyes. What she saw there eased the tension that had taken hold of her from the moment Jarvis had joined the party. Though she had once thought Manningford irresponsible, she knew now that she could count him as her friend, to stand by her and help her with whatever came her way. Had anyone asked how she knew, she could not have said, but she knew. She said quietly, "Nothing can happen quickly, can it, sir?"

His hands came gently to rest upon her shoulders, and he gazed into her eyes in much the same way she remembered his having done once in her dreams. "Some things happen quickly, Nell, but not the business of a chancery court. We have time on our side." His gaze held hers, and she waited hopefully, but a moment later one of the others spoke, and the spell was broken.

That there was not so much time as they had thought was brought home to her the next day. Lady Flavia having gone to visit Mrs. Prudham, she was working at the escritoire when Sudbury entered to announce a caller.

"Deny me, if you please," she said without turning. "I cannot come just now, so ask whoever it is to leave a card, Sudbury, and extend my excuses. Or tell them that Lady Flavia will be at home after one o'clock."

Sudbury cleared his throat and said gently, "The gentleman is not an ordinary morning caller, Miss Nell."

Hearing a familiar chuckle, she turned sharply to see her brother's laughing face just beyond the butler's shoulder.

"Nigel! Oh, Nigel, my dear, how delightful! That is," she amended as she leapt to her feet, "it is not delightful at all! What are you doing here? Are you out of your senses?"

Lord Bradbourne, a slender young gentleman of medium height, whose auburn locks and dark blue eyes gave him to look so much like his sister that people who knew one were frequently able to recognize the other, stepped past the fondly smiling butler and gathered Nell into his arms, giving her a crushing hug. "Nellie, Nellie," he said when she burst into tears, clutching at his lapels, "gently, my sweet. This coat was made for me in Paris, and I'll not have you crushing it to bits."

She gave a watery chuckle. "You sound very much like a gentleman I met only last evening," she said. "Paris has turned you foppish, my dear."

"The deuce you say! It's done no such thing. I'm a Corinthian perhaps, but never a fop."

"I do not suppose there can be any difference. They are all the same to me."

"Good God! To you, perhaps, but to no one else." He held her away and looked at her searchingly. "You're looking hagged, Nellie. Been going the pace too much, I'd say."

"Then you'd say wrong," she retorted. "We are still in mourning, though you don't look as if you'd remembered the fact."

He shrugged. " 'Tis a hard thing to recall in Paris, when the music is so lively and the young ladies so beautiful."

"You do not change," she said with a tolerant sigh. "I had thought you would play least-in-sight, and avoid anyone who might know you, but I daresay I ought to have known better."

"Yes, sweet Nell, you ought."

"Well, this past week is the first I can claim to have done anything out of the way. Which is not to say that I have had no cause for apprehension, and do not have more now, you wretched creature. What can you mean by coming to Bath, of all places? You will turn my hair white with worry!"

He shrugged, glancing over his shoulder to be sure Sudbury had gone and had shut the door behind him. "I hope he brings me something to wet my whistle, Nellie, but he can take his time if he likes. Now, smile, for I've done nothing to put you in such a pelter. Indeed, I begin to think I never have done.''

She gripped his arm. "I know you did not. You *could* not! Oh, but Jarvis told us that you had fired before time, and no one has denied it, Nigel, so I do not see how you can hope to clear your name. The risk! If you fail, you will be hanged!''

"Perhaps I deserve hanging,'' he said, his expression heavy. "I killed my own father, after all. I cannot tell you what it was like to learn of his death, and to be so far away, but I dared not return. Not then, in any case.''

"I understand. But, Nigel, you are not to say such a thing.'' She grabbed both his arms and gave him as much of a shake as she was able. "Papa killed himself. His is the blame.''

"Had I not—''

"No, hush, I'll not hear it. You went to try what you could do to straighten out a tangle of his making. He ought to have gone himself. And however that man Bygrave died, I will never believe that you turned and fired before the signal.''

"You know, Nellie,'' he said as he gently disengaged himself and moved to lean against the mantelpiece, "in all the confusion there was nothing else to believe but what Jarvis told me.''

"He said you were inebriated, Nigel. How came you to drink so much at such a time as that?''

"Well, I did not go there to fight a duel, after all! Bygrave was not there when we arrived, so we had a glass or two while we waited. I must have had more than I thought, for I was dashed muzzy by the time Bygrave came in. I know I asked him to tell Jarvis the truth about the wager, and he said flat out that Jarvis had the right of it. Showed me that damned book and said he remembered as if it were yesterday that Papa staked Highgate against that damned brewery. Jarvis said later that I called the man a liar, and I must have done, but I'd never have been so cork-brained as to fight him on the spot if he hadn't insisted. I ask you! It might have done well enough for our grandfathers, but the law frowns heavily on such doings nowadays.''

"When did you come to see the matter differently?''

"I thought about it often, and bits kept coming back to me. Something dashed havey-cavey about Bygrave. I can see that now."

"Someone else said the same thing about the whole affair," Nell said. "I think Jarvis had a hand in it."

"What, him?" Nigel shook his head. "I never much liked him, but I don't see how he could have done, you know. There's no making any sense of it."

"Well, don't try. Tell me instead how you managed to get into England without being taken in charge, and how you mean to look into the matter without being hanged."

Grinning at her matter-of-fact tone, he said, "I met a marquess in Paris and attached myself to his entourage. The whole group travels under his passport, you know, so there was no difficulty about it at all once he vouched for me with customs."

"A marquess?" Nell looked at him. "Not Axbridge!"

"The same," Nigel said. "But how did you guess? You cannot know him, though I daresay you will before this is done, for he's here in Bath, as a matter of fact."

She nodded. "At Manningford House in Royal Crescent. I visit the house nearly every day. You will not like to hear this, Nigel, but I have been reduced to working for my living."

"To what?" The look of astonishment on his face was all that she might have expected it to be, but he seemed to accept her glib explanation of her work, and did not ask any awkward questions about how she had come to discover such a position.

# 11

To Nell's amusement, Lady Flavia accepted the arrival of her grandnephew with her customary composure, merely expressing at the dinner table that evening her hope that he would not be too uncomfortable in the bedchamber that had been allotted to him, just as though, Nell thought, there were nothing at all out of the way in his return to Bath. Her ladyship's reception of the information that the Marquess and Marchioness of Axbridge were presently in residence in Royal Crescent was a different matter.

"We must lose no time in paying our respects," she informed Nell with a decided nod. "Sybilla is quite a favorite of mine, for I knew her best of all Sir Mortimer's children. I shall be pleased to see her and to renew my acquaintance with Axbridge. We will call tomorrow."

Declining to serve herself from a dish of scalloped oysters that Sudbury offered her, Nell said, "I had thought to wait a few days before returning, ma'am. I doubt Sir Mortimer will want to see me while Lady Axbridge is visiting him."

"If you think he will let such a small matter as that weigh with him, then you cannot have learned much about the man," her great-aunt said. "If he has so much as communicated with her since her arrival in Bath, I will own myself surprised. Do you not recall, my dear, that until Mr. Manningford forced him to accept you as his scribe, he had refused to see anyone but his manservant for nearly a quarter of a century?"

"But he has allowed me to visit him nearly every day," Nell protested. "Surely he will no longer insist upon keeping himself to himself, for I have seen for myself how lonely he has become, particularly since he can no longer occupy his hours with his work. Indeed, I think his circumstance quite pitiful.''

"He would not thank you for saying so," Lady Flavia said, accepting a serving of stewed celery. "Only think of the blow it would be to his dignity to have to beg for company now. He will not do it. He might be lonely, my dear, but after all this time, he would not know how to accept kindness, or even to recognize when only kindness is meant. Mortimer is a proud man. 'Tis bad enough that he has been forced to admit Mr. Manningford, the doctor, and you to his chamber. He must not be forced to admit any more persons, so don't get to thinking that all you have to do is to encourage Sybilla to ignore his orders and barge into his room to effect a more normal relationship between them.''

After a moment's reflection Nell said slowly, "You are right. Until his first attack, he controlled his own life and the lives of his dependents with no help from anyone. Now that he is dependent and must look to others to help him, it must be dreadful for him.''

"So much so," Lady Flavia said, "that one actually wants to help him, and 'tis the oddest thing, for I am certain that such a notion has never entered my head before. But now that it has, I suppose I must speak to Sybilla before she takes the matter into her own hands, and it will not do to be putting off the business out of nonsensical scruples or misguided notions of propriety, for she might attempt to beard him at once, thinking to do him good. The excellent Borland will be unable to prevent her, of course, and although it is possible that Mr. Manningford may do so, one must not leave the matter to chance.''

"Goodness, ma'am, do you think Mr. Manningford would even think to attempt such a thing?''

Lady Flavia's eyes twinkled. "I do not know for certain, of course, but I do not believe that at this point he will encourage his sister to take the reins from him.''

"But until quite recently he has been in the habit of letting others manage things for him, has he not? And I think, from all that he has said of her, that Lady Axbridge must be something of a managing woman, Aunt Flavia.''

Lady Flavia chuckled. "Sybilla has always been one to think that if a thing needed doing, there was no one so capable as herself to do it. As the eldest of Sir Mortimer's motherless children, she quite naturally assumed leadership over the others, particularly since Charles, though heir to Sir Mortimer's title and estates, has not got a forceful character. When Sybilla married Axbridge—Earl of Ramsbury he was then—for a time she tried to rule over two households, her own and her father's. It did not answer, of course. Such arrangements never do. One heard rumors of some rather exciting fireworks between Axbridge and Sybilla before that business was settled, but now that she has got children of her own—four of them—she has little time to spare for the household in Royal Crescent. Nigel, dear," she added briskly, "pray do not eat all the mushroom fricassee. Your sister is partial to that dish."

Nigel grinned. "She's partial to anything with nutmeg in it, or hadn't you tumbled to that fact, ma'am? But I've left a bit, for I mean to have another helping of the roast chicken; and you needn't think I mean to eat you out of pocket, either, for Nell told me how things are, so I slipped Sudbury a few sovereigns to pass along to the missus."

"That was kind of you, dear, but truly, not necessary. Thanks to dear Nell's wages—most generous—and Jarvis' entirely unexpected contributions, we do very well now. You ought to have kept your money, for I cannot doubt you will need it."

Nell looked up at him in surprise as she helped herself from the dish of mushroom fricassee. "You had sovereigns in your pocket, Nigel? I must say, I didn't expect that."

"Fact is," he said, "that I had a bit of a run of luck in Paris, and Axbridge wouldn't accept a sou from me for the trip home. He's a great gun, you know. I can't even remember how it came about that I told him about myself. Just began talking one night at some rout or another—both being from England and finding that we both had aunts in Bath. Though everyone has at least one of those," he added with a grin at Lady Flavia. "At all events, by the time we'd met one another at several more such affairs, I'd told him more and more, until he'd grasped pretty nearly the whole of it. Said straight out one night that I didn't seem to be the sort to get mixed up in a duel, let alone one who'd fire before time. I snapped back that of course I'd never do such a thing. Well, until that moment I hadn't questioned what had happened, but then I got to thinking about it more and more, and the devil of it is that I have so *little* memory of what happened. I want to discuss the whole with Jarvis, of course, though I daresay he won't be best pleased to learn that I've come back after he thought he'd got me safely out of the country.''

"But surely," Nell said, "it cannot be safe for you here."

He looked at her with defiance. "I don't care about that now, or not so much as I care about finding the truth if I can do so. If I didn't kill Bygrave in the manner Jarvis said I did—"

"Then you didn't kill him at all," Nell finished for him. "I tell you, Nigel, Jarvis is the villain, first to last."

He grimaced. "I know you do not like him. Nor do I, but what reason could he have?"

"To get control of Highgate, of course. He has always coveted what he constantly calls 'the seat of the Bradbournes.' Why, whenever he sets foot on the place, one can see the calculating look in his eyes, as though he is mentally scything lawns, counseling tenants, and generally refurbishing things."

"Well," Nigel said, flushing, "I know he has long held our father—and me—in contempt for our neglect of the place, but he cannot have had any notion that killing Bygrave might benefit him in any particular way."

"At the least, my dear," Lady Flavia interjected gently, "he might have counted on ruining your reputation; and Nell's chances to marry, you know, were not high even before that night, since your father continually refused to allow her to have so much as a single Season in London. She has suffered a good deal from his suicide, and although nothing much seems to be known hereabouts about your affair, Jarvis has made it clear enough that he can alter that situation with no more than a word. He desires, for some reason, to marry her himself, you see."

"What?" Nigel glowered at his sister. "Don't tell me you thought of doing such a thing, even for a moment."

"No, of course I did not," she retorted, her own temper rising, "but had Aunt Flavia not been willing to take me in, and Sir Mortimer not willing to pay me an excellent wage to . . . to work for him, the case might well have been different, for neither Papa nor you had made the least arrangement for me, you know. Both of you just left me to . . . to Jarvis' mercy."

Nigel grimaced. "Out of fairness to Jarvis," he said, "I should tell you that I did ask him to look after you."

"Yes, he has told me so," Nell retorted. " 'Tis his constant litany that he wants only to shield me and to protect the family name. He pretends to be all that is noble, and I detest him."

"Well, you needn't marry him, after all. I do not suppose he can force you, not now that I am returned, at all events."

"Yes, but you cannot show your face, certainly not to Jarvis, not unless we can clear your name. Do you remember nothing of use from that night? Surely you had seconds."

"Oh, to be sure, but I don't know their names, and their faces are lost in a fog of brandy."

"Well, then, what do you recall?"

"Only what I told you before." He hesitated, gathering his thoughts, then said slowly, as though he were seeing a mental image of the action in his mind, "I remember thinking when we arrived that Kingsmeade Square was rather too near the rougher edge of town for my taste, but inside, the place looked like any proper gentlemen's club—a porter at the door, old men dozing in chairs, and a card room. A little shabby, perhaps, but then, so is White's in London. Bygrave —he was the club secretary then, you know—was not on the premises when we arrived, but he was expected, so Jarvis suggested we have a glass of brandy while we waited. We must have had several, for by the time that damned fellow showed up and announced that the wager was what Jarvis had said it was, I was castaway and hardly knew what I was saying."

Nell frowned. "How came you to fight the duel at once? I thought such things were generally arranged for dawn."

He grinned. "They are, and one is expected to be sober. I cannot tell you why it happened as it did. I've a hazy memory of thinking we ought to wait a bit, and of being pressed to finish the thing, but that's well nigh all I do remember. If I didn't think they'd call up a constable the instant I set foot in the place, I'd pay the Bees-waxers' a visit to see if being there again would stimulate my memory. But Ned—Axbridge, that is—says I mustn't do any such thing until he discovers what charges have been laid. He has sent a fellow to his man of affairs in London to see if a charge has been laid against me there, and he'll set someone else onto it here in Bath."

"It is kind of him to take an interest," Nell said.

"Lord, yes, for when a marquess requests information, you know, no one tries to fob him off with a lot of nonsense. And the best of it is that Ned believes it cannot be so big a tangle as we had thought, else the circumstances would be more widely known. They are not, he says. Not at all, in fact."

"No," Nell agreed, "I must own that it surprised me when Aunt Flavia told me that no one here in Bath seemed to be aware that Mr. Bygrave was killed by a Bradbourne. Certain gentlemen here, and elsewhere, are aware of the fact that he was killed in a duel in the club, for Mr. Manningford knew before I told him so, but even that much is not common knowledge."

Nigel did not seem inclined to discuss the matter at greater length, then or later. He was restless, and she knew it chafed him to be tied by the heels in Laura Place, wondering what was happening elsewhere. He had given his word to Axbridge to stay put until the marquess had a more exact understanding of the situation, but patience had never been one of his more noted virtues. Thus it was that Nell, hoping to discover what was occurring and report back to him, put forth no more argument against calling in Royal Crescent the following day, and willingly accompanied Lady Flavia to pay their respects.

They traveled to the crescent in a pair of chairs, but they were not carried to the garden gate in Julian Street. Being set down at the front door gave Nell quite a new perspective of the place, and she paused for a long appreciative moment to gaze at the distant prospect before they were admitted by the porter.

He stood tall, carrying himself with nearly arrogant pride, and Nell hid a smile, certain that he had altered his demeanor in accordance with his notion of what was due to the increased consequence of a household containing a marquess. He handed the callers over to a tall, unfamiliar footman who guided them up the stairs to the drawing room, where he announced their names with the air of haughty dignity to the four occupants of the room.

If Nell had feared that their hostess might be as high in the instep as her servants, she soon discovered her error. The moment their names were announced, Lady Axbridge, who had been idly playing a melody on the pianoforte, pushed back her stool and rose gracefully to her feet. Her russet-silk afternoon frock set off her copper-colored curls to admiration and clung so becomingly to her curvaceous body that Nell found it difficult to believe her the mother of four children. Her figure, though voluptuous, was youthful, and she moved with a lightness and grace that most matrons of her age had already forfeited. She was taller than Nell by several inches and built on more generous lines, but her hazel eyes twinkled and her manner when she stepped forward to greet them was cheerful and warm.

"Lady Flavia, how kind of you to call so soon. And, Miss Bradbourne, I am quite delighted to make your acquaintance. My reprehensible brother has just been telling us of the miracles you have wrought with my father. You must be sure to tell us the secret, for I own I cannot imagine how you induced him to let you go to work as you have with him. Oh, but do let me make you known to Axbridge, for this is he, you know," she added, gesturing toward the tall dark-haired, rather harsh-visaged gentleman who had broken off talking to Manningford and Mr. Lasenby by one of the tall front windows when they entered.

As she made her cursty, Nell glanced briefly at Manningford and saw that he was regarding her rather narrowly. Since she could not imagine what he might have told his sister, she made no effort to reply to her observations, but rising, smiled at the marquess and said, "I am told that I stand in your debt, sir, although I confess that at this present I am not entirely convinced that I ought to thank you."

Axbridge's smile lightened his severe countenance considerably, and his voice was gentle when he said, "I cannot blame you for your doubts, ma'am, but I have influence in certain quarters, you know, and I believe that I may be of help."

"Indeed he can," Sybilla said brightly, "so you must place your trust in him, Miss Bradbourne, and think no more about it, for as it happens, a new worry faces us just now— concerning my father's ridiculous novel, you know—and 'tis one that puts every matter but your own completely in the shade."

Nell turned abruptly to Manningford, to discover a rueful twinkle in his eyes. "She knows all," he admitted. "It was not my fault, but Borland's, for he now reads all letters held at the receiving office for Clarissa Harlowe before deciding if he will trouble my father with them. One arrived today that he decided must be given to me, and when Sybilla told him I'd gone out, his distress aroused her suspicion. She demanded an explanation, and the idiotic man found it impossible to snub her."

"So I should hope," Sybilla said. "He would have been most ill-advised to set his will against mine. Indeed, I should hope any servant in this house would know better than to do that."

"Most of them do not know you, my dear," Manningford said gently, exchanging a look with his brother-in-law, "though I cannot doubt that they soon will."

"Well, you are mistaken if you think I am going to stay here to run this household for you, dear brother. There was a time, to be sure, when I should have felt obliged to do so; and I own I was astonished to find you here when we arrived, and even more astonished to learn that you have taken some responsibility for once in a way. Though if you are responsible for hiring the excellent servants I have so far been privileged to meet—"

"You must credit Borland for most of them, my dear, not me."

"Ah, that explains their quality. But I shall not tease you. The fact is that since we do know your great secret—Papa's secret, I should say—and since Lady Flavia and Miss Bradbourne were actually favored before I was— No, no, Ned," she added in a laughing aside to her husband when he made a sound of protest, "I am not finding fault, for I should not have wished to know and, indeed, would prefer that no one else ever discover that my own father, not content with acting the part of Bath's greatest eccentric all these years, has now added color to his role by making it known that he has written I don't know how many lurid romances for the amusement of young ladies who ought to be spending their time more wisely than by reading them."

"Gently, Sybilla," her husband recommended. "You will recall that Miss Bradbourne is at present attempting to complete just such another tale. It will not do to be condemning her labor before your father may reap its benefits."

Sybilla turned her merry face toward Nell. "Indeed, and I hope you are not one easily to take offense, for what I must condemn in a man who ignored the existence of his family merely to amuse himself by writing such things, I can only admire in one who has been so kind as to assist him in this crisis; however, I must tell you about the letter that came, for you will nev—"

She broke off with a comical grimace when her footman and two of the maids entered just then with refreshments for the visitors. The conversation turned to desultory matters while the servants were in the room, and Nell could not help but notice that Mr. Lasenby took little part in it. Indeed, as she realized, he had spoken scarcely a word since their arrival and seemed to be paying heed only to the excellent view from the window. The moment the servants departed, she took advantage of the fact that Manningford had moved to her side to ask if all was well with his friend.

"Oh, no," he said, chuckling, "he is quite cast down, I'm afraid. You will recall that he decided to follow your

*Amanda Scott*

advice and write to Miss Wembly to beg her forgiveness."

"Yes, of course. I still think it was an excellent notion. Surely she was not refused to forgive him!"

"Oh, no, for there has been no time for her to do so yet; however, she has broken off their betrothal."

"Oh, dear, what a coil," Nell said, looking sympathetically at Mr. Lasenby. "But surely she will change her mind once she receives his letter and understands how truly sorry he is."

Manningford's eyes gleamed with amusement. "Well, I suppose she might have done, had he remembered to post the thing."

Nell stared him suspiciously, and then, when she was quite sure he was not roasting her, turned her astonished gaze upon Mr. Lasenby. Since Manningford had made no attempt to lower his voice, everyone in the room had heard him, and Mr. Lasenby looked guiltily back at Nell.

"Too true, ma'am," he confessed. "I had laid the confounded thing on m' dressing table and must have let it fall behind. The maid, suffering from an excess of zeal, brought on, no doubt, by the presence of a marchioness in the house, pulled the table away from the wall today for what must be the first time since she began working here, and there was the dashed letter, lying all unbeknownst! You cannot imagine my chagrin. I posted it at once, of course, but I cannot suppose it will make the least difference at this late date."

"Of course it will, if your sincerity is clear, sir. She could not be so cruel as to refuse to grant you another chance."

"Wembly might now allow her that choice, however," Manningford said, the glint of laughter in his eyes more pronounced than ever.

"Wembly?"

"Her father. 'Twas he who wrote the letter informing Sep that the betrothal was at an end. I am afraid he was not kind."

"Her father?"

The others had been listening, and Lady Flavia said now, " 'Tis not at all unusual that her father should write such a letter, my dear. Mr. Lasenby has behaved very badly."

Nell looked from her to Manningford, bewildered. "Yes,

but how could he? Her father, that is. Surely he is dead.''

"No such thing," Mr. Lasenby said with a dismal sigh. "Unless . . . It is possible you read of his demise in the *Gazette*, ma'am? I might have missed it m'self, you know, but dash it, not even m' grandfather can expect her to renew our betrothal if the whole family's gone into mourning!''

"I saw no such thing," Nell said, "but unless I am mistaken, you told me that Miss Wembly is already in possession of her fortune. I had thought her father *must* be deceased.''

"Oh, I see how it is," Mr. Lasenby said in a deflated tone. "You was thinking she had her wealth from him, but it comes from her brother, Alfred, you see. He had it from a nabob uncle, and when Alfred was killed at Waterloo, the fortune, by his will, went to Miss Wembly. Had he not willed it to her, it would have gone to his father—as his next of kin, don't you know—and she would not have got it so soon as she did.''

Sybilla said suddenly, "I am sure Mr. Lasenby's difficulties must be quite fascinating to us all, of course, but now that the servants are unlikely to return, we really must decide what is to be done about Papa's letter.''

Her husband, who had moved to a seat beside her on the claw-footed sofa against the wall, said gently, "All of us, my dear?''

"Well, certainly. Why ever not? Mr. Lasenby knows quite as much as anyone else does—in point of fact, he knew about Papa's books before I did—and Lady Flavia and Miss Bradbourne are part of the whole now, are they not? Surely they ought to be told about the Regent's wanting to meet Papa!''

The silence that followed her statement was due to the fact that both Nell and Lady Flavia were stunned and everyone else in the room had been expecting them to be—except Mr. Lasenby, who had been abashed by the latter's comment and was now lost in contemplation of his own difficulties. Lady Flavia recovered first. "Let me understand you, Sybilla," she said carefully. "Are you telling us that his royal highness desires to meet Sir Mortimer, or that he desires to meet that Gentlewoman of Quality whose skirts and pen have so long hidden your irascible parent from public view?''

Manningford grimaced. "As usual, ma'am, you have nicked the nick precisely. It is indeed a lady Prinny expects to meet, and the problem before us now is whether to reveal my father's secret or—if we decide we must continue to keep it—provide his highness with an impostor. I think you will agree that to return a flat refusal to his request is not an eligible alternative."

"Good gracious, no. That cannot be thought of. When does he come to Bath? I had heard nothing of this."

"He is to stay one night only at Bathwick Hill House with Sydney and Carolyn Saint-Denis. He visits them from time to time, you know, to ask Sydney's advice when he intends to purchase some new piece of Oriental bric-a-brac. They have been acquainted for donkey's years. The plan, according to the letter from his highness's librarian, which Murray forwarded to our Miss Harlowe, is that Prinny desires to have his author presented to him at Bathwick Hill House early in the afternoon. He will then attend the races at Landsdowne, where he has a horse called High Flier running—a slug, I'm told—before they dine and attend the new production at the Theater Royal. I can't think how to manage the thing, for even if Miss Bradbourne were to agree to carry her assistance with the subterfuge so far—"

"I couldn't!" Nell exclaimed.

Lady Flavia said calmly, "No, to be sure you could not, my dear, for there is no way you could make anyone believe you had been writing books for nigh onto thirty years."

Manningford said, "One could perhaps claim that only a few of the books were written by this particular Gentlewoman of Quality, you know. I daresay there are any number of—"

"Don't be foolish, Brandon," his sister interjected. "I spoke with Borland at length once he told me about Papa's books, and he said that although Papa has remained anonymous, the notation is made in each book that it was written by the author of *Cymbeline Sheridan*. Thus the prince must know perfectly well how long Papa has been writing. I do not think it would be wise to try to fob him off with Miss Bradbourne."

Nell said weakly, "Truly, I could not."

Manningford placed a reassuring hand upon her shoulder. "No one will ask you to do any such thing," he said calmly. "It would be infamous. If the worse comes to the worst, we shall simply have to tell Prinny the truth."

"No!" Sybilla exclaimed.

Quelling her with a look, Axbridge said, "I cannot think it would be at all wise to distress Sir Mortimer by revealing his secret to the Regent, whose ambitions arouse in him nothing but ill temper, or by insisting that he meet him. Either course would distress him, which cannot be good for his health."

"Perhaps, sir," Lady Flavia suggested, "Mr. Manningford might ask Sir Mortimer's publisher to explain to the Prince that the author is ill."

Axbridge frowned. "It is an alternative, of course, but would it not result in drawing even more unwanted attention in the end? The quicker and cleaner we bring a conclusion to this business, the better it will be for all concerned, especially in view of your grandnephew's difficulties, ma'am."

There was another, longer silence, during which Nell racked her brain to think of a way to honor the Regent's request without betraying Sir Mortimer. She could think of none, however, and could only hope that the others would agree with Manningford that she must not attempt to deceive his royal highness.

Just when it seemed that no one had been able to formulate a possible solution to the problem, Lady Flavia said calmly, "You know, my dears, I have thought and thought, and I can conceive of no good reason why I should not pose as Miss Clarissa Harlowe."

# 12

Lady Flavia's proposition was met with stunned silence. Nell looked from her great-aunt's untroubled countenance to the others, seeing a reflection of her own astonishment in every face but one, since Mr. Lasenby, still apparently deaf to their discussion, continued to gaze absently out the window.

Axbridge, watching Lady Flavia now with a glint of amusement in his eyes, seemed the least affected, though he flicked an occasional glance at his wife or his brother-in-law, as though he expected sparks to fly between them. Sybilla looked thoughtful, Manningford disturbed.

It was Sybilla who spoke first. "Such a plan might work, ma'am, but we could never ask it of you."

"Certainly not!" her brother agreed.

Lady Flavia cocked her head a little to one side, regarding them quizzically. "But why should you not? No one can deny that I am sufficiently stricken in years for the imposture; and surely I can lay claim to being a gentlewoman of quality."

Nell saw that Manningford, like his brother-in-law, was beginning to see humor in the situation, but he still shook his head as he said, "We do not doubt your capability, ma'am, but there would be a considerable risk, and we must not ask you to—"

"Oh, piffle," she said, cutting him off without apology. "One does see certain obstacles in one's path, I'll grant you, but none that cannot be overcome with a certain amount of sensible forethought. It is quite out of the question, for example, that my presentation be in any way public. Indeed, no one but ourselves and the Saint-Denises must know of it, since I am by far too well known in Bath to expect anyone here to swallow any pretense on my part to literary accomplishment. Also,'' she added with crisp candor, ''I doubt I can maintain such a deception for longer than half an hour.''

Axbridge smiled lazily at her. ''I believe you are equal to anything, ma'am, and I for one applaud you, but Sybilla is right, you know. We ought not to take advantage of your good nature.''

''I say 'piffle' again, sir, if you will permit me the liberty, for if the truth be known, I expect I should enjoy myself enormously. My scruples are no more delicate than those of most folks of my generation, you know, though one does draw the line at making a public display of oneself. When does he arrive, if you please? No date has been mentioned.''

With a resigned look on his face, Manningford said, '' 'Tis set for next week, ma'am, but you cannot have thought the matter through. You would be deceiving a prince of the realm—not a matter to take lightly, I think. Outrageous, in fact.''

''One must be practical, however,'' she pointed out, ''and if you desire to keep your father's secret, which I must assume you do, you require a woman of my years to assist you. I am utterly available, not to mention perfectly willing, and furthermore, you have been kind enough to entrust me with the secret. Too many people know it now, if I may say so, and it will not do to be making a gift of it to many more, or there will soon be no point whatever in continuing any deception. Moreover,'' she added in the tone of one having the last word, ''I have read nearly all of your father's books, I believe, so should his royal highness ask me a question about one, I shall not be made to look no-how, which is not a thing you may depend upon in just anyone you might ask to play the part, you know.''

When he still hesitated, she added dulcetly, ''It is no more outrageous than other rigs you have run before now, dear boy. At least there are no live bears involved.''

His eyes opened rather wide at that, and he looked at Nell. ''Been telling tales of me, my girl?''

''No, sir,'' she said.

Axbridge chuckled. ''She has no doubt heard about the horse coper you sent to Bedlam.''

"Did he do so?" Lady Flavia asked, with an appreciative look at the rueful Manningford. "I did not know. The tale I heard involved a bear introduced to the Pump Room."

Sybilla, who had been paying them no heed, said suddenly, "You know, Brandon, I fancy we must consider how we are to divulge Papa's secret to Sydney." When he did not instantly respond, she added firmly, "We will have to do so if Lady Flavia is to play her part, for he knows perfectly well who she is and that she is no mysterious authoress. Moreover, he is completely trustworthy. You know he is. And since I agree that Lady Flavia cannot meet the Regent anywhere other than at Bathwick Hill House, Sydney—and no doubt Caro too—must know the whole."

Manningford replied, "You are right, of course, but even if we make Sydney a party to the deception, how is he to carry the thing off in anything like a private manner? Prinny will expect a certain amount of pomp and ceremony, you know, for he does like a proper audience when he condescends to confer any extraordinary civility upon one of his subjects."

Lady Flavia's eyes twinkled. "But, my dear boy, that part of the business is simplicity itself. Mr. Saint-Denis has only to tell his highness that the author is shy beyond reason, which is already known to be the truth, after all, and that she will not agree to any but an absolutely private meeting. Even his highness will find, one dares to think, that his consequence is increased by being admitted to the ranks of the few who know the identity of so popular but so mysterious an author."

"Dash it, ma'am," explained Mr. Lasenby, his attention caught at last, "do you mean to say that you write books too? If that don't beat all! I should never have guessed it, you know."

Several persons began to speak at once, to explain his error to him, at which point Borland entered, bowed, and said to Sybilla, "Begging your pardon, ma'am, but Sir Mortimer, having learned that Miss Bradbourne is on the premises, desires that she should step upstairs for a few moments, if it be convenient."

As Nell arose and smoothed her skirts in preparation to accompany him, Sybilla raised her eyebrows in surprise and said, "You put us all to the blush, Miss Bradbourne. This must be quite the first time in many, many years that my father has actually requested that someone visit with him."

Manningford, having got up when Nell did, prevented her from attempting to respond to this daunting comment by saying briskly to Borland, "You may tell my father that Miss Bradbourne will be along directly. I'll take her upstairs myself, however, for there are several matters I want to attend to in the study."

When the manservant had gone, he held out his arm to Nell, but she had heard an edge to Sybilla's voice that she recognized at once, and she turned to her to say gently, "I have no true understanding of your father's behavior, ma'am, but I believe that for some reason known only to himself, he finds it more comfortable now to communicate with a stranger than with the members of his family. It is quite his own fault, of course, that he does not know you all better, but you must not think this a sign of particular favor toward me, for it is no such thing. He dislikes me quite as much as he dislikes anyone, I believe, but he presently finds himself in a position where he must depend upon someone. Only think how dreadful it would be for him now, after having ignored you all so assiduously for so many years, to have to admit his need of you."

The glint faded from Sybilla's eyes. "You are kind to explain his situation in such terms, Miss Bradbourne." Turning to her husband, she sighed and said, "I begin to think the sooner we return to Axbridge Park, my love, the better it will be. I quite long for the sight and sound of my children."

His charming smile lit his face again as he reached out to squeeze her hand. "We will go as soon as I receive word from London, sweetheart. Sooner, if you insist, but I think matters here will arrange themselves more sensibly if we linger for another day or two."

Manningford touched Nell's arm then, and she allowed him to guide her from the room, but she was thinking about

Sybilla and Sir Mortimer. She could not fancy that the marchioness owed her any debt of gratitude, since the entire absurd situation must be most uncomfortable for Sir Mortimer's family; and just then, as she knew full well, her presence on the scene did nothing to help them. Indeed, the more she thought about it as she accompanied Manningford up the stairs, the more disturbed she became.

On the upper landing he stopped, turned toward her, and said quietly, "Something has distressed you. What is it?"

She replied in an undertone, "Only that I am truly coming to realize what an abominable situation your father has created."

"He has," Manningford agreed, "but you can have no cause to blame yourself. Indeed, if you want to disassociate yourself from the whole affair, I will arrange for you to do so at once."

She stared at him. "But how could you think that I—?"

"Come." He glanced toward the door to Sir Mortimer's room and took her arm again. "We'll talk in the study."

"But he is waiting."

"Let him wait." He opened the door and drew her into the room, shutting the door again behind him. "He might hear our voices but not our words, and although Borland might come out while we stand on the landing, he will not interrupt us in here." Then an unfamiliar stern note entered his voice. He said, "Tell me the truth, Nell. Do you want to end this nonsense right now?"

She drew a long breath, staring at the top button of his waistcoat, trying to sort her feelings. Despite her concern for the effect her relationship with Sir Mortimer might have on his family, she knew she didn't want to stop what she was doing. Still, the thought that Manningford would end it for her when it was in his own best interest for her to continue was a warming one. She wondered if he truly believed he could stop it all so easily. Wanting to believe in him but knowing she had no real wish to test him, she looked up at last with a rueful twinkle in her eyes and said, "Will you think me irrational if I tell you I have no wish to end it?"

He smiled. "Not in the least. I should be most relieved to hear it, but understand me quite clearly. The moment you desire an end, I will tell him. I'll not allow you to be troubled by an agreement to which you are held against your will."

"I am not unwilling, sir," she said, warmed beyond reason by his words and the tone in which he spoke them. "I will own that the Regent's involvement has me in something of a quake. Despite Aunt Flavia's assurances, I cannot believe that we might not find ourselves in the suds if we attempt to deceive him."

"Will you trust me to deal with the Regent?" he asked. Then, before she could reply, he added gently, "Your great-aunt has the right of it, you know. With no more than a certain amount of care we ought to brush through that whole business unscathed. You need not let it distress you so."

She hesitated, then said, "To be truthful, sir, though I feel a certain apprehension regarding his highness's visit—because Sir Mortimer's secret might be revealed, you know, which would affect his health adversely—that aspect of the matter does not concern me personally, and so it does not distress me quite so much as I might have led you to think."

"But something has done so. Tell me."

She glanced up at him, opened her mouth, then shut it again and looked away.

He frowned, stepping back. "If you feel you cannot confide in me, of course there is nothing more to be said."

For reasons that she could not explain, even to herself, it was imperative to her to assure him that she had no qualms about confiding in him. Quickly she said, "I did not mean to seem secretive, sir, but the matter is one of some delicacy, and I should not wish you either to think ill of me or to believe that I am imagining things. If I am troubled, it is by the fact that your father seems likely to continue to demand my frequent presence in this house while your sister is here. She cannot like my growing relationship with him, and I am sure I do not blame her."

"You need not let Sybilla's megrims fret you," he said.

"Oh, but I look at her and feel such sorrow that she has never known the sort of companionship I knew with my father. My mother died when I was not much older than she must have been when yours did, but I had Papa's love to sustain me, and though he was not a sensible man, his disposition was most affectionate. I adored him and still miss him very much.'' Tears welled into her eyes, but before they could spill down her cheeks, she pulled her handkerchief from beneath her sash and wiped them away.

He took an impulsive step toward her, and for a moment she had the pleasing notion that he meant to take her in his arms to comfort her, but he did not. Instead he stopped directly in front of her and said firmly, ''My sister's emotions need not concern you. In fact, she is happy in her marriage and takes care that none of her mischievous brats shall lack the love and affection that were denied to us by our father. For that matter, if you will consider the matter judiciously, you will see that our childhood was not unusual, and that of the two parents, it was yours rather than mine who was the rarity.''

''Why, what can you mean, sir?''

''Only that is is quite customary for children of the *beau monde* to be strangers to their parents. Had my father spent his time in London at his club, leaving his brats at his country home to be raised by servants, no one would have thought it at all odd, for most of the gentry do precisely that. What makes my parents unique is that we lived in the same house with him until we—Charlie and I, at least—were sent off to school. Even if our mother had lived, we still would have been raised by nurses and governesses, just as most children are. My sisters are hardly the only women of our world, you know, who retain a stronger affection for Nurse than for Mama or Papa.''

It was true. She knew it as well as he did, but she had not thought about it in that way. She did now, and realized that she had been refining rather more upon Sybilla's tone than she need have done. Having recognized Sybilla as a managing woman, she knew now that a portion, at least, of her attitude stemmed from the fact that Nell had accomplished something with Sir Mortimer that his daughter never had.

''Perhaps I might induce him to—''

"No," Manningford said. "You will only upset him and do no good by it. In any case, you ought to be thinking about your own difficulties and not bothering your head about ours. One reason I came up with you is that Ned told me he brought your brother home with him. He thinks well of him, and I respect his opinion. Even before this, I had meant to get to the bottom of the business with your cousin. Now it becomes more pressing, and I want to have a closer look at that betting book. If there is anything out of the way about the manner in which the wager was entered, I'll rout it out. It is possible that Jarvis, after his father's death, might have found a way to alter the wording."

"But such books are practically sacred, are they not, sir, and you forget that Mr. Bygrave was the one to inscribe the wager in the book. He said himself that he wrote it down precisely the way Papa and Reginald commanded him to do."

"Or so Jarvis told your father," Manningford reminded her. "Recollect that your brother had already left for the Continent by then and could neither confirm nor deny the tale."

"But he has confirmed it now," Nell said, then corrected herself at once. "Or at least he remembers nothing to contradict any of what Jarvis told us then. His recollection of the whole business is dim, since he was so odiously foxed at the time."

"Oddly so, Ned thinks, and I agree with him."

"Oh, no, for Nigel is—or I should say, was—sadly unsteady in that way, sir. He was frequently quite . . . quite sodden with drink, for I saw as much myself, often and often. Why, even when they were at home together, both Papa and Nigel were used to drink as many as two or three bottles of port, between them, after dinner. And if you think I cannot know, sir, let me tell you that it was I who kept the house-keeping books, not Papa."

He chuckled. "I don't doubt your word, but I still intend to look into the matter closely. I have been party to too many outrageous schemes in my lifetime not to recognize the framework for one when I trip over it. Your cousin's error, I think, is in having thrown too many ingredients into his stewpot. One might believe in a wager gone wrong, a host of convenient corpses, even a duel, but someone cheating in the duel, then a disappearing heir . . . Nell, I ask you, even in the sort of books my father writes, so many bits and pieces could never add up to a tidy whole. Jarvis has overdone it, and therein lies his undoing.''

She sighed. ''Perhaps, sir. I confess to a hankering of my own to see that betting book, but despite what you may think of him, if Jarvis did do something dreadful, I doubt we will find him out. He can be devilishly clever when something matters to him. No scheme of his will unravel at a touch.''

''Perhaps not, but I wish you will trust me to try my luck. I think you see more of your father and brother in me than I deserve. No, no, don't poker up,'' he added when she moved to protest. ''I don't mean to offend you. I know I must be absurdly easy for one in your position to assume from the tales you have heard about me that I am cast in a similar mold.''

''Oh, no,'' Nell said, but the words sounded weak in her own ears, and she was not surprised when his expression indicated clearly that he did not believe her. From the moment, weeks before, when he had so casually told her he was abducting her, she had seen in him many of the same traits she identified with the two men she knew and loved best, but although she had known all along that she had an inclination to compare him to them, she had had no idea that he had been aware of the fact.

''I know that my reputation for outrageous behavior must appall you,'' he went on, ''for I have frequently been careless, certainly irresponsible, and at times even downright foolish. But I am older now and capable of better things, and so I shall prove to you. In the meantime, my dear, if we are not to have Borland hammering upon the door, you had better get along to the old gentleman now.''

She stood where she was, staring at him, wishing she might contradict him; but she could not. So it was that when he grasped her elbow lightly and gave her a little push toward the door, she nearly went without speaking; however, as he reached to open the door, she turned in his grasp, almost without thought, stood on tiptoe, and reaching her hand up to clasp the back of his head, pulled his face down and kissed him hard on the lips.

Then, smiling mischievously at him, she turned and ran from the room, down the corridor to Sir Mortimer's door. When she reached it, she looked back over her shoulder to see him grinning at her with such elation in his eyes that she knew without a word having been spoken that he read the thoughts racing through her mind and was delighted by them. When he took a step toward her, however, she recollected herself at once, and turning away with a jerk, reached for the door handle and pushed open the door, resolutely erasing all thought of Mr. Manningford from her mind and fixing her attention upon Sir Mortimer.

To her surprise, for she had thought him very ill indeed, the old gentleman was sitting up against his pillows, and his eyes lit with welcome at the sight of her. Borland got up from his chair by the window at once and said, "Most impatiently he's been waiting, miss, if I might take the liberty to say so. He's got a wee surprise for you."

"Indeed?" She turned to the gaunt figure in the bed, smiled, and said, "I wonder what that might be, sir. I adore surprises."

"Good," he said, if not clearly, at least more forcefully than she had heard him speak in several days. "Sit." His eyes shifted toward the chair by the bed that she generally occupied while she read to him.

As she moved to obey, Nell said, "I hope you will not be vexed with me, sir, for I have brought no pages to read today. I had thought you would not wish to continue our work while her ladyship and Axbridge were here, and so although I accompanied my aunt to pay our respects, I did not anticipate being asked to visit with you."

He grunted, cleared his throat, and said carefully, "Flavia here?"

"Yes, to welcome Lady Axbridge, you know, for your daughter is quite a favorite with her. But I must tell you, sir, I am delighted that you are beginning to recover your power of speech."

Sir Mortimer's odd half-smile touched his lips, and Borland said, "He's been that determined to speak, miss, though I was by no means certain it were good for him to keep trying as he did. Still, I thought it better to allow him to have his way than to vex him further by sniping at him. Then too," he added with a sigh, "it was never of the least use to do so. But I must say, I was quite as astonished as what I can see you are yourself. And that's not the whole of it," he added, smiling as he held out a sheaf of papers to her. "He's been hard at work, he has."

"Oh, indeed?" Nell took the papers with some reluctance, for although she was not by any means confident of her ability to mend his book by herself, she was oddly averse now to interference from anyone in what she was doing, and though she shrank from submitting work to Mr. Murray that was not entirely Sir Mortimer's, she dreaded the old man's criticism.

As she glanced at the top page, Borland said diffidently, "An you can make head or tail of it, miss, I'll own m'self surprised, for he was unable to speak at any length and I made no attempt to write more than what he did say. I take leave to tell you, I don't know, myself, what he meant in some instances."

Nell nodded, but she scarcely heeded his words, for she was having all she could do to hide her immediate opposition to what she was reading. Clearly because of his disability, Sir Mortimer had been brief to the point of curtness, but his comments were nonetheless pithy for all that. The first thing Borland had written was "Elizabeth insipid," followed by "Percy a stick." Impulsively she opened her mouth to defend the two characters, but she repressed it and read the next comment, "lives before." Her imagination stirred, for although the note was a brief one, she knew suddenly what he had been trying to tell her.

Elizabeth still had not come to life, and Sir Percy was no more than a stick figure. Only their villain had life. She looked up from the page to find the old man staring at her, his eyes narrowed as though he would measure her reaction.

She sighed. "I didn't know what was wrong. Whenever

I read what we had written, I knew that certain passages—
particularly ones I had altered—made me uncomfortable, as
though something were amiss. You are right about Elizabeth.
Try as I will, I cannot like her. She is so . . . so . . .''

He took a deep breath and sputtered, "S-saintly!"

"Exactly so, but I suppose it is always the case with a
heroine, for she must be an example to the reader of all that
is good and noble, must she not?''

Sir Mortimer snorted.

Nell grinned at him. "Dear sir, are you attempting to tell
me that she can have faults? I own, one of the things I
particularly enjoyed in Miss Austen's *Emma* was the fact that
even the title character was not flawless, but that book is
unique, I think, for in my experience, heroines of most
modern romantic novels are very sweet and good. And
indeed, you said yourself that your books are quite different
from Miss Austen's.''

With difficulty Sir Mortimer gave her to understand that
small faults gave the characters something to rise above. The
conversation after that was distinctly one-sided, as Nell
continued to read the list of brief comments and question him,
but after a time she discovered that she could anticipate some
of what he wanted to say from what little he had communicated to Borland, and by the time his eyelids began to droop,
she was feeling much more confident about their story. He
had obviously listened carefully to all she had read to him
and had had some excellent notions, including several ideas
regarding minor characters that would enliven the action and
enrich the plot.

When she arose to take her leave of him, he was looking
very tired, but she thought he was pleased too, and she knew
the time had been well spent. Not only did he believe that
once again he was contributing substantially to his novel,
but she believed she had gained enormously from his help.
Bidding them both a good day, she tucked the notes she had
made into her reticule and took her leave. Her mind was alive
with new ideas as she made her way downstairs again.
Unconsciously drawn to the sound of a concerto being skill-
fully played upon the pianoforte in the drawing room, she

nearly passed Mr. Lasenby on the landing without seeing him.

"Miss Bradbourne!"

Startled, she exclaimed, "Oh, dear, what you must think of me, sir! I beg your pardon. My mind was in the clouds."

"Been waiting for you," he informed her.

"Have you? Oh, and I have been such a time, too. My aunt must have long since given me up."

"Gone home," he said. "Said you was not to concern yourself with her, but to look after the old gentleman, because she meant to stop in Queen Square to visit with a friend."

"That will be Mrs. Prudham, I expect," Nell said. "She was set upon by footpads not long ago, in the middle of town, right at the top of Avon Street. I expect Aunt Flavia wishes to assure herself that she is completely recovered from her ordeal."

"Avon Street," Mr. Lasenby said, shaking his head, "is a black slum and not a good place at all, ma'am, though it ain't the center of town but the lower part, you know, and without you count the new development across the river, it would be the very edge of town, to my way of thinking."

"True enough, for my great-aunt has said the place is flooded, like as not, at least once a year. But what did you wish to say to me, sir? You said," she prompted when he appeared to be at a loss, "that you had been waiting for me. Surely it was not only to tell me that Aunt Flavia has gone home."

"No, no, it was something else altogether, but dash it, I cannot call it to mind," he said. He looked toward the drawing room. "Must ask Bran. He might recall."

Nell thought she had begun to understand Mr. Lasenby's particular shortcoming a trifle better in the past weeks, and she said gently, "Had it something to do with Miss Wembly, sir?"

His expression cleared. "Aye, that'll be it, I expect. Dash it, of course it is. Wanted to ask . . . that is . . . you said you thought she might forgive me for forgetting her deuced ball, ma'am, that my letter'd turn the trick."

He paused, and something in his demeanor gave her clearly to understand that, for reasons known only to himself, he was hoping she would deny it, but she said, "I believe it might, sir, if you explained the matter clearly. Anyone may be expected to suffer a lapse of memory from time to time, and by now Miss Wembly must realize that you suffer rather more than most. And she will not know, after all, that you forgot to mail your letter."

"Bound to know," he said despondently. "Put the date on it when I wrote it. Always do."

"Oh, dear," Nell said, struggling against an irresistible urge to laugh. "But it does not do to repine before the fact, sir. You must strive to keep your spirits high and hope that fate will reward you. Goodness," she added in dismay, "I sound just like a character from a novel, do I not?"

He nodded. "Comes from working so hard to put words in characters' mouths, I expect, in that one you and the old gentleman are writing."

"No doubt you are right. Is that Lady Axbridge playing the pianoforte in the drawing room? I must say my farewells, I'm afraid. I've a deal of work to do."

"Daresay it is," he said. "At all events, she's in there with Axbridge and Bran. Not musical m'self. Think I'll step down to Meyler's Library for a bit, look at the papers, don't you know. Tell Bran, will you, ma'am?"

She agreed, and he took his leave. When she entered the drawing room, Manningford got quickly to his feet, and Sybilla, seeing him do so, stopped playing and turned on the stool.

"Oh," Nell said impulsively, "please do not stop! You play amazingly well. That was Mozart, was it not?"

"It was," Sybilla said, smiling at her, "and I thank you for the compliment. I have not been able to play as much as I like these past weeks, while we have been on the Continent, and I am glad to have the opportunity again. Are you leaving us now, Miss Bradbourne?"

"Yes, I must go. Your father seems rather better, but I think he is tired and wants to sleep."

"Good gracious," Sybilla said, "have you been working

all this time on his book? I thought he could not speak, and surely you did not bring work with you.''

"He has recovered some part at least of his power of speech," Nell told her. "Borland said he worked very hard to do so. I am not surprised, though, for I daresay it was particularly trying to him not to be able to communicate.''

Sybilla held out her hand. "I spoke out of turn a while ago, Miss Bradbourne, and I want to apologize. It is not your fault that my father behaves so dreadfully, and I was wrong to speak as I did to you.''

Nell's gaze flew to Manningford, but he shook his head, and she turned back to her hostess and said, "You have nothing for which to apologize. I took no offense, I assure you, and I do understand that your father's eccentricities must be extremely difficult to live with.''

Sybilla laughed. "You may say so," she said, "but I want you to know that I look forward to your visits. You must come as often as you wish—or as he wishes—and do not be thinking you must run away afterward. I know that after having been such a time today, you will not want to linger, but do come again soon. Ring for someone to see her to the door, will you, Brandon?''

"No, for I mean to see her home myself," he said.

"That is not necessary, sir," Nell said, rather shaken.

"Nonsense," he retorted with a quizzical gleam in his eyes. "You cannot be walking unattended across Bath.''

"Oh, piffle, as Aunt Flavia would say," she said, giving him look for look. "I can very well hire a chair, you know, and even if I did choose to walk, 'tis broad daylight.''

"Women cannot always be certain of being allowed to go unmolested, even in Bath," he said, and since she could not, in view of Mrs. Prudham's recent experience, argue the point, she said no more, having, in any case, no real desire to dissuade him. And when he informed her that since Max had returned to Bath they might as well take him along to protect them both, she laughed at him but made no objection.

# 13

A warm breeze was blowing soft white clouds across an azure sky when they stepped outside, and the only thing to mar the peaceful afternoon was Max's vociferous determination, once Manningford had freed him from confinement, to gambol ahead of them, straining at the lead. Ruthlessly calling him to heel, Manningford apologized to Nell for the dog's bad manners.

"I sent him down to Westerleigh, you know, to my brother, but he refused to eat, Charlie said, and Clarissa insisted he be sent back to me, so I am quite puffed up in my own esteem, for I am sure no one has ever cared so much for my company before as to starve without it. Still, I suppose, it is the outside of enough to foist his company onto you, particularly since our respective visitors' arrival has postponed, for the moment at least, our plan to see more sights and take that ride on the downs."

His casual attitude giving her instantly to know that he had no intention of teasing her anymore about her outrageous behavior in the study, Nell smiled at him, tucked her hand into the crook of his free arm, and said, "I assure you, sir, I have not the least objection to Max's company, though he is not the sort of dog one is accustomed to see on the streets of Bath. Generally, such animals are the fat, spoiled, very rude companions of dawdling elderly ladies. Max is worth any number of them."

"He is, isn't he? Yes," he added when the dog's ears perked up, "we are discussing you. Try, if you will, at least to affect the manners of a gentleman, and do not disgrace me." They walked in silence for some minutes after that until, upon reaching the top of Gay Street, Manningford said,

"There was one small matter I wished to discuss with you, if you don't mind."

She glanced up at him and said warily, "No, of course not, though I hope I have done nothing to vex you."

He smiled and said, "Not in the least, my dear, though you have certainly given me food for thought. But that is not the point at hand," he added when she blushed and looked away. "As you know, I've been looking after my father's private affairs since I arrived here, and because of that, something occurred to me this morning that I ought to have realized some time ago. You once told me that your father's cousin had made a number of changes at Highgate, did you not?"

"Yes." She looked up at him curiously. "But I must tell you, sir, that the alternations he has made are nothing less than commendable. One of Jarvis' more vexatious traits, in fact, is that he frequently does admirable things, especially where the family is concerned, that make it difficult to continue to detest him as thoroughly as one wishes to do. Of course, one instantly wonders why he does them."

"Well but that is precisely the point," Manningford said. "If he has been putting his own money into the estate, there is nothing more to be said, though anyone would be curious about why he would do such a thing when the land is not yet his own."

"Oh, but he has not," Nell said. "I know, for he is quite puffed up over having shown, as he believes he has, that good management makes all the difference. Moreover, I am certain that the allowance he makes me is from Highgate money, for he said so, and he must know that I should refuse to take any of his."

Manningford nodded. "Then it is as I suspected. I daresay you know nothing about this sort of thing, for I didn't myself until recently, but one cannot simply take over another man's affairs so easily as that. My father had to provide me with his power of attorney before I was able to attend properly to his affairs or to those of the house, and I have had to produce it on more than one occasion before being allowed to act. Jarvis must likewise have got your brother to provide him with one."

"He did get some sort of authority," Nell said. "I thought I had told you. 'Twas only a note of hand and not sufficient for all he wants to do, but he has had it since that fatal night, for he told me it was a good thing he had had the foresight to get it before Nigel left the country."

"But why should it have occurred to him then that such a document might be necessary?"

"Why, surely because—" Nell stopped short on the flagway and stared at him in dismay. "Good God, Papa was still alive then, and Jarvis could not possibly have known that he would kill himself! The only reason he could have had for demanding Nigel's permission to act on his behalf was that he knew he would need it. Jarvis *did* murder Papa, just as I have long suspected!"

"Gently, gently," he said, urging her onward. "Not only are you leaping rather impulsively to conclusions, but you'll soon have all the quizzes ogling us. No, Max, you may not cross the square. We are turning toward the bridge now, if you please."

"It is of no more use to try to silence me, sir," Nell said grimly, "than to try to convince Max that he should walk tamely at your heel. If that odious man killed my father, I mean for the entire world to know about it."

"I'd have thought, in the event that Jarvis had murdered anyone, he'd have been more inclined to have murdered your brother," Manningford said in a musing tone, "for with Nigel dead and Jarvis the heir, your father would have been unlikely to have argued with him any further over that idiotic wager. Indeed, I have been wondering about that for some time now. I cannot think why he didn't kill him."

"Well of all the things to say!"

"I meant no insult to your brother, but since Jarvis did not kill him, one must think it unlikely that he killed your father either. Indeed, his having exerted himself to get your brother out of the country makes no sense at all."

"It would if you had a single ounce of family feeling," Nell said tartly. "No one can be surprised that you have none, of course, but you might at least try to understand those of us who do. For all his faults, Jarvis has a proper sense of his duty to protect the family name."

"If that is indeed so," he said thoughtfully, "one begins to wonder if your father's death was not even more of a shock to Jarvis than it was to everyone else."

"Well, I don't believe it was," Nell retorted. "You may talk round the point all you like, but now I am convinced that he killed Papa. Or can you tell me why he might have got that paper from Nigel before Papa had killed himself?"

Manningford did not reply at once, and when he did, it was to say slowly, "Your brother may well have an explanation for that, you know, but if he doesn't and Jarvis didn't commit a murder, I am rapidly coming to agree with you that we shall be unable to prove it at this late date."

Sobered by a conviction that he was right, Nell debated the point no further, but when they reached Laura Place to find Nigel alone in the drawing room, solacing boredom with one of the more lurid gothic tales in his great-aunt's collection, she demanded as soon as she had performed the introductions to know if he had given Jarvis his power of attorney.

"Some such thing, certainly," he said, watching Max flop gracelessly to the carpet and begin to lick his paws. "I say, does Aunt Flavia allow you to bring large dogs into this room?"

"Of course she does," Nell said. "Nigel, Jarvis must have murdered Papa, and that's all there is about it."

"Good God," he exclaimed, staring at her in astonishment, "what makes you say such a thing?"

"Because he had no reason to ask you to provide him with authority to act until after Papa was dead and you had become master of Highgate," Nell said. "Until then, you had nothing to do with the affairs of the estate."

Relaxing, with a glint of amusement in his eyes, Nigel said, "There was, however, the small matter of my affairs in town. Even such a nipshot as I was, my dear, had a flat and horses to dispose of, servants to pay, and a banker and creditors to placate."

"Oh," Nell said, deflated, "then I suppose it was not so odd of him to ask for a note of hand before you boarded the packet."

"Well, no, particularly inasmuch as he also gave me every farthing he had on him—a considerable sum, I might tell you. Dashed generous I thought him, too, for I need scarcely tell you that my pockets were all to let at the time."

Anger flashed in Nell's eyes. "Do you mean to tell me that Jarvis has been franking you all this time, that in fact, though he has insisted he had not the least notion of your direction, he has known where you were all along?"

"Of course he has not been franking me all this time!" Nigel said indignantly. "A pretty fellow you must think me!"

"You needn't snap her head off," Manningford said sharply. "Not only has your cousin continued to insist that your direction was unknown to him, but it was certainly unknown to your sister. Before you take offense, Bradbourne, you might at least admit that you ought to have written to inform her of your safe arrival and to notify her of your whereabouts."

"Jarvis thought it better that I write to no one," Nigel said, glaring at him, "so I did not."

Nell thought his excuse a weak one, but he had never been a good correspondent; and, in fact, she had fastened upon another point. She said, "Nigel, you cannot have had enough money to have kept you these eight months past, certainly not in such style as you appear to have commanded."

"Well, it ain't so difficult as you might think," he said sulkily, "for I had more than one run of luck at the tables, and I scarcely ever dined in my own flat. A single gentleman, you know, is always welcome somewhere or other. I doubt Jarvis realized how well I should contrive, especially since he'd advised me to stay clear of Paris, but that would not have suited me, for there is nothing to do anywhere else, so to avoid any more jobations, I simply neglected to tell even him my exact whereabouts. Thus, you see, he told you no more than the truth."

"I begin to think," Manningford said, "that it was just as well for you that he did not know where to find you."

"Good God, do you think he'd have tried to murder me? I doubt it. It would not have disturbed him to have learned of my death, I daresay, but I doubt he would have actively sought it.''

Nell glanced at Manningford to see that he was looking thoughtful, but if he had more doubts about her cousin's behavior, he said no more about them then. Nor did she have the benefit of his counsel the following day when the Marquess of Axbridge's man returned from London to inform his master that after a full but necessarily discreet inquiry he had been unable to discover a single charge laid against Lord Bradbourne with the chief magistrate at Bow Street. Even more surprisingly, none had been laid against him in the county of Somerset.

Axbridge carried the news to Nigel at once, and so although Nell had spent her usual time with Sir Mortimer that afternoon, it was from her brother, at home, that she learned of it. She wished she might have discussed it with Manningford, but since she had spent a good part of her time in Royal Cresent attempting, unsuccessfully, to induce Sir Mortimer to admit Sybilla to his bedchamber, she rather thought it as well that she did not encounter Manningford at all that day. In any case, she had more opportunity than she wanted to talk about Axbridge's news, for Nigel seemed unable to discuss anything else and continued to speculate long after his great-aunt and sister had tired of the subject, without arriving at any new conclusions.

''I should like to know just what Jarvis thinks he is about,'' he snapped suddenly halfway through dinner. ''In point of fact, I should like to know where he is hiding himself, for there is more than one home question that I should like to put to him.''

It was not the first time he had made either statement, and since neither lady wanted to encourage him to list his questions, Lady Flavia said matter-of-factly, ''Dear boy, one knows just how you must feel, but I remind you once again that it will not do to be seeking him out. We know you are not mentioned by name in any charge; however, we know, too, that his lordship's man, fearing that to mention the incident so soon after naming you might link the two in someone's mind, did not inquire into the known details of

Mr. Bygrave's death. And you promised his lordship that you will remain quietly here until he has had time to set additional investigations in train.''

"Well, I'd just like to speak to Jarvis, that's all.''

Nell, tired after her long afternoon, roused herself to say, "I told you before, Nigel, that he has gone to London to see about getting the wager honored by a court of chancery.''

"Well, I can stop that nonsense,'' he retorted.

"Perhaps,'' she agreed, "if we discover that you need not fear the hangman. But I am beginning to wonder if the chancery court has been only a bogey to frighten me into agreeing to marry him, for I cannot believe he sets as much store as he pretends by that wager. And you need not snort like that,'' she added tartly, "for having taken it into his head that my life was ruined by Papa's suicide, if not your exile, I think he really did believe that accepting his offer of marriage was the only way left me to protect my good name. It ought not to surprise you that he might think that way, you know.''

"What surprises me is that no word of my supposed doings appears to have got about, even here in Bath. At all events, I can scarcely be said to have ruined you.''

Lady Flavia said, "But, my dear Nigel, no one has said that; however, people do know that your father blew his brains out, and that alone is enough to make them look askance at your sister, even if they do not know why he did it. Indeed, that they do not know may make it all the worse, for then insanity must be suspected, you know, and no man of sense wishes to ally his house with one of tainted blood, particularly where there is no great fortune to offset the risk.''

Nigel could not remain interested in Nell's problems when his own seemed to him to be much more pressing, but though he might rail at his cousin's continued absence and deplore his own forced inactivity, she was grateful to discover that he had no immediate intention of flouting Axbridge's advice. He did refuse the marquess's invitation to enjoy the hospitality of Axbridge Park until the whole business might be resolved, however, declaring that he was not going to allow Jarvis to send him into hiding. And since she was certain that he still wanted nothing so much as to confront his cousin and demand explanations from him, she could only be grateful that Jarvis continued to remain absent from Bath.

In the days remaining before Lady Flavia's presentation to the Regent, Nell continued to spend a portion of each afternoon in Royal Crescent, but though she frequently saw Manningford, neither he nor Axbridge had additional news to disclose. She did manage at last, however, by the simple means of declaring her refusal to sit with Sir Mortimer again until he had admitted his daughter to his presence, to convince him to do so.

Having told Sybilla only that he had asked to see her, not why, and then having left them alone together, Nell had second thoughts about the wisdom of interfering when she discovered that Sybilla was greatly shaken by the meeting.

"He is so very altered," she said when Nell, having wondered if all was well, came upstairs again to find her, much subdued, sitting on the padded bench on the landing. "He did not even shout at me, Nell. Indeed, he apologized for being such a paltry parent—his very words, and though they are true, I found I did not like to hear them upon his lips. I have made of him a sort of beast behind a cage door, you see, for I have rarely seen him since Ned and I sorted out our own troubles and I agreed to put my marriage ahead of my duties here. Now, for all Father tries to seem the same, he speaks so haltingly and looks to be such a sickly old man that it is quite dreadful. I own I never looked for a responsible thought in Brandon's head, and was astonished—perhaps even resentful—to learn that he had taken control of this household, but now I am grateful that he has done so, and even more grateful that Ned is to take me home again tomorrow. I do so long to see my children."

Sir Mortimer appeared to be no more thankful for their reunion that Sybilla was. In fact, he did not speak of it, and when the Axbridge party departed the following day, Nell was more relieved than sorry to see them go—and not only because Axbridge had promised to go on to London as soon as he had got Sybilla settled, to see if he could discover what Jarvis was up to.

Having arrived as they were departing, she found herself, some minutes later, alone with Manningford in the front hall. Encountering a speculative look that made her remember rather guiltily that he might have cause to be vexed with her, she was not surprised, when the porter and a young footman came in behind them, to hear him suggest gently that she accompany him upstairs.

She remained silent until they reached the library, but when she heard him shut the door behind her, she said without turning, "I know you must be displeased, sir, but indeed, I had to try what I could do, for both their sakes."

She felt his hands on her shoulders, and when he turned her to face him, she could see no anger in his expression, only resignation touched with amusement. "What I think," he said, still in that gentle tone, "is that you simply have not yet learned to trust me."

"You are not vexed?"

"No, my dear, only a little disappointed."

He did not look angry, nor even distressed, but his words shook her, and when he said that he perfectly understood that she had done only as she thought best and that perhaps she ought now to go to Sir Mortimer, since he was no doubt impatiently awaiting her, she went, wanting to cry and not knowing precisely why.

She collected herself before she reached the top floor, and was able to present a cheerful face to Sir Mortimer. She had managed each day to find time for her writing, knowing that he looked forward to hearing her read what she had written, and to discussing it with her as well as he was able. And contrary to his daughter's opinion, he appeared to be regaining more strength each day. His speech had improved, he was able to sit up against the pillows in his bed again, and he began to speak of getting out of bed one day soon to sit in a chair by the window; however, the doctor had so strongly warned them all about the dangers of allowing him to exert himself that there could be no thought of his attempting to do more just yet.

He seemed content to let Nell do all the writing, merely to advise her; however, as a result of his newfound stamina,

he soon insisted upon reading his own correspondence—
letters collected from the receiving office for Clarissa
Harlowe and his personal letters, as well—and it was one
of the latter that nearly led to their undoing.

Nell had long since discovered that his vast personal
correspondence was responsible for his seemingly uncanny
knowledge of what went on in the *beau monde,* and it was
just such a correspondent who saw fit, in a letter delivered
two days later with the afternoon post, to inform him of the
Regent's visit to Bath. Having obeyed a surprisingly sharp
command to enter his bedchamber when she arrived, Nell
found the old gentleman sitting bolt upright, with Borland
trying unsuccessfully to persuade him to lie back against the
pillows.

"What is this?" Nell demanded. "Be calm, sir, I beg of
you, lest you bring on another of your attacks. Only tell me
what has occurred and I will do what I may to set it right.
Borland, do you stop pushing at him and fetch a glass of his
tonic at once. And do not you, sir, attempt to tell me anything
whatever until you have drunk it down and lain back peace-
ably again, or I shall not listen to a word you say to me."

These severe words having their effect, she waited several
minutes until the old man was calm, then said, "Now, tell
me."

"The Regent," he muttered. "Coming here!"

"Why, yes, so he is, sir, to visit Mr. Saint-Denis and his
wife at Bathwick Hill House. I am told he frequently does
so."

"Encroaching fellow," he muttered. "Popinjay. He'll
want to meet his pet author, damn him. I won't!"

When she tried to reassure him, he grew so agitated that
she finally decided there was nothing to be done but to
confess that such a request had already been made. Borland
gasped when she added matter-of-factly that Lady Flavia was
to pose as Miss Harlowe, and since Nell had feared nearly
as much as he did that the news would bring on one of Sir
Mortimer's attacks, she was equally astonished when, with
a bark of laughter, the old man fell back against his pillows
instead.

"Flavia?" he said a moment later. "She agreed?"

"It was her own notion, sir, and she has been rereading your every book, in fear that his highness might catch her out with a question about some scene or character she does not remember."

"Don't remember 'em m'self," he muttered. "Tell her not to fret." He paused. "You'll be there?"

She had not planned to make one of the party, for she had no wish to draw the notice of the Prince Regent, whom she cordially despised for his treatment of his wife and daughter, as well as the scandalous flaunting of his aged and corpulent mistresses, and his unending extravagance; however, Sir Mortimer insisted, and by agreeing at least to confer with the others, she was able to persuade him to work for a time. As she was preparing to take leave of him, he informed her that the manuscript would soon be ready to send off to London.

"Oh, surely not yet!" she protested.

Clearly tired now, he glanced at Borland, who said, "It is necessary for Mr. Murray to be getting on with his part of the business, Miss Nell. Indeed, a letter from him arrived at the receiving office only this morning, containing a draft of the title page and wording for the dedication, and wondering when he might be privileged to see the manuscript."

She still could not imagine that what she had contributed was of such a standard as to impress Mr. Murray, but neither could she reconcile it with her conscience to debate the point with Sir Mortimer, who was by now having difficulty keeping his eyes open. Accepting Borland's suggestion that she take with her the proposed title page to put with the rest of the manuscript, she took leave of both men and made her way downstairs to the drawing room, looking for Manningford.

Mr. Lasenby was alone, however, reading a newspaper. He put it down and got up at once. "Bran's gone out, ma'am. Your humble servant would be delighted to walk beside your chair if you would not despise the company."

"Not at all, sir, though I warn you, I mean to walk. It

does not suit me to be cooped up in a chair on so fine an afternoon, but you may certainly accompany me, if you like. Dare I ask if you have had word from Miss Wembly?''

''Devil a bit,'' he replied. Though he did not seem cast down by that fact, he grimaced as he added, ''Had a scrawl, however, from m' grandfather. Says he's had a visit from a pair of dashed impertinent tipstaffs, looking for me. Now the betrothal's been called off, they ain't so patient as they was, and m' grandfather said if I don't wish to find m'self in the sponging house, I'd best post up to London at once to placate Miss Wembly.''

''Then she has returned to town,'' Nell said. ''But you sent your letter to Brighton, did you not, sir?''

''Did I, by God?'' he replied, much struck. ''Forgot, you know, but that would account for her not replying, would it not? Daresay the thing's been lost.''

''But surely they would send it on after her,'' Nell said.

''Do you think so?''

''Oh, yes. In fact, if she did not receive it in Brighton, it must be because she left some time ago, in which case the letter ought to have reached her, even in town, by now.''

''I daresay you are right,'' he agreed with a sigh. ''Nothing for it, then. M' grandfather says I won't like the sponging house, so—though I daresay one life sentence is much the same as another—I suppose I shall have to post up to town next week to see what is to be done.'' He held out his arm. ''Shall we go?''

Nell swallowed the laughter that threatened her in response to his notion of ''at once,'' and accepted his arm, but they got only so far as the hall, where they encountered Manningford. Lasenby seemed very glad to see him.

''I say, Bran, your pockets are flush again, ain't they?''

Manningford regarded him wryly. ''They are. How much?''

''A monkey. I've had a devilish good notion.''

''You terrify me, but I'll give it to you later if you play least-in-sight now.''

When Lasenby had gone, Nell lost no time in telling Manningford that Sir Mortimer now knew of the Regent's forthcoming visit. The information did not please him, but he agreed when she had explained the whole that it was probably just as well. As to her making one of the party, he had not the least objection, since Lady Flavia had already said she would require support. He was to escort her to Bathwick Hill House himself, and he could not think it would pose any difficulty for Nell and Lasenby to be included in the party. "Sydney knows the whole," he said, "So he can simply tell Prinny that the author, being notoriously bashful, requires the support of her niece and her friends to see her through the ordeal of being presented."

And so it was the following day when the four of them arrived at Bathwick Hill House. Mr. Saint-Denis, having taken the trouble to greet them in the spacious hall, said to Lady Flavia, "Prinny knows many people are frightened by the ceremony that surrounds the royal family, and while he don't insist upon all that when he travels, he is aware that he is a figure of awe, and rather pleased by the fact, so he don't think it at all odd that his author wants her family at her side. In point of fact, he never objects in the least to meeting a pretty young woman," he added, smiling at Nell. "You should continue to wear lavender after you put off your half-mourning, Miss Bradbourne. The color becomes you mighty well."

She blushed, for though she had known the simple muslin dress became her, Mr. Saint-Denis was an authority. His attention to sartorial details was respected throughout the *beau monde,* and he was always precise to a pin himself. Beside Mr. Manningford, whose careless elegance did not include precision of any kind, and Mr. Lasenby, whose taste was exquisite but lacked something that Mr. Saint-Denis had in abundance, Sydney, dressed in a black coat and cream pantaloons, without a touch of color except for the enormous emerald nestled in his snowy cravat and the gold trim on his quizzing glass, was magnificent.

Lady Flavia, in wide silver skirts and a staggering amount of frothing lace, had chosen to enhance her eccentricity with three pink ostrich plumes waving in her headdress. She carried a lorgnette in one hand, a lace reticule and her cane in the other, and had said in the carraige—for Mr. Manningford had insisted upon taking them to Bathwick Hill House in style—that had she bethought herself of it earlier, she would have borrowed a lapdog to carry with her.

"Of course, one might have brought dearest Max along," she had told her companions, "but I daresay the effect would not have been quite what one desired."

Chuckling with the others at the vision thus brought to mind, Nell had said, "For myself, I only hope that poor Sudbury can constrain him to remain in the kitchen while we are away."

"Oh, indeed, he promised Max a marrow bone, and we must hope it serves the purpose, but it would not have done, you know, to have had him baying at the Prince Regent from the carriage, and one cannot help but think that Mr. Saint-Denis might object to our bringing him into his house at such a time."

Nell, remembering that moment as she followed the others upstairs to Carolyn Saint-Denis's drawing room, found it necessary to suppress an all-too-familiar urge to laugh. Thus she was not nervous at all when she discovered their hostess and her chief guest awaiting them.

The Prince Regent, fatter even than Nell had expected him to be, was gracious enough to rise, corsets creaking, to greet them. Mr. Saint-Denis performed the honors, and Lady Flavia, soon put at her ease by the Regent's famous charm of manner, was able to carry off her role with all her usual flair.

Indeed, so adept was his highness at putting his companions at their ease that as they were taking their leave of him twenty minutes later, Mr. Lasenby was moved to speak to him as he might have done to any chance-met acquaintance.

"Daresay you might not have thought of it, sir," he said casually, "but while you're fixed in Bath, you might like to take a look-in at the Bees-waxers', don't you know. Made a bit of history for the club thirty-five years ago, putting your name down in their book like you did. Daresay it'd gratify some o' those sleeping old gents—even wake 'em up a bit—if you was to take another look-in on your way home from the theater tonight."

"Damme, sir, if I can make head or tail of what you're asking," the Regent said, shaking his head, "but what with that nag of mine running this afternoon—and at thirty to one against, damn their impertinence—then the theater tonight, I've no time for more appearances. What club did you say that was?"

"Bees-waxers', though now I come to think about it, probably had another name when you was there, but your signature is set down in their betting book, for anyone to see who cares to look. Thirty to one, sir?"

"Aye." The Regent frowned. "Damme, but that can't be so. Don't say I've never signed a betting book, for I have, and more than once at that, but not in Bath. Damme, sleepiest town I know. Never set foot in the place before I began visiting Saint-Denis now and again. M' mother was used to come, but not I, and not thirty-five years ago. Prefer the south coast."

"Don't like to contradict you, sir," Mr. Lasenby said, sticking to his guns, "but the fact is, seen it m'self. There's a date, too, though I'm dashed if I can remember what it is."

"I can," Manningford said, regarding the Regent somewhat fixedly. "The fifteenth of December, eighty-five."

"I wasn't there," the Regent said flatly.

"But dash it, sir," Lasenby protested, "how can you be so certain? I mean to say . . . Well, thirty-five years ago!"

The Regent said to Manningford, "You certain of that date?"

"I am, sir. Five years to the day before my own birth."

"My memory is equally acute," the Regent said, his naturally florid face turning an even deeper color. "I know for a fact I was nowhere near Bath that evening, damme if I don't."

His expression was so forbidding that even Mr. Lasenby did not dare to question him further on the subject. Manningford remained thoughtful, however, and back in the coach he said, "The time has come to find the truth, Sep. We'll visit the club again tonight, while everyone who is anyone is at the theater."

Mr. Lasenby, saying that he had some business to attend to during what remained of the afternoon, left them at Laura

Place, but Manningford accompanied the ladies inside to describe to Nigel the meeting with his highness, and when the matter of the Prince's signature and the betting book had been explained to him, he was instantly alive to certain possibilities.

"We know now that that book is anything but sacred," he said. "Perhaps Reginald found out and somehow got Bygrave to alter the wager, or . . . Wait! Bygrave wrote it down, did he not? Suppose Reginald forced him to alter it by threatening to reveal the fact that the Regent's signature was false? Oh, but Reginald would not have done such a thing, and though I begin to think Jarvis might, he was not there when the wager was made."

Nell frowned. "Reginald was a jokesmith, Nigel. Suppose he never meant the wager to be taken for real. If he told Jarvis—"

"Jarvis," Nigel said grimly, "is entirely capable of having taken advantage of an intended joke to get his hands on Highgate. I'll not be left out of this business any longer, Manningford. If you go tonight, I go too, and afterward I mean to find Jarvis and shake the truth out of him!"

# 14

When the gentlemen had gone, Lady Flavia announced that she had things to do if she was going to be ready to depart for the Theater Royal once they had dined.

"Are you certain you wish to go, ma'am?" Nell asked. "Perhaps we ought to remain at home tonight."

"Nonsense, my dear. It has been a long time since I have felt wealthy enough to treat myself to a play, and by tomorrow the whole world will be talking about the Regent's visit. You may depend upon it that if we do not go to the theater tonight, one of us will be bound to let slip something that will prove we have seen him. Only think how it would be if we could not say we had done so at the theater."

Agreeing that such reasoning was sound, Nell made no further objection; however, when she sat down at the escritoire to read over the scenes she had last discussed with Sir Mortimer, she found it difficult to concentrate, for she kept wondering what Manningford and the others were doing and what, if anything, they would discover. Managing at last to stifle these thoughts, she had no sooner set her mind to work than Sudbury entered.

"Mr. Jarvis is here, Miss Nell. I have told him that you are not receiving, but he insists upon speaking to you."

Fighting to keep her voice calm, she said, "Very well, Sudbury, show him in."

She was surprised to see that Jarvis looked just as he always did, for although her imaginings had endowed him with all manner of villainous characteristics, he was dressed in his usual sleek fashion, and made his bow with customary flair.

"I trust I see you well, my love," he said smoothly.

"Very well, thank you," she said, ignoring the endearment. "No doubt you will forgive me if I express my hope that your business in London did not prosper. Do sit down," she added hastily when he moved nearer, his expression sharpening to curiosity when he saw the manuscript. It was all she could do not to put her hand over it, but he moved obediently to a chair.

As he took his seat, he said, "My business is going so well just now that I felt confident in leaving it to see how Bath has been treating you. It occurred to me that by now you must have discovered how unfortunately you are placed and might be more willing to discuss a future with me."

"I am not, however."

He leaned forward. "Surely you will not tell me that either Manningford or that ass Lasenby has offered for you? I am certain you have met no other eligible gentlemen here in Bath."

"Neither has offered for me," Nell said, smiling as the thought of Manningford brought a vision of that gentleman to her mind's eye and a glow to her heart.

Jarvis stiffened. "Do I take it that you are in expectation of receiving a declaration? By my oath, I cannot credit it."

"You need not do so, for it cannot signify. I wish you will believe me when I tell you, sir, that I shall never marry you. If I have no better offer, I shall continue to reside here."

"I should dislike to compel you, Nell."

"You cannot."

"Nonsense, I have only to threaten exposure of Lady Flavia's true pecuniary circumstances to the quizzes to force you—"

"You know?"

"But of course. Good gracious, her jointure is set out in her husband's will, a document of public record. I read it years ago, and prices being what they are, it took no great feat of mathematics to deduce that by now she must be feeling the pinch. She conceals it well, but I confess to having feared the truth might be discovered if your coming to her were to exact too heavy a toll on her purse. Hence, your allowance."

"I see," Nell said, getting to her feet in her agitation.

"Well, I know nothing about wills, Jarvis, but I do know you would never betray her. Concerned as you are with the Bradbourne name, you could never want people to know her real circumstances, for they would only want to know why you did not assist her."

"True," he said. "I make you my compliments, my love. But there is still the wager, you know, and our reprobate Nigel."

"One wonders," she snapped, "why you have not mentioned the fact that no one in London or Paris or even right here in Bath seems to know it was he who killed that man, Bygrave, or the fact that no charge has been laid against him anywhere at all."

Her words brought an arrested look to his eyes. "And one wonders," he said gently, "how you know these things. But lest you think it might be good to send for Nigel, my dear— even supposing you know how to reach him—let me warn you to do no such thing. If no one has spoken against him, 'tis only because I persuaded those who know to hold their tongues. Should he become a nuisance to me, I have only to persuade them to speak. Their words will hang him, Nell."

It had been on the tip of her tongue to tell him Nigel was in Bath, but now she pressed her lips firmly together.

Jarvis went on smoothly, "As to the wager, to prove its existence and have title to Highgate transferred to me, I need only produce the betting book in court. 'Tis irregular, perhaps, but without Nigel here to dispute the claim, the court will have no other choice."

"The Regent once signed that book, Jarvis, and may, now he is in town, be asked to do so again. Surely the club will not let anyone remove so famous an object from its premises. 'Twould be to jeopardize its integrity, would it not?"

"There is no time for Prinny to sign it again; he leaves tomorrow," Jarvis said, but she knew from his expression that she had hit a nerve. He went on, "And if the court requires to see the book, the club will have no choice. Indeed, I mean to collect it at once. You do not like my plan, Nell—I see that—but since you have been so cruel as to spurn my offer of marriage, you cannot expect me to continue to protect

Highgate for your brother's sake. And if you are honest, you must admit that the estate will be safer in my hands than in his.''

Nell did not waste words telling him she would admit no such thing, for her thoughts were racing. She knew the others would agree that the betting book ought not to find itself in Jarvis' possession, and she could not doubt that by her reference to the Regent and the book's integrity in much the same breath, she had spurred his decision to obtain it. Even worse was that if he went to collect the book before she could warn them of his arrival in Bath, he might well meet them all, including Nigel, when he did. With this fear in mind, she smiled ruefully and said, "Perhaps I simply do not understand all you are trying to tell me, Jarvis. Won't you stay to dine with Aunt Flavia and me, and perhaps accompany us to the theater afterward? If we send Amos out at once, I daresay he can procure a ticket for you.''

He gazed back at her searchingly, but when she maintained an innocent expression, he relaxed and said, "I am not properly attired for the theater.''

"Nonsense," she said, turning away at once to pull the bell. "You are precise to a pin, Cousin, as always.'' When Sudbury entered, she requested that he set another cover for dinner and send Amos at once to the Theater Royal to see if one more ticket for the evening's performance might be obtained for Mr. Bradbourne. "Tell him to order a box, if necessary," she added.

"Yes, Miss Nell," Sudbury bowed and left the room.

"Well, well, well."

She whirled sharply at hearing the softly spoken words, to find that Jarvis had got up from the chair and moved to the desk, where he stood holding pages of the manuscript in his hands.

Looking up with a gleam of triumph in his eyes, he said, "So you are turned authoress, my dear! I wondered how you thought you would go on if ever I tightened the purse strings. But I see by this letter and title page that you have represented yourself to the publisher as the author of *Cymbeline Sheridan.* That, one feels, was a mistake, for how amazed he must be to learn your true age, particularly since he seems to have persuaded his royal highness to permit you to dedicate this work to him!''

"Put that down, Jarvis. It is none of your affair."

"Ah, but I think I can now persuade you to do as I wish, my dear Nell. You did not choose to believe I would betray Lady Flavia, and I doubt you believe I'd allow any Bradbourne to be hanged, but you must know I should have no qualm whatever against informing John Murray that his supposed Clarissa Harlowe—what a romantic pen name, my love—is but one-and-twenty years of age."

She could think of nothing to say that would not reveal more than she dared let him know, but she could not chance his writing to Mr. Murray, lest Sir Mortimer's secret be revealed. At last she bit her lower lip, sighed deeply, and said, "You have learned my secret, sir, but I beg you will do nothing horrid until I have explained it all to you. Now I must change my gown for dinner, but let us attempt to have a pleasant evening, to discover if we can manage even to be friendly toward one another, and tomorrow, when we have both had time to think, we can discuss the whole matter calmly and with reason." She held out her hand.

To her relief, he set down the papers and grasped it. She had meant only to squeeze his hand in a spurious gesture of friendship, so when he bowed over hers and kissed it, she had all she could do not to jerk it away. When he released her, she turned quickly to gather up her manuscript, and said, "I will tell Sudbury to bring wine for you, sir. It was remiss of me not to have ordered it before."

Then, whisking herself out the door before he could attempt to delay her, she rushed down the stairs and, to her great relief, found the butler talking to young Amos in the hall.

"Oh, Amos, I am so glad you have not gone yet!"

"I were out, Miss Nell, a-fetching of some haddock from the fishmonger's for Mrs. Sudbury ter poach fer yer supper, but 'is nibs 'ere were just a-tellin' me I'm ter fetch a ticket fer ye."

Sudbury said grimly, "I doubt there are any to be had,

Miss Nell, what with his highness attending, and all.''

"Well, Amos must try, that's all. Perhaps there will still be a box, but, Amos, do not go yet. I must write a note for you to take to Mr. Manningford in the Royal Crescent on your way.''

"Miss Nell," protested the butler, "it is not on the lad's way at all, but quite another direction altogether.''

"Well, the note is more important than the ticket, Amos, so be sure you deliver it first," Nell said. Moving toward the little front parlor, where she knew she could find notepaper and a standish, she paused to say over her shoulder, "Oh, and, Sudbury, please take up some wine to Mr. Jarvis. I do not want him growing restless." It took only moments to write her message, and she handed it to Amos with a feeling of relief, confident that Manningford would know exactly what to do.

It was as well for her frame of mind that she did not see him twenty minutes later when the note was delivered to him in the library at Royal Crescent, where he and Nigel had retired to devise a plan for the evening ahead. Since neither was any too sure of what, exactly, he hoped to discover at the club, their discussion had reached an impasse, which they had sought to ease with the help of some of Sir Mortimer's best Madeira.

Manningford, having possessed himself of the two main facts in Nell's note—that Jarvis threatened to reveal her association with the manuscript and that he might try to remove the betting book from the club—sat for some moments in silence, thinking.

Nigel, watching him, said at last, "Not bad news, I trust.''

Manningford blinked, made his decision, and said mildly, "I hope not, but you will have to excuse me for a few moments. I must speak with my father. Help yourself to more wine.''

"Well, I will," Nigel said, "for I don't mind telling you it's a most tolerable vintage, but look here, oughtn't I to know what's going forth?''

"You will, I promise you, but my father does not receive visitors, so I must handle this part of it myself. I'll explain it all as soon as I can." He got to his feet, shoved Nell's note into his waistcoat pocket, and went quickly up to Sir Mortimer's bedchamber, entering without ceremony.

The old man was propped against his pillows, and to his son's surprise, his expression was welcoming. Manningford nodded to Borland, who sat in his usual place by the window, and pulled up a chair to the bed.

"How are you feeling today, sir? You are looking a trifle better, I believe."

"I'll hold. Tell me . . . Flavia and Prinny?"

Realizing that the old man had been anxiously awaiting news of the imposture, Manningford experienced a rush of remorse. "I apologize, sir," he said. "I ought to have come up as soon as we returned, but something else has occurred that distracted me. The meeting went off very well, for Lady Flavia was in her element and carried it off with a high hand, but no doubt Nell—that is, Miss Bradbourne—will want to tell you everything that was said and done. Just now, there is another matter which we must discuss. I need your help."

"Mine?"

"Yes, sir. The matter is urgent, or I'd not ask you."

"S'prised you would. Nell, of course."

"If you mean did she ask me to come to you, she did not. If you mean does it involve her, it does. Someone has seen the manuscript and threatened to expose her as a false Clarissa Harlowe. She has no thought for what it might mean to her, of course, only that it might lead to your own exposure."

"Foolish," Sir Mortimer growled.

"Exactly so. I'm afraid sir, the time has come for you to reveal yourself to Murray, if to no one else." He waited tensely for the reaction he both expected and feared.

But Sir Mortimer's eyes began to twinkle. "Still a step ahead of the devil," he said. "Murray knows."

Manningford was astonished. "He knows your identity?"

"Not that." The old man glanced at Borland. "Tell 'im."

The manservant smiled and said, "Wrote Mr. Murray a letter, we did, Master Brandon, telling him the novel would be a trifle delayed; and with the master's permission, I took the liberty of explaining that, being ill and having no plans at present to write more books, the author wished to bring to his notice the fact that in this instance assistance had been rendered by a most promising young writer. Miss Bradbourne was not, I need hardly say, mentioned by name, but what the master is telling you, sir, is that, should the dastardly person threatening her go so far as to inform Mr. Murray that she is involved with the present novel, the information will come as no great surprise to him.''

Manningford smiled at his father. "Promising?''

"Talented,'' Sir Mortimer muttered. "No confidence.''

Borland said, "He felt it best, the master did, to say nothing to Miss Bradbourne about the letter, fearing, sir, that such news might make it more difficult for her to finish the present work. If she should next like to write one of her own, however, the letter should serve her very well with Mr. Murray.''

"Never mind that,'' Sir Mortimer said tersely. "Who threatened 'er?''

"I'll tell you all about it,'' Manningford said, and proceeded to do so. His father listened carefully, stopping him only when it was not clear to him how it had been possible for the previous Lord Bradbourne to stake land that had been in his family for generations and again when Manningford mentioned Jarvis' threat to take the matter before a court of chancery.

"Nonsense,'' the old man said.

"Not nonsense at all, I'm afraid,'' Manningford replied. "Even without that damned wager, all he has to do, you know, is allow it to be known that the present Lord Bradbourne committed murder. Hanged or exiled, it won't matter where Highgate is concerned, for Jarvis stands next to inherit.''

Sir Mortimer shook his head. "Entail gone,'' he said. "Jarvis not next to kin.''

"But certainly he is, so far as the title . . .'' He broke off, realizing what his father was saying. "Good God, sir, no wonder he has pressed Nell to marry him! As things stand now, she, not Jarvis, will inherit Highgate if anything happens to her brother, and Jarvis wants Highgate as much as he wants the title. No wonder he has not yet actually taken the matter before a court!''

Sir Mortimer nodded. '' 'Nother thing,'' he said. ''You ought to know . . .'' He paused, tiring but determined. ''Reginald Bradbourne an owner . . . Bees. Didn't like to tell her. Not the thing. Gentleman don't own . . . such places.''

Frowning, Manningford added this interesting piece of information to the rest and thought he began to see a larger portion of the whole. Looking rather grimly at Sir Mortimer, he said, ''But you might have told me before now, sir.''

''Might. Didn't know you. Know you . . . you like her.''

''I . . .'' But he was not ready to tell Sir Mortimer how he felt about Nell Bradbourne, that he had been fascinated by her from their first meeting, that although he had briefly taken her for precisely the sort of managing woman he liked least, he had quickly come to realize that she was a deeply caring one instead. And that now, certain she cared for him, he wanted nothing more than to solve her problems for her and keep her safe forever.

''Ought to marry her.''

He had not realized that his father had been watching him so closely, but he looked up at these words and felt warmth rush to his face. Instead of obeying a familiar impulse to deny his wish to marry anyone, he said frankly, ''Well, I will if she'll have me, but then you'll look no account, sir, for if you think you can continue to hide in this room with Nell, and, no doubt, at times, even Lady Flavia in the house, you'd better think again.''

To his astonishment, Sir Mortimer gave his crooked smile and said, ''Full o' spunk, Flavia. Like to see her again.''

Grinning back at him, Manningford took his leave and went back downstairs to tell Nigel all he had discovered, and discuss how they might go about removing the betting book from the club to study at their leisure before Jarvis got his hands on it.

''But why,'' Nigel demanded, ''would he even want the thing? That book was useful to him only so long as everyone believed it was treated as sacredly as the book at White's or any other reputable club. Once it's known that they've played tricks with it, no court will support a single wager it contains.''

"He cannot be certain we've discovered that," Manningford pointed out, "but he does know his only hope of getting Highgate now is that wager, so whatever qualms he had about producing the book before must now be put aside, and quickly."

"Well, I say we tell him what we know," Nigel said flatly.

"Are you willing to risk your life to that end?"

Nigel slumped back in his chair. "Would you believe I forgot about that? But look here, do you believe there is anything to it? There can't be any witnesses, I tell you, who would tell the tale he wants them to tell."

"What I think," Manningford told him, "is that all Jarvis has been interested in from the first is that wager, so we want to get our hands on that book. Nell writes that she can keep him at her side all evening, so we'll chance waiting until there won't be anyone at supper, for that's the one time you can count on any club being a bit lively. Since we'll have the new secretary to deal with, if not Jarvis himself, the fewer members we encounter, awake or asleep, the better. We'll do better with three of us, too, and Sep will be back by then."

A footman entered just then to inform him that two persons were below, inquiring for Mr. Lasenby.

"What sort of persons?"

"Bailiffs, sir, if I know the look o' such."

"Well, we don't want to see them," Manningford said with a grin. "Deny any knowledge of his whereabouts."

"I do not know where Mr. Lasenby may be found, sir."

"That's the dandy. Tell them just like that."

The footman left, and Nigel said with a chuckle, "They'll catch up with him, you know. Bound to. Always caught up with me. Have to mend my ways now that I'm a lord, or . . . I say," he exclaimed, "they can't pen up a peer, can they?"

"You'll mend your ways, in any case," Manningford told him. "I mean to marry your sister."

Nigel raised his brows. "Do you? And does she know this?"

"I think she does; however, I shall make certain of it before we're any of us much older—in fact, just as soon as we've put this cousin of yours out of the way of making more mischief."

Mr. Lasenby came in twenty minutes later, a newspaper tucked under his arm and a stunned expression on his face.

Manningford demanded, "Where the devil have you been? The tipstaffs are nipping at your heels, my lad. Had a pair of them here not an hour ago, but they've gone now, so you can sit down and have some wine while we tell you what we're going to do."

"I'll take the wine," Mr. Lasenby said, but he made no move toward the Madeira. "I'm in shock, Bran, true as I stand here. Look at this, will you?" He held out the newspaper. "*Gazette*. Look here." He pointed. "Miss Wembly to marry the Earl of Cardhall. Can you beat that?"

"Good God, Sep, I'm sorry. We must get you out of the country, that's all. Just as soon as we get Bradbourne's affair settled, he can help you do the trick."

"Certainly," Nigel said. "Expert, that's what I am."

"Oh, but that won't be necessary," Mr. Lasenby said, reaching into his waistcoat and withdrawing a roll of bills. He peeled off several of these and held them out. "Here's the money you lent me, Bran. Can't remember the full amount I owe you, though. You'll have to tot it up and tell me."

Manningford stared at the money. "Where the devil—?"

"Races," Mr. Lasenby said. "Knew instantly—highest race course, High Flier—couldn't miss, could he? Decided days ago. But thirty to one!" He sighed appreciatively. "And now Miss Wembly to wed Cardhall. Astonishing how everything can come right once fate takes a hand in one's affairs, ain't it?"

"You put the whole money on the Regent's sorry nag? By God, Sep, I ought to thrash some sense into you. I never heard of such a thing!"

"Don't suppose you have," Mr. Lasenby agreed. "Vision,

that's what it was, sure as check. I'll have that wine now. Daresay after that, I'll put up my feet and count my money.''

The other two gentlemen quickly disabused him of that notion by explaining that that very night they meant, one way or another, to discover the truth about the wager and Nigel's duel.

After hearing all they had to say, Mr. Lasenby nodded and said, ''Well, I daresay you'll need me along to see if all comes right. Angel on my shoulder today, dashed if there ain't!''

Shaking their heads at him, the other two bore him off to the dining room to fortify themselves for the ordeal ahead, and it was dark by the time they left the house. They encountered their first obstacle, however, when Manningford's phaeton was brought around from the stable with Max perched on the seat next to the groom. The dog flatly refused to comprehend that his master desired him to remain behind.

''Daresay we'd better walk, after all,'' Mr. Lasenby said.

''Not on your life,'' Manningford retorted. ''You, for one, won't want to be walking about where those bailiffs can see you, for it won't matter to them that you can pay your debts. They've got orders to collect you, and that's all they'll care about.''

''Doubt they know my face, but if they do, can see me just as well in your phaeton. Sooner, with that hound up between us.''

''No, they won't, and we'll need the phaeton to go round to the inns afterward to find Jarvis and confront him with whatever we discover at the club. Nell didn't say where he is putting up, but I daresay it will be the York House or the Swan. You won't want to be walking from Kingsmeade Square all that distance and back to the crescent, and if you think we shall find chairs for three of us anywhere near Avon Street, you're wrong.''

''Don't suppose we shall. But dash it, we don't want the dog. Here, groom, take him.''

''Beggin' yer pardon, sir, but he's got no lead, and he don't want ter come.''

''Never mind,'' Manningford said. ''He'll stay under the seat, and if I tell him to stay in the phaeton when we go in, he will.''

Nigel looked on in amusement, offering no comment, but Mr. Lasenby protested. ''Dash it, Bran, he'll create a ruckus in the street, is what he'll do.''

''No, he won't, Sep. You must not have noticed, but he hasn't done so for some time now. He'll behave, won't you, boy? Smartest hunting dog in all England, remember, Sep?''

But Mr. Lasenby only shook his head. Max was agreeable, however, to curling up under their feet, and the three gentlemen made themselves as comfortable as they might on a seat built to accommodate two persons. When they reached Kingsmeade Square, Manningford looked about unsuccessfully for a linkboy to hold the horses, but there didn't seem to be one about.

Chuckling, Nigel said, ''Perhaps it's as well you brought the damned dog. He'll at least deter would-be thieves. Or should one of us stay with the rig?''

''No,'' Manningford decided. ''Best if we all go in. This pair will stand readily enough if I tie a line to the area railing. Impedes the flagway somewhat, but we'll not heed that. There are times, though, when one wishes this city were more accommodating to carriages.''

The porter, opening the door to them, recognized Manningford and Mr. Lasenby if not Nigel, and let them in without comment, although he did look askance at the phaeton. ''Want me to send a lad to take that rig round to the stables, sir?''

''No, I don't,'' Manningford said, ''We'll not be long.''

The porter nodded and moved back to his chair, and the three went up the broad stair at the far end of the entance hall to the floor above, where Manningford knew an office was located. They passed the supper room, closed now, and moved on past a card room, where four elderly gentlemen sat over a game of whist. A short distance farther, they came upon a door that was shut.

''This is it,'' Manningford said. He tapped on the door, and a voice from within bade them enter.

When he opened the door, they found themselves confronting the club secretary, a heavyset, well-dressed man, who sat behind a large desk in the spacious office. "Name's Wolsey," he said, getting to his feet. "How can I help you, gentlemen?"

They stepped inside and let the door swing to behind them before another voice was heard. "An excellent question, Wolsey," Jarvis Bradbourne said, stepping out from behind the door and smiling as the three turned sharply to face him. "Good God," he added, the smile vanishing, "is that you, Nigel? How very foolish, dear boy!" He gestured meaningfully with the pistol he held. "Put your hands in the air, all of you."

Nigel glared at him. "I'm very glad to see you, Jarvis."

"Are you? And here I thought your sister was to have kept me away from here tonight. Unfortunately, she reckoned without the extreme curiosity of the lower classes to gawk at their betters. Not a single ticket to be had, nor a box. Indeed, she ought not to have suggested the latter, for it was bound to arouse my suspicions, you know. And if it had not, her spirited attempt to keep me at her side must have done so. She insisted that I accompany them all the way to the theater, but that is only a few blocks from here, so I did not mind in the least. Now, please do as I ask and put up your hands, all of you. I should very much dislike having to shoot anyone."

"It would do you no good," Nigel said. "Your game is up, for you cannot possibly think I would sign over Highgate to you now, and no court in the land will honor a wager set down in this club's betting book once it's known that some if not all of the contents have been falsified."

"Do you know," Jarvis said, "I doubt his highness would willingly present himself in a chancery court to testify on your behalf, but it really does not signify, for I believe I hold all the cards at the moment, and you will do just as I ask."

"I won't," Nigel said, "and you can hardly think that shooting me will change that."

"Ah," Jarvis replied, "but will you be so sanguine about my shooting, say, first Lasenby and then Manningford? I think not."

Mr. Lasenby said indignantly, "Well, I should think not, as well. What a thing to suggest! You must be mad, man."

"If I am," Jarvis said, shifting the pistol in his direction, "it will make no difference to you."

# 15

Nell, having failed in her determination to keep Jarvis at her side, found it impossible to fix her attention on the play, and so, before the first act was over, she and Lady Flavia hired a pair of chairs and left the theater. There was a brief discussion about the route they would take back to Laura Place, Lady Flavia pointing out that to go by way of Beauford Square and the Borough Wall, though a hilly route not beloved of chairmen, was perhaps safer than Monmouth Street, which passed through the northeast corner of Kingsmeade Square at the top of Avon Street.

"Now, ma'am," Nell said, "you know 'tis the route you usually take. You are perhaps afraid of what we might find in Kingsmeade Square, but 'tis early yet, and I promise you, I mean only to discover if there is anything to be seen, nothing more."

She was sincere in making her promise, but when they reached that part of the square opposite the Bees-waxers', to see, tied to the area railing across the way, a phaeton with a large familiar-looking hound perched on the driver's seat, looking for all the world as though it meant to gather up the reins and drive away, Nell called to the bearers to set down their chairs.

"Aunt Flavia," she said as soon as this had been done and the men dismissed, "that is Max. They are still here, and I cannot help but feel that Jarvis must be here too, which cannot be a good thing for Nigel or anyone else. We must do something."

"But what can we do, my dear?" Lady Flavia demanded, casting a suspicious glance at a pair of loafers leaning against an area rail across the square. "Ladies do not enter gentle-men's clubs."

"I shall not let such a trifle as that dissuade me," Nell said resolutely. "Only think how we should feel if anyone were hurt merely because we refused to conquer some silly scruple!"

"But, really, Nell—"

"Will you abandon me, ma'am?"

"No, certainly not, but how shall we gain entrance? I daresay there is a porter, you know, and if he bars the door to us, that will be that. We could not threaten him at the point of a gun, after all."

"Not even if we had my pistol," Nell agreed, smiling at her.

"Well, we do have it," Lady Flavia said, hefting her reticule. "I took the precaution of bringing it because of Maria Prudham's having had that most distressing experience."

"My pistol?"

"Well, yes. Botten knew where you kept it, you see. I should have mentioned it to you, perhaps, but I did not want you to fret. I have borrowed it once or twice before when I have gone out to pay calls. So sensible, I thought. Such a comfort, knowing it is there in one's reticule."

"But, ma'am, you do not even know how to fire it!"

Lady Flavia shrugged. "One points and pulls the trigger, does one not? I confess, I did not know if you had loaded it."

"I did," Nell said with a chuckle. "You are the most complete hand, ma'am. You must keep it, too. My bag is too small to conceal it. I suppose I ought to have wondered why you were carrying that great cloth thing. But come, we must try what we can do to gain entrance to that place, and without, I think, flourishing the pistol. We will make enough of a stir as it is."

Mounting the steps, she pulled the bell, and when the door was opened, she said with an agitated manner, "Sorry to trouble you, but I must find my brother, and I believe he is within."

"No females," the porter said staunchly. "What is his

name, madam? I'll send someone to fetch him out to you.''

"No, no, that will not do! I cannot be standing here upon your step. It is not at all the thing, my good man. This area is not safe. Only look at those two ruffians across the way! You cannot leave two ladies standing here like this.''

"Ladies oughtn't to come here at all,'' he said, looking where she pointed. "Them men be harmless. Came and wanted to look over the place, they did, but we don't allow just anyone in, you know. Didn't know 'em at all, and the fellow they be asking about ain't a member here. Still and all, been a-standing there this past twenty minutes and more, they have, just a-watching.''

"Well, you cannot leave us standing out here.''

He showed no sign of giving way, however, and the argument might have lasted a good deal longer, had another party not been heard from. But Max, recognizing a familiar voice, accepted it as an invitation to leap down from the phaeton and, baying in delight, came bounding up the steps to greet Nell.

"Oh, Max! Down, sir!'' she cried as the dog tried to jump up to lick her face.

At the same time, the porter snapped, "Here, get that hound out of here! Fine goings-on. Scat, you!''

Not liking his tone, Max turned toward him and growled, and when the man stiffened with alarm and stepped back away from him, Max took the movement as a sign of encouragement and growled louder, showing teeth.

"Here! Hold that dog! Looks vicious to me.''

"Well, he is,'' Nell said instantly, "and I cannot hold him. As you see, he has no lead, and he is much too strong for me, in any case. You will simply have to let us in.''

"Oh, no, I will not,'' he said, beginning to shut the door.

Seeing the prey about to disappear, Max leapt at the door, pushed it open, and sent the porter sprawling. Making no further effort to defend the place, the man scrambled out of his way, and the two ladies passed unmolested into the hall.

"Find the master, Max,'' Nell said urgently. "Find him!''

Max pricked up his ears, wagged his tail, and turned toward the stairs, with Nell and Lady Flavia following in his wake. Until he reached the landing and turned down a corridor, he moved at no more than a trot, sniffing the air as though casting about for a scent, but when he had passed the card room, a sound from farther up the corridor galvanized him suddenly into action. Racing ahead, he flung himself at a half-open door.

His entrance was greeted by an uproar of male voices, but Manningford's was heard above all the others when he roared, "To heel, Max! Now, sir!"

Nell, having passed the card room without drawing so much as a glance from its four murmuring inhabitants, reached the doorway in time to hear next her cousin's soft voice saying, "Very wise, Manningford. I should have disliked killing him. Really, the porter was very careless to have let him in. But now, Nigel, I do hope you will get on with signing those papers. My patience is wearing a trifle thin."

From where Nell stood, she had an oblique view of the room and could now see Manningford and Mr. Lasenby, but not Jarvis or Nigel. Then, as she stepped forward, she caught a glimpse of another, unknown man, seated at a desk, and stepped hastily back. She knew Manningford had seen her, but thought Mr. Lasenby had not. Glancing at Lady Flavia, she hesitated uncertainly.

Lady Flavia looked up and down the empty corridor, tiptoed back to peep into the card room, nodded in satisfaction, and came back, silently taking the pistol from her reticule.

Nell's eyes widened and, frantically, she shook her head.

Putting a finger to her lips, Lady Flavia moved up beside her, close to the doorway. Nigel's voice could be heard now.

"Before I sign anything, Jarvis, I want to know the truth about that damned duel. I am quite certain now that that affair did not proceed as you described it to me."

"Perhaps it did not, dear boy, but if you expect me to say anything different at this late date, much less before witnesses, you are quite beside the bridge."

"It is my belief you shot Bygrave yourself in order to keep him from telling the truth about the wager."

"And what—just out of curiosity, you understand—does your fertile imagination suggest might be this truth you speak of?"

"That your father, knowing the betting book had already been falsified—and he must have known, since he was one of the owners of the place—decided to falsify it again to serve his own end, by bribing Bygrave to change the wording, either to cheat my father, or merely as a joke. You took advantage of it after Reginald died and then decided you had to shut up Bygrave rather than chance his revealing the truth later."

Jarvis shrugged. "If I made a mistake that night, it was in getting you out of the country. You can have no notion what a deal of trouble that caused me. I'd no idea your father would shoot himself, and afterward there was probate to be got through before anything could be done about the wager, and I hadn't a notion where you were and no real wish to try my luck with a chancery court, though I did think that threat would encourage Nell to look favorably upon my suit. If she had, I might have bided my time, knowing it would all come to me in the end."

"I might have married," Nigel said.

"Oh, my dear boy, surely not with a cloud over your head. Careless you have always been, but you know as well as I what is due to your name, just as I fancy you know you must honor your father's wager, for it was quite real. If your irresponsible parent did not read the thing before signing it, that does not make it any the less binding, between gentlemen."

Manningford said sharply, "Hardly a gentlemanly thing to try to cheat a member of your own family out of his birthright."

Coldly Jarvis said, "I think I will shoot you first, Manningford. You have been something of a thorn in my side."

Impulsively Nell stepped forward, but even as she did, she was shoved aside by Lady Flavia, who pushed past her into the room, brandishing the pistol wildly in Jarvis' direction as she snapped, "You ought to be ashamed of yourself, sir!"

Involuntarily he swung his weapon toward her;

whereupon, startled by the movement, she pressed her trigger, discharging the pistol and sending a bullet whistling past his right ear. Wolsey, still seated behind the desk, yanked open a drawer and reached inside; and Manningford leapt into action. Flinging a nearby small chair at Wolsey, he did not so much as pause to see if it struck him before turning his attention to Jarvis.

One quick stride closed the distance between them. Then, grabbing Jarvis' pistol hand before the astonished man had recovered from the shock of Lady Flavia's shot, Manningford gave it a twist. To everyone's amazement, Jarvis seemed to turn a somersault in midair before crashing to the floor, where, since his head hit with rather a bang, he lay like one dead.

Taking advantage of Wolsey's surprise at having a chair flung at him, Nigel had dealt roughly but effectively with the man, while Max, teeth bared and clearly believing he was helping, held a furious Mr. Lasenby quite motionless.

Into the sudden silence that fell, Manningford, gently taking the pistol from Lady Flavia's hand, said, "You never cease to astonish me, ma'am."

"But I didn't really do a thing," she protested. "It simply went off! And what on earth did you do to Jarvis? Is he dead?"

"No, he seems to be breathing well enough," he said, gazing dispassionately down at his victim. "It was a little trick I learned from Sydney Saint-Denis, but I still haven't quite got it right. When Sydney or that man of his does it, whoever goes flying always gets up again straightaway. I shall have to ask them what I did wrong."

"Bran," Mr. Lasenby said grimly, "call this devil off, will you? Dash it, he's got rats in his belfry."

"Max, come," Manningford commanded. Then, chuckling as Lasenby, freed at last, moved to gaze down at Jarvis, he added, "Look here, everyone, we've got to get out of here. Someone is bound to want to find out what all the noise was about."

Nell said, "But we didn't see anyone but a porter and four men playing cards in the card room. They didn't even look up when Max ran past, so they must be pretty deaf, I should think, and the porter is afraid of Max.''

Manningford grinned at her. ''So that's how you got in. I wondered. But . . .'' He broke off. ''Quiet, someone's coming.''

Even as he spoke, two rough-looking men came hurriedly into the room. ''What's amiss here?'' the burly, grizzled one in the lead demanded. ''Heard shots, we did.''

Manningford said casually, ''Pistol misfired, is all. Two men fainted from the shock. Nothing to worry you.''

''Well, I'm glad to hear it, for it ain't none o' our business, sir. Just stepped in, finding the door ajar, ye see, ter discover if one Joseph Lasenby might be on the premises.''

Mr. Lasenby stiffened, drawing the man's attention, but Manningford said instantly, ''No use to protect the man, *Giuseppe*. It would be wrong to impede these gentleman in the course of their duty. That's your man, gentlemen, on the floor. Here, Sep,'' he said, pulling rather clumsily at Lasenby's coat and then bending over Jarvis, ''help get him up. Fellow ought to pay his bills, you know. Not the thing, to cheat his creditors.''

''That's right, sir,'' said the spokesman. ''A pleasure it is to find someone so understanding, sir. We've been a-searching of this cove all the way from Lunnon, we 'ave, but once we learnt there were a club here, we knowed where to look. A gamester, he be, by what we've been told. But we won't be requiring yer assistance so long as you be sure he's Lasenby.''

''Sure as can be, my friend, but he's no doubt got a card case on him, you know. You may see for yourselves. In his waistcoat pocket, it would be, I don't doubt.''

And to Nell's surprise, not to mention Mr. Lasenby's, the card case was found there, just as Manningford had suggested. She held her breath when the man opened it, but let it out again when he nodded and said, ''Just as you say, sir, 'the Honorable Joseph Lasenby.' That's our man. We'll just be taking him along now. Not to worry,'' he added, looking at Mr. Lasenby. ''He's only to pay off his debts and he'll be free as a bird in a twink.'' Then, laughing, he bent to Jarvis' shoulders while his companion took the feet, and a moment later they were gone.

The others looked at one another, and when Nell's gaze encountered Manningford's, she began to chuckle and then to laugh until tears streamed down her face. Then he laughed, and Mr. Lasenby, who had stood staring at the doorway as though he expected the men, at any minute, to discover their error and return for him, looked first at Manningford and then at Nell. Smiling doubtfully, he said, "I shall never ignore the duns again, dash it. I couldn't think what you were doing when you snatched at my coat, Bran. My best card case, too."

Manningford chuckled again. "I had the greatest fear that you might have forgotten to put any cards in it."

"Oh, no," Mr. Lasenby said. "I don't forget such things as that. One never knows when one might need his card. Oh, but look, that fellow is waking up."

"Yes," Manningford agreed, "and that means Jarvis may be doing likewise below, you know, so it will be as well for you to play least-in-sight, Sep. Since I took the liberty of removing his card case when I put yours in his pocket, we must hope that our friends will detain him for some time, though not, one fears, for as long as he deserves. Here, you, Wolsey," he added, as the secretary tried to sit up, rubbing his jaw where Nigel's fist had connected with it, "that fellow you helped is a rogue, as I think you know, and I doubt the affairs of this club can stand much examination. What with all that's been going on, you'll likely have the magistrates here any minute, so if you know what's good for you, you'll get out."

The man needed no further invitation. He was gone.

Manningford then regarded Nigel. "I think your problems are over. We'll take the betting book with us, and I think the best thing to do with it is to turn it over to the nearest magistrate, for you can depend upon it that if one entry is false, others are, as well, and that will be enough to shut this place down for good. The affair of Bygrave, as of now, is unsolved, and likely to remain so. I doubt there was a duel at all, but whether Jarvis killed Bygrave because the man meant to kill you or to silence him on his own account, we'll never know. At present, I think, the important thing is to get your sister and your great-aunt away from this place. Did you ladies keep your chairs?''

"No, we sent them away," Nell said. "We didn't think the men ought to see us going into a gentlemen's club.''

He grinned at her. "Certainly not. This is no place for a lady. Very well, then, Nigel and Sep, take her ladyship to the Monmouth Street corner of the square and call up a chair for her. I am going to allow the pair of you to accompany her to Laura Place while I drive Miss Bradbourne there in the phaeton. I've a few things I want to say to her.''

Nell looked at him rather doubtfully. "If you are vexed with me for coming in here, sir, I must warn you that I cannot be sorry for something I would do again.''

"We must hope that you never find it necessary to do such a thing again, my dear, but I am not vexed in the least.''

"Oh." She saw that her brother was regarding her quizzically, and said, "Perhaps Nigel will object to my driving alone with you at this hour of the night, sir.''

Nigel shook his head. "You'll have Max for a chaperon,'' he told her with a teasing grin. "Couldn't ask for a better one.''

Manningford murmured for her ears alone, "Afraid you'll ruin your reputation, my dear?''

"I wish you would stop that," she said.

"What?''

"Calling me your dear in that odious way. It is just what Jarvis always called me, and I dislike it enormously.''

"Very well," Manningford said, "come along with me, my love, and we will discuss the matter at some length.''

Feeling suddenly in that instant very much more aware of him, and in a way she had not been before, she said hastily, "What about this place? Should we not do something?''

"What would you have us do?''

"But what about Jarvis? He will prove that he is not Mr. Lasenby soon enough, you know.''

"Yes, well, we shall have to discuss that. I cannot look forward to a future with Jarvis Bradbourne constantly on my doorstep, so we shall have to dispose of him more permanently.''

"I knew it," Lady Flavia exclaimed. "I suggested it at the outset, you know. You must tell him, Nell. From the very beginning, I said Jarvis deserved to be murdered. And really, you know, if he did kill that man Bygrave—"

"But we do not know that he did, ma'am," Nell protested. "We know only that he might have done."

Chuckling, Manningford urged Lady Flavia toward the door. "We are not going to murder him, ma'am. I had something rather less violent in mind. It will take some thought, but I rather believe he can be persuaded to make his home in the future on the Continent. He must be made to see that his reputation will suffer if he remains here, and since he cares for it so much, I believe he can be made to see reason."

"Oh, yes," Nigel said sweetly, "we can convince him."

"Yes," Manningford agreed, "you take my meaning well. And now, my love," he said to Nell, "you are coming with me."

Not until they had passed by the house in Laura Place and continued up Great Pulteney Street did she realize that she was being abducted again, but she made no objection. And when he drew to a halt at the gate to Sydney Gardens, got down, and held up his hands to help her, she said only, "You do not intend to drive me through the gardens again, sir? You are losing your touch, I believe."

Sternly commanding the dog to stay where he was, Manningford tucked her arm in his, extracted a shilling from his waistcoat pocket, and handed it to the gatekeeper. Only when they had passed inside and were walking along the gravel path together did he say, "I suppose I must be losing my touch at that. I was certainly clumsy with Jarvis."

"I was astonished when you gave him to those men in place of Mr. Lasenby," she said, chuckling.

"Well, I couldn't help but think that we should all get out of it more cleanly if we did not have to deal with Jarvis just then. He'd have been bound to make a nuisance of himself over the fact that you and Lady Flavia were present, and while we've learned to detect some of his empty threats, I wasn't in a mood to hear them. My action was purely impulsive, but I think it answered our purpose. I must talk to Axbridge to see if there is anything more we can do to bring him to justice, but I think we will find there is not. Will that distress you?''

"To own the truth," she said, "I should just as soon not have a felon running about with the Bradbourne name. What with Papa's suicide, that would put us quite beyond the pale, and I believe I care about that quite as much as Jarvis does.''

"But you will not carry the Bradbourne name yourself much longer, you know," he said gently, stopping her in the middle of the path. They were some distance from the rear of the hotel now, and there was no one nearby.

"I won't?" She gazed up at him. "And why is that, sir?"

"Do you not know I love you? Must I say the words?"

"I like to hear them. I know you have never thought my father's death a matter over which to concern yourself, but I hope you have thought about what it would be to have a wife whose father killed himself. People might—''

"People," he said firmly, "can go to the devil. I have never concerned myself over what others say of me, except you, and I know you think me irresponsible, but—''

"No, sir, not for weeks. I love you with all my heart."

"Then, will you marry me, sweetheart?"

"Willingly, sir. Oh, good heavens, I have just had the most appalling thought! Your father's book! Jarvis will certainly betray us to Mr. Murray. Whatever can we do?"

He smiled. "Father has already written to tell Murray about the promising young authoress who has so kindly helped the Gentlewoman of Quality. You, my love, will become a far more famous authoress than she, and I shall live long and prosperously on my wife's income. Shall you mind living with him, Nell?"

"Not at all, sir. I like him."

"Surprisingly, so do I." Then, grinning, he demanded, "Are you sure I am not too old for you?"

She stared at him. "Too old?"

"You once said—"

"I have said any number of idiotic things in my life," she

said, laughing. "If you mean to hold them all against me—"

"The only thing I mean to hold against you," he said, drawing her into his arms, "is my unworthy self."

Tilting her head up so that he might kiss her, she said softly, "I have known you only as a man of worth, sir, a man who would protect me without wrapping me in cotton wool, a man who loves me without trying to change me from what I am. You did not turn a hair when you saw me in that club. My own brother would have gasped with dismay, but you did not so much as blink."

He kissed her then, gently at first, but discovering with delight that his kisses were even nicer in reality than in her dreams, Nell responded with enthusiasm, and he was quick to follow suit. It was some few minutes before he set her back on her heels again, but then he said, chuckling, "I didn't react, my sweet life, because I was terrified that Jarvis would see you. He had a gun, and I, for one, did not know whether he would use it, but I did know I didn't want you in the line of fire if he did. And then that crazy great-aunt of yours—and do not tell me she is not crazy, for I should be most disappointed to hear it—jumped in with her pistol blazing, so to speak, and pandemonium reigned." He paused, then said, "I really must ask Sydney to show me that throw again."

"Perhaps he will show me, as well," Nell said thoughtfully. "It seems to be a very good thing for a woman to know, and I believe Aunt Flavia would like to learn, too. I don't know why you are laughing, sir. I daresay Mr. Saint-Denis would quite like to give us all lessons."

"Ah, Nell," he said, still chuckling, "I doubt that our life together will ever be boring."

"No," she said, "I don't believe it will."

# Author's Note

Readers whose curiosity has been aroused by the Regent's certainty that he could not possibly have been in Bath on December 15, 1785, or by his reluctance to explain that certainty, will be interested to learn that at six P.M. on that date, in her drawing room, Park Street, Park Lane, London, he was secretly married to Maria Anne Fitzherbert before witnesses and according to the rites of the Church of England. The witnesses were Mrs. Fitzherbert's uncle and her brother. The Reverend Robert Burt officiated. The marriage certificate, placed with Coutts Bank for safekeeping and kept there for nearly 175 years before being discovered in a general filing reorganization, is now in the Royal Archives.

The Royal Marriage Act of 1772 required the king's consent to any royal marriage, with the penalty for disobedience being forfeiture of one's right to the throne. Also, the Act of Settlement of 1662, which established the Hanoverian claim to the throne of England, flatly disqualified any claimant whose spouse was Roman Catholic (as Mrs. Fitzherbert was). Therefore, the Prince Regent did everything in his power (including going through with a bigamous marriage to Caroline of Brunswick) to keep secret his marriage to Mrs. Fitzherbert. It is not likely, therefore, that even so many years later he would have forgotten the date and time of the wedding.

With regard to Sir Mortimer's comparison of his work to Miss Austen's, he is no doubt right in his estimation. The total revenue from all Austen's books during her lifetime was about one-third of what Maria Edgeworth (1767-1849) made on any single one of her romance novels.